Keepsakes
from the
Cottage
by the
Loch

BOOKS BY KENNEDY KERR

LOCH CAMERON

The Cottage by the Loch

A Secret at the Cottage by the Loch

The Diary from the Cottage by the Loch

A Gift from the Cottage by the Loch

An Invitation to the Cottage by the Loch

MAGPIE COVE

The House at Magpie Cove

Secrets of Magpie Cove

Daughters of Magpie Cove

Dreams of Magpie Cove

A Spell of Murder

Kennedy Kerr

Keepsakes from the Cottage by the Loch

bookouture

Published by Bookouture in 2024

An imprint of Storyfire Ltd.
Carmelite House
50 Victoria Embankment
London EC4Y 0DZ

www.bookouture.com

Storyfire Ltd's authorised representative in the EEA is Hachette Ireland
8 Castlecourt Centre
Castleknock Road
Castleknock
Dublin 15 D15 YF6A
Ireland

ISBN: 978-1-83525-850-7
eBook ISBN: 978-1-83525-849-1

For the ones we love and lose

FRASER AND BALLANTYNE SCOOP
NATIONAL PRIZE

Highland Dancing champions Ramsay Fraser and Tara Ballantyne received perfect scores from the judges at Inverness yesterday in the finals of the National Scottish Dance Championship.

Fraser and Ballantyne, both from the tiny village of Loch Cameron, wowed the crowd with a faultless Highland Fling. Both are on track to compete at the international competition next year.

Fraser said,

'We are absolutely delighted to have won the Nationals – it's been a personal goal for us both for many years. We worked really hard, and I'm so grateful to have Tara as a dance partner. She makes everything fun, even when our legs feel like jelly.'

Ballantyne said,

'I'm so proud of both of us. This is such an achievement, especially as we're both about to go off to university. We still plan to compete, but this is a perfect way to finish the competition cycle this year.'

Fraser plans to study engineering, and Ballantyne is set to follow her dreams to teach. We hope that they can still find time to represent Scotland on the international stage next year.

PROLOGUE

We were inseparable.

I don't remember the day that we met, but my mum told me that it was the first day of nursery school. On that day, Ramsay was playing by himself in a corner. He had a dark bruise on his cheekbone, Mum said.

Ramsay always had bruises.

Apparently, I went over to him and gave him a hug. Maybe it was the bruise that made me do it, even though I wouldn't have known what a bruise was at that age. I certainly wouldn't have understood why he had one on his face.

We started playing together, and we were best friends from that day on.

Then, when we were in high school, Ramsay was walking me home one night – we'd gone for a walk up on Queen's Point – and he kissed me. It felt like the most natural thing in the world. I had loved Ramsay Fraser for as long as I could remember.

I was his safe place. That was what he told me, over and over, as the years passed. My family was his real family. The family of his heart. He spent as much time as he could at my house, helping my parents at the Inn on weekends, just happy to be there. He always said, *one day, I want a family of my own. Just like yours.* I felt the same, and I never imagined having that family with anyone else other than him.

We toured Scotland as Highland dancing champions. We were never apart. I thought we would be together forever. He was the other part of me. With Ramsay, I felt whole.

But, just before we went to university, we argued. I think that I was afraid of letting him go: we'd never been apart, and, suddenly, he was going to Edinburgh, and I was going to Glasgow. He had said, *don't worry, hen, we'll still see each other. You'll always be the home in my heart.*

But I was so afraid that I'd lose him, I told him that I wanted us to end things. I said that we should both be free at university. We shouldn't be beholden to each other in a time when everything was new. I was stupid, and proud.

I'll never forget the look on his face. *If that's what you want, hen,* he said. *But please know that I'd wait for you. I'd wait forever.*

That first Christmas, we both came home, and I couldn't stand it anymore. I'd missed him so badly, that whole first term. I'd hated being away.

We got back together again: he'd missed me too. We'd both been stupid to believe that we could ever be apart. Even if we had to be at different universities, then we could still see each other when we could, and talk, and email, and be the other's missing half.

That New Year's Eve, Ramsay proposed to me on Queen's Point, overlooking Loch Cameron. He reached up to his neck and took off his half of a heart pendant we'd both worn since we were teenagers, or even before then. It was the first time, to my knowledge, that he'd taken it off: he handed it to me solemnly and said, *now you have my whole heart. I'll get you a ring, though. As soon as I can.*

Of course, I said yes. I was so full of love for him, and in love with the idea of our future together. We both wanted the same things: we wanted to win the international Highland dance competition, travel, then get good jobs – structural engineering for him, teaching for me. I fantasised about teaching at the same little primary school in the village that we'd both gone to. Then, a home in Loch Cameron. Two children. All the simple happiness that anyone wants.

To me, a ring wasn't the goal. The simple gesture of him giving his half of the necklace to me was what I still remember, all these years later. That meant so much more to me than any size of diamond.

Yet, three months later, Ramsay Fraser disappeared from my life, never to return.

I was heartbroken. The centre of my whole life had fallen apart, and no one could give me an explanation.

It was a betrayal of all our dreams – everything we'd planned for our future.

And, though I never said it to anyone, I knew it was my fault. And knowing that – the secret I've kept ever since – broke my heart, savagely and completely.

ONE

'Miss?' the little boy asked, shyly. He was the last of all his classmates, and Tara had just said goodbye to them all individually as they'd filed out for the day. The rule was that you could choose how you wanted to be greeted as you came in, and choose how you wanted to be bid goodbye to – a handshake, hug, high five, a hello with no touch or a little dance.

The idea was simple but effective: it gave the power to the child to choose what they felt comfortable with. Tara knew that consent was important: all too many children had grown up being forced to kiss and hug people they didn't want to. Becoming accustomed to having to endure unwelcome touch wasn't a good message for children to take on board.

Tara stood just inside the classroom door with Andrew, the last of her Primary 4 class to leave for the afternoon.

'Yes, sweetheart?' Tara tucked a tendril of auburn hair behind her ear. Most days, she tended to wear her shoulder length hair in a ponytail, but today she'd done it in a severe twist at the back of her head – and she was regretting it. It was pulling on her scalp, due to the amount of grips she'd had to put in it.

'Can I have a hug today?' Andrew asked.

Tara made an effort not to look surprised. Andrew was a child in foster care, with a history of traumatic abuse. He didn't usually like to be touched at all, for obvious reasons, and Tara understood why. Andrew always went for a hello or goodbye with no touch. Not even a high five.

'Are you sure?' she asked, doubtfully. 'Not just a goodbye today?'

'No, Miss.' Andrew looked nervous, but hopeful. 'I think I'll try a hug today.'

'All right, then.' Tara leant forward slightly and gave Andrew a light, brief hug. Even though it wasn't a bear hug like some kids gave back to her – it was adorable when they did – the action brought a tear to Tara's eye, and she felt emotion well up in her throat. She swallowed. 'How was that?'

'Good,' Andrew said, simply, and gave Tara a little nod. 'See you tomorrow, Miss.'

'See you tomorrow,' she said, watching him as he trotted off down the corridor. *Oh, my heart*, she thought, closing the class-room door and resolving to tell her colleagues what had happened in the staff room tomorrow.

This was one of the greatest parts of being a teacher. Children were unpredictable. Yes, they could be a pain sometimes, but Tara had never lost her amazement at how sweet they could be. They surprised her every single day, and she loved the fact that every one of her work days was different to the one before.

That night, when her flatmate Carla got home, Tara was watching TV, having just finished some marking and a microwave meal for one.

'Hey.' Carla stuck her head around the living room door; her short pixie cut framed a pretty, heart-shaped face with deep brown eyes and long lashes.

'Hey.' Tara looked up and smiled. Carla was a good friend; they'd lived together for two years now, and apart from Carla's clumsiness – she was prone to breakages from over-enthusiastic washing up, and knocking things over with the hoover – Carla was a good flatmate. She was also a teacher, although she taught English at the large local secondary school.

Tara guessed that, if Carla could criticise *her* living habits, she could be accused of leaving piles of schoolbooks on the living room floor and half-read books all over the flat. But Carla had never mentioned either of those things, which made Tara appreciate her even more.

'G&T?'

'Go on, then.'

The flatmates had developed a routine. If both of them were at home on a weeknight, they'd share a bottle of wine or pour themselves a couple of large gin and tonics and watch the soaps on TV. Most nights, there was a solid three-hour block of soap opera programming on one channel or another – or, they'd pick up where they'd left off on a reality TV show they both liked, featuring a gang of extremely glamorous, bitchy estate agents selling luxury homes in Los Angeles.

Carla returned, carrying two tall tumblers full of clear liquid, with a lemon slice in each. She handed one to Tara.

'Good health,' she said, taking a sip of hers and picking up the TV remote. 'What's it going to be tonight then? I feel like we need to know what happened to what's-her-face. You know, the pub landlady with the heavy eye makeup.' Carla tutted. 'All this time and she had no idea she had a secret half-sister. It's a tragedy waiting to 'appen, darlin',' she said, in a stereotypical Essex accent, and raised a humorous eyebrow at Tara.

They had their own set of phrases they liked to use when watching their trashy TV, all delivered in their mothers' voices. Tara would imitate her mother, Dotty: Scottish, gossipy and judgemental. Carla's mum voice was Essex, loud and addicted to scandal.

'Aye, she's no better than she ought tae be,' Tara replied, giggling.

'She's gonna lose that nice 'usband of 'ers if she's not careful.' Carla sucked air between her teeth, mock-disapprovingly.

'Aye well, she only has herself tae blame,' Tara added, thinking of her mum, who actually *was* a pub landlady. Well, it was an Inn in a small Scottish village called Loch Cameron, but close enough.

Tara and her mum, Dotty, had a loving relationship, but they were very different people. Tara was quiet and bookish, and her mum was outgoing and gregarious: the centre of Loch Cameron's gossip mill.

He's just a lad, her mum had said, when Ramsay had disappeared, all those years ago. *We'll miss him too, darlin', but you shouldnae let him stop ye doin' what you want tae in life.*

But Tara couldn't be that hard-headed. Ramsay was part of her, and when he disappeared – without warning, totally and completely – it was worse than losing a leg or an arm. She was utterly destroyed. She couldn't dance anymore, and she had thrown herself into her studies, and into books. Dotty had tried to push her to go back to dancing, and, after a few months had passed, had tried to set her up on some dates with young men in the village, but Tara had refused both.

Ye cannae find love in books, Dotty had sniffed disapprovingly, after Ramsay had left. All they'd had was a brief letter, a couple of weeks after the last time Tara saw him.

Dear Tara

I'm okay. Don't worry about me. Nothing bad has happened, but I have to move away from the village.

I can't tell you why, but I'm leaving, and I'm not coming back.

I love you, but I can't be with you anymore. Please don't be angry with me: I couldn't stand it, though I know you will be.

Ramsay

No one had heard of him after that: he'd dropped out of university, according to the couple of uni friends of his that Tara knew. He didn't have any family that she knew of.

That was a whole other story.

'So. Are you set for Berlin?' Carla turned to Tara expectantly. 'I found good flights, and I've got a twin room for us, so that's all sorted. The rest of the gang are booked in the same place.'

'Yeah. Term finishes a couple of days after your school, then I'm all yours.' Tara grinned. 'I can't wait!'

They were heading to Berlin for a week at the start of the summer holidays with a gang of teacher friends from Carla's school, a large local comprehensive in what was deemed the roughest part of the city, but which had a brilliant drama department and a team of young but dedicated teachers who really cared about the kids they taught. Carla and her fellow teachers had taken Tara under their wing as an honorary addition to what they called the St Clare's Massive. Carla made sure that Tara was invited to all of their pub nights, which invariably involved drinking games, ridiculously competitive quizzes and loud but well-meaning arguments about 90s sitcoms.

By contrast, the staff at Tara's school weren't exactly gregarious. She loved the kids there, but, if she had to measure the social temperature in the staff room on any given day, it was relentlessly glacial. Her school – a normal state-run primary school – had what Carla described as *all the pretensions of a private school with none of the skiing trips*. Lomond Primary had a local reputation as the state primary that parents wanted their children to go to if they didn't want to pay for a private school, but still wanted something on their child's record that looked good to prep schools.

Tara had been there for under a year, and she hated it.

She had been headhunted from her previous school – a lovely, slightly under-performing village primary on the outskirts of Glasgow. It hadn't been anything fancy. They hadn't had anywhere near the budget that Lomond Primary had, which was entirely due to the fact that the school were constantly asking parents for money for anything from costly school trips to France, to new playground equipment, to tablet computers for every child in the school. What was amazing to Tara – who was used to communities where families were often struggling to make ends meet – was that the parents paid whatever was asked. It had evolved into a game with Carla: every week, Carla would try and guess what new thing the affluent parents at Lomond Primary had paid for.

'I bet you can't wait. I don't envy you having to be at Loaded Primary every day.' Carla opened a bag of crisps and stuffed a handful into her mouth.

'Lomond. But, yeah. It'll be nice to get a break,' Tara sighed. 'Guess what it was this week. The last week of term, mind you.' She rolled her eyes.

'Agh. Wait.' Carla placed her crisp-crumbed fingers on her temples and closed her eyes, mimicking a fairground psychic. 'I see... two live zebras and a wombat for a petting zoo?'

'No. Though I wouldn't put it past them,' Tara chuckled.

'Hmm. A G&T vending machine for staff? And a chocolate fountain.'

'You would want to work there if they had one of those,' Tara rebuked her flatmate.

'True. I could look past the snootiest of colleagues for endless cocktails.'

'Guess again.'

'Okay. If it's not an end of term celebrity appearance by a minor royal, then I'm out of suggestions.' Carla shrugged.

'Actually, you're not that far off.' Tara opened the cupboard and reached for a packet of biscuits, taking one and biting into it. 'The end of term summer fair is being opened by Melinda Blessed. You know, that celebrity chef from the TV.'

'Melinda Blessed? The really posh one that always makes those thinly veiled sexual innuendoes?' Carla started laughing.

'Yeah. She calls everything "plumptious".' Tara giggled. 'Apparently she's one of the PTA's old friends from school and she's in the area shooting her new TV show. She's popping in to judge the cake competition.'

'Dear lord.' Carla looked scandalised. 'Nice bit of pressure for anyone entering a cake.'

'I know. I was going to do some brownies but I don't think I'll bother now. You just know that all the hyper-competitive yummy mummies are going to be magi-mixing into the wee small hours in preparation. Stress baking.'

'Ugh. Hard pass.' Carla yawned. 'The lads are going to be beside themselves that she's coming to your school, though. They all fancy her, or they want to be her best friend.' Carla's gang of teacher friends comprised the drama, languages and PE departments, for some reason.

'Well, I'll try and get an autographed cookbook or something,' Tara chuckled. 'Not that anyone's going to give me any kind of important task to do. They still don't like me.'

'Well, anyway. In just over a week you'll be on a plane to Berlin.' Carla nudged past Tara into the lounge, where she slumped onto the sofa. 'Craig's excited that you're coming.' She raised an eyebrow.

'Craig?'

'PE.' Carla shook her head, mock-disapprovingly.

'What's wrong with PE?'

'Narcissists.'

'Right. I'll avoid him, then,' Tara chuckled.

'Well, you might just be unlucky.' Carla shrugged. 'He'll probably try and sit next to you on the plane. Ask you about your fitness routine.'

'Who do I want to sit next to, then?'

'Me, naturally. Or, failing that, anyone from the Drama department. Solid laugh.'

'Right.' Tara nodded, faux-seriously. She was looking forward to six blissful weeks of no lesson planning, no resource-making, gluing and laminating, no getting roped in to random fundraising projects and, most valuably of all, no having to make small talk with colleagues that apparently looked down on her.

Tara was also excited to have a week to explore a city she hadn't been to before. Plus, she and the rest of Carla's friends had planned to visit a couple of ritzy restaurants, the Berlin Wall and there had been some talk about visiting one of the more alternative Berlin nightclubs. Once upon a time, Tara would have loved the opportunity to go and dance the night away somewhere like that. Nowadays, she didn't think her body would manage it.

'I can't wait,' she said. 'I've put ten books on my kindle. I'm going to read in coffee shops, go for walks, go to some museums.'

'Ten books?' Carla laughed. 'I'd struggle to get through one in a week. The holidays is the one time I don't have to study books. I'm going to eat my own body weight in sausage, though. That's what I am going to do.'

'I know, but I love it.' Tara grinned. 'I won't miss school, but I will miss the kids. I know that's pathetic, but it's true.'

'No, it's sweet. You care about them,' Carla said. 'I don't miss mine, but that's because they're louts,' she said, affec-tionately.

Tara remembered Andrew, the little boy in her class, asking for a hug. Changing the subject, she told Carla the story.

'Aww. Bless his heart.' Carla shook her head. 'Poor wee man, though. Having had such a hard start in life.'

'I know. It's heartbreaking. But I'm glad that he trusts me, at least. Or, he's starting to.' Tara sipped her drink.

'You're a fab teacher. It's lovely that he gets to be looked after by someone that cares as much as you do.' Carla tapped her on the knee. 'I'm so proud of you.'

'Thanks.' Tara blushed. There was something to be said for living with a friend, Tara often thought. She had long ago had her heart broken by Ramsay Fraser, and she had avoided romantic entanglements ever since. Tara had remained single, but she liked it that way. All in all, life was predictable, but also, not terrible. She knew what terrible felt like, and had absolutely no inclination to fall in love ever again.

Yet, Andrew also made her think of Ramsay, when they were children: he had also come from an abusive family, even though, at the time, no one ever talked about it. It wasn't the done thing.

Perhaps that was something to do with why she loved being a teacher. She loved helping children discover new ideas and develop their skills: she loved it when that *aha* moment hit, and she'd see it in their faces. But, more than that, she had always been attuned to the fact that some children needed help. Ramsay had taught her that.

In the end, she hadn't got to spend the rest of her life with him, like they'd planned. But she'd never forgotten him, and despite the fact that he'd broken her heart, she still knew what it was to want to be a safe place for someone. She had been that for Ramsay Fraser once, and the least she could do was to be that for the children that she worked with now, if they needed it.

Tara's phone rang: she frowned, wondering who was calling her at this time in the evening. Probably a sales call.

Yet, the screen showed Mum & Dad. She pressed Accept.

'Tara? It's Dad.' Tara's dad Eric never called her: it was always Dotty, her mum. It wasn't that Tara wasn't close to her dad – she was. He'd always been loving and steady. He just wasn't much of a chatty person on the phone, compared to Dotty, who, when she wasn't running the Loch Cameron Inn, seemed to have the phone virtually glued to her ear.

Tara could immediately tell from her dad's tone that something was wrong; instinctively, she put her hand on the arm of the sofa. 'Dad? Is everything okay?' Her tone alerted Carla, who looked up from her phone in concern.

'Everything's fine,' her dad began in a placating tone that he only ever used when something was definitely not fine. 'How are you, hen?'

'Dad. Why are you calling me?' Tara's heart sank, and an oily wave of dread pulsated in her belly. 'What's wrong?'

'It's yer mum, hen. I'm afraid I've got some bad news.'

TWO

'Mum's not feeling too good, I'm afraid.' Eric sounded cagey. Tara could hear her mother's voice in the background. 'What? Hang on, she's talking to me... Dotty, I'm talking to Tara,' he said. Tara could tell that he was holding his phone away from his ear. She heard her mother's voice saying something in her no-nonsense tone.

'Eric. For goodness' sake, just put the speakerphone on,' Dotty, Tara's mum, said, her voice muffled. 'The button that looks like a speaker. Dear me, must I do everythin'?'

'Mum?' Tara was relieved to hear her mother's voice: she wasn't dead, then. For a moment, she had thought the worst.

'Hello, darlin'.' Dotty's voice sounded strained, but Tara was relieved by its familiarity. 'It's all right. But I've broken my leg. I fell over on the kitchen floor. My own fault: I spilled a glass o' water and forgot to mop it. You know what those tiles are like when they're wet.' She tutted, presumably at herself.

'Oh, no. I'm sorry, Mum! When did you do it?' Tara wondered, but didn't say, at what age falling over turned into "having a fall". Her parents were in their mid-sixties and were very active, running the Inn and involved in various community activities, but Tara had noticed that they were starting to slow down just a little, here and there.

'Yesterday. I was up tae the hospital an' had an x-ray, then they put me in a plaster cast an' gave me some pills, so I'm all right. It's a bit o' a tricky break, though, the doc says. I've got to be laid up fer weeks.' Dotty sighed. 'It's no' very convenient at all. We're booked solid fer weeks because it's the summer holidays.'

'Oh, no. Can you get someone in to help?' Tara had a sneaking suspicion of what her mother was about to say, and she didn't want to hear it.

Please don't ask me to come home.

Tara willed her mum to say that someone from the village had volunteered to do everything Dotty normally would: take the bookings at the Inn, work behind the bar, cook the breakfasts and do the lunches and dinners, order in food and drink as well as the cleaning. Dotty was and always had been someone who loved to live at a frantic pace, and still found time to keep the Loch Cameron gossip mill running.

'I need you tae come home and help oot until I'm back on my feet, sweetheart.' Her mother said the words she'd been dreading. 'I know yer aboot to go on your summer break, so ye won't have tae take any time off school. It should only be a few weeks, but your dad just cannae cope on his own.'

'Oh.' What kind of daughter did it make her, not to want to go back to her home town and help her parents, who needed her? But she'd been so looking forward to her holiday. Last year, she hadn't gone anywhere, and at the end of the six weeks she'd vowed that she wouldn't ever squander that lovely stretch of time again.

But, it wasn't just that. Tara had avoided going to Loch Cameron ever since Ramsay had disappeared without a trace; ever since she had done the thing that she had regretted ever since. It was something that she tried not to think about, but it often kept her awake at night, even now.

I'm supposed to be going to Berlin for a week with Carla. And, I don't feel comfortable coming home. Not with reminders of what happened everywhere I look.

She wanted to say it, but she knew she couldn't. It wasn't her mum's fault that she'd broken her leg, and Tara knew her mother well enough to know that she wouldn't have asked for Tara's help unless there was no other option.

'Tara? Are ye there?' Dotty asked. 'You'd really be helpin' us oot, hen. I know it's no' what you planned for the holidays, but we need ye. Can ye come?'

Tara had hardly ever heard her mother sound this way: she was normally so strong, brisk and friendly. It shook Tara to hear Dotty sound so vulnerable.

'Of course, Mum.' Tara made her voice bright, although she felt anything but positive. 'I'll be there on the weekend. Okay?' She met Carla's eyes and mouthed *I'm sorry*. Carla gave her a quizzical look.

'Thank you, darlin'.' Dotty sounded relieved.

'Are you all right, Mum?' Tara's heart clenched at the thought of Dotty being in pain.

'It's a wee bit sore, aye,' her mum chuckled, but Tara could hear the stress in her voice. 'I cannae lie, I almost passed out on the kitchen floor before your dad came an' found me lyin' there like a lame sheep. But I'm takin' the pills, an' they help. Doc says I can have occupational therapy in a while, when it's healed enough.'

'Oh, Mum.' Tara felt a wave of anxiety wash over her. It sounded awful. She hated to think of Dotty lying on the cold kitchen floor of the Inn, calling out for Eric, with her leg bent under her at an awful angle.

'Ach, don't worry, hen. I'll be okay, I just need your help for a bit. I just dinnae trust anyone else with the Inn. And it'll be good practice for ye. You'll inherit this place one day.'

Tara berated herself again for even thinking about the Berlin holiday, when her mum was in so much pain. It was hardly important.

'I'm a teacher, Mum,' Tara reminded Dotty. 'I don't plan to run the Loch Cameron Inn.'

'Aye, well,' Dotty replied, airily. 'Ye never know. Things change.'

'All right, well, I'll see you on Saturday, then.' Tara repressed the urge to sigh. But, what choice did she have? Dotty needed her, and she had to go.

Well, I guess I'm going to Loch Cameron this summer, Tara thought.

THREE

Tara drove into the little village of Loch Cameron, taking in the beauty of the loch that spread out in front of her. It was a sunny day and the warm, golden light glinted on the surface of the water, setting off a thousand sparkles that made the loch appear enchanted. A few boats bobbed on the side of the loch, tied to a few moorings that belonged to a handful of local families.

Tara had gone to school with a girl whose father had owned one of the boats; she racked her brain to remember the name of it. *Voyager? Vision?* She thought it was something beginning with a V, but she couldn't be sure. The girl had been called Emma, and she and Tara had been good friends all through school. But, even though Tara came home at Christmas and at other times when Dotty absolutely demanded it – usually only for a couple of days, refusing her parents' requests to stay longer – she didn't tend to socialise in the village anymore, because of what had happened. Because of what she'd done. The guilt nagged at her.

Still, Tara found herself wondering if Emma still lived in Loch Cameron. It was likely, because many people never left. People were born, raised, lived and died here: it was that kind of place. Objectively, Loch Cameron was a great place to live. Tara knew that. It was quiet, calm, the views were stunning and the high street was full of good, independently-run local businesses. People were, on the whole, kind, if a little gossipy. Also – as Dotty and Eric had told her repeatedly – there were new affordable, sustainable houses being built up on Gyle Head, which sat above the village and along the headland from the old, whitewashed cottages on Queen's Point, which overlooked the loch. Tara knew that was a not-so-subtle hint: her parents would be overjoyed if she came back to live in Loch Cameron. But, despite all its lovely qualities, Tara couldn't live here again. The past was too painful.

Driving along the narrow road that ran alongside Loch Cameron's quaint little high street, Tara noted the familiar shops and small businesses: a bookshop, a hairdresser's, the whisky shop which had been there for as long as she could remember, a bakery, a butcher. There had once been a funny little café with multicoloured glass windows which had closed after the owner, Myrtle, died: Dotty had been good friends with Myrtle, and Len, the man who had run the place before. When Myrtle had run the café, it had been stuffed full of knickknacks and oddities, and had been a nice spot to drop into for a coffee and a cake. Tara knew that her mum really missed her time spent gossiping with Myrtle in the café, overlooking the loch.

Yet, years before, when Len had run it, the place hadn't been a café: Tara thought that it had been a barber shop, but she also remembered her mum getting a new kettle from Len once, and then a sofa at another time. So, she wondered whether she was remembering it right.

As she took the turn into the car park for her parents' Inn, Tara thought about the walks around Loch Cameron and Gyle Head she'd used to take as a teen, often taking a book with her, to a selection of secret, beautiful outside spaces to read until nightfall. Then, when it got too dark to read, she would sit and watch the stars come out in the vast black sky that stretched across the horizon like a velvet blanket.

Loch Cameron by night was magical. Because it was quite remote – you had to drive, as the nearest train station was twenty miles away, and the local buses were few and far between – it was still relatively unpopulated. Ten years ago, it had been possible to walk out at night under the stars and see no one for hours.

And, you were safe in Loch Cameron – or, so she had believed, then. Everyone knew you, and there was little risk of anything bad happening to you if you did slip out at night to watch the moon rise over the loch. The biggest hazards were natural: falling down a cliff in the dark, twisting your ankle on a hillock or unexpected dip in the grass.

Queen's Point, a promontory that overlooked the loch, had been one of Tara's favourite places. There were a number of quaint cottages up there, but there were also quiet nooks where she could sit unobtrusively amongst a circle of oak trees, her back against a comfortingly solid trunk, and gaze up at the sunset through a canopy of leaves, or listen to the wind in their branches.

Tara had loved being a competitive dancer, but reading and being in nature were her ways to unwind and be alone. Sometimes, though, she had taken those walks with Ramsay, and on those walks, she hadn't read, but they'd talked into the night. About their future, about dancing, about what they both wanted.

She didn't want to think about Ramsay Fraser now.

Tara parked her car in the Inn car park and waved at her dad who had appeared at the Inn's back door. She got out of the car and opened the boot, hauling out her suitcases, wellies and rain mac. One of the suitcases was a third full of books. She'd thought, when she was packing, that she would at least use the time in Loch Cameron to attack her towering "to be read" pile:

she never felt like she got any time to read novels when she was teaching. She would help out at the Inn, spend time with her parents and read. Perhaps she'd revisit some of the little hidden spots around Loch Cameron that she hadn't been to for years.

One of her favourite places was a narrow stretch of sandy beach that lay alongside the side of the loch, which you could get to if you followed a muddy footpath around the loch for about an hour from the Inn. Technically, the beachy strip was on Loch Cameron Castle land, but the Laird, Hal Cameron, didn't mind people using it as long as they were respectful – didn't leave litter or camp there. Tara thought about walking over there one evening to watch the sunset over the loch: it had been a long time since she'd done that. The thought filled her with a sudden excitement.

She was still sad about missing out on Berlin with Carla, but maybe a summer in Loch Cameron wouldn't be so bad.

'Hi, Dad,' she called out, as he approached.

'Ah, ye made it okay then?' Eric enveloped his daughter in a bear hug. 'Drive all right?'

'It was fine.' Tara nestled her head gratefully into her father's shoulder, taking in the familiarity of his handknitted jumper, the scratch of his grey beard on her ear, and the gentle timbre of his accent. He wasn't a tall man, but he had always made Tara feel safe and protected. 'How's Mum?'

'Up tae high doh.' Eric tutted as he released Tara from the hug and took one of her suitcases. Tara smiled at the phrase: Loch Cameron was one of those places where people would sometimes drop old Scottish sayings into conversation. She knew that *up tae high doh* meant her mum was stressed out. Other favourites that Eric and Dotty sometimes used was *what's fer ye will non' go past ye* and, one she used to hear a lot as a child, *a lie's halfway round Scotland afore the truth's got it's boots on*.

'Poor Mum,' Tara sighed.

'Ach, ye know what she's like. She hates no' bein' able to get on wi' things.' Eric gave his daughter a world-weary look. 'Anyway, come in, come in. I've made up yer auld room. I'll make us some tea and we can all have a blether.'

Eric led Tara into the Inn, which, though she knew her parents were very good at keeping everything clean and tidy and updating the décor when it needed it, seemed never to change in her eyes.

The door from the car park led into a short, dark, wood-panelled hallway that opened onto the Inn's reception area, where Dotty usually received guests, standing at a dark wood desk where she kept her laptop for bookings, a pot of pens and a stack of leaflets for local attractions: tours of Loch Cameron Castle and the Loch Cameron Whisky Distillery, walking tours of the local countryside and around the loch, and for some things further afield, like a lovely farm a little drive away that had a small petting zoo, flower gardens, and further again, Loch Awe and Loch Lomond and Trossachs National Park.

In the entryway, her parents had also placed a tall container that held spare umbrellas for customers, and there was a tall coat stand for customers on the frequent rainy days that befell Loch Cameron. This area led into the main bar of the Inn which featured a cosy fireplace, which Eric had usually got going with a crackling wood fire, except on the very warmest days of the year, various leather sofas and upholstered chairs with low tables where customers could relax and chat, and a long, dark wooden bar where Dotty and Eric usually served drinks, lunches and hearty dinners, either for anyone who popped in, or for customers who were staying at the Inn. Tara knew that her mum also provided breakfast for residents, either in the bar, or would take it up to their rooms on request. She started to realise how busy she might be for the next few weeks, taking up her mother's daily schedule, which was considerable.

Not as much of a holiday as you thought, maybe, Tara thought.

Dotty was enthroned in one of the comfy upholstered chairs, and held out her arms as her daughter walked in.

'Tara, darlin',' she called out, and Tara walked over and gave her mum a careful hug, avoiding her leg, which was in plaster. Dotty was wearing one of her pleated tartan skirts in grey and purple, and a grey cardigan which was buttoned to the chin. She still wore her customary string of pearls and had done her hair, but Tara could see that she wasn't her usual self, and that she was tired and in pain.

'Mum, I'm so sorry about your leg.' Tara kissed Dotty's cheek. 'How's it feeling?'

'Ah, not so bad,' Dotty said, in her customarily breezy manner. 'How are you, dear? Drive okay?'

'It was fine,' Tara said. 'The usual.'

Carla had been initially devastated that Tara had bowed out of the trip. *But who am I going to share a room with?* she'd asked, wide eyed, when Tara had told her about her mum. *Oh, god. Craig's going to be disappointed. He was planning to romance you, I'm sure of it.*

Tara had apologised, but Carla had rallied quickly. *That's all right, love. Of course you've got to help out your mum and dad. Give them my best, and wish me luck in Berlin with the Drama department. I'll keep you posted.*

'Good, good.' Dotty shifted in the chair, an expression of discomfort crossing her face. 'We so appreciate you coming tae help us oot, hen.' She leaned her head back in the chair. 'Eric! Tea, when you're ready,' she called out, imperiously. Tara stifled a smile. Her mother might have broken her leg, but she was still the reigning queen of the household, it seemed.

'It's okay.' Tara sat down. Her dad set a tray with a teapot, cups and saucers and a jug of milk on the table. He poured a cup of amber liquid and stirred in some milk and one sugar and handed it to Tara, then did the same but with no sugar for Dotty.

'Because yer sweet enough, aye,' he said to his wife as he handed her a cup and saucer.

'Ach, get away with ye.' Dotty took the cup from her husband with a frown, but then shot Eric a loving look.

'Well, we appreciate it.' Dotty sighed, sipping her tea. 'We're fully booked an' your dad just cannae do it on his own. Now. Before we get into all that, tell us what you've been up tae since we saw ye. It's been too long,' her mother chided. 'Ye hardly come home. I know, I know.' She waved away Tara's remonstrations. 'I know you're teachin'. But ye could still pop home on a weekend, now and again.'

'Mum. It's not as easy as that,' Tara protested.

'Aye, well. We miss ye.' Dotty pursed her lips, though not unkindly. 'So, how's school?'

'Good, thanks.' Tara briefly told her parents the story of little Andrew Fairlie in her class, and how he'd asked for a hug for the first time ever.

'Aww. Poor little mite.' Dotty looked thoughtful. 'That reminds me of Ramsay Fraser, ye know.' She sighed. 'We thought of him as our own. We always said, *ye've a home here.* He didnae have tae leave.' She shook her head. Dotty reached for Tara's hand and patted it.

'I don't think about him much,' Tara said, shortly. *Because if I do think about him, my heart feels as though it's breaking,* she thought, but didn't say. *Still. And I wonder if it will ever stop.*

'Hmm. Ah well,' Dotty sighed.

'Tell me what needs doing, then.' Tara changed the subject. She didn't want to talk about Ramsay Fraser. 'How many guests are staying at the moment?'

'Ten guests, so that's four doubles and a twin, which is two friends. Lovely ladies. Here for the walkin'.' Dotty ticked them off her fingers.

'Two o' the couples leave on Friday and there's a quick turn-around fer two new bookin's on Friday night,' Eric interjected. 'I can help you make up the rooms and check people in and out, so you remember how it's done.'

'All right. What about the food, and the bar?' Tara asked.

'I've asked one of the lads from the village tae help me on the bar,' her dad said. 'If ye can do the breakfasts, that'd be grand. I'll say we're only doin' sandwich lunches at the bar, an' I can deal wi' those. Dinners, we'll have tae see. I might see if I can rope in one of your friends from the crochet group, darlin',' Eric said to Dotty.

'Hmm. I expect Sheila would help ye out. Mina would love tae get her hands on the kitchen I'm sure, just so she could tell everyone she saved the day.' Dotty rolled her eyes. 'I'd ask June but I think it'd be a bit much for her. If Kathy's free, ask her first. She's waitressed up at the Fat Duck, so she knows how it works. I think she's a decent cook. Ye just need tae do a casse-role or a lasagne, and a vegetarian option every day. Nothin' fancy. Enough for thirty people, I'd say.'

Just two dinner dishes, enough to feed thirty people a day, plus breakfasts and making up rooms, Tara thought with some panic. *So, not much.*

Dotty caught the look on her daughter's face.

'Aww, hen. It'll be okay, I promise. You'll get the hang o' things.'

'I know. It can't be harder than doing phonics,' Tara said with a wry smile. But, she was wondering how on earth she was going to get everything done – and, more to the point, how her mother managed to do it all.

FOUR

There is a knock on the door and Tara opens it. It's her birthday, and a party is bubbling behind her, in the bar of the Inn which is closed for the night for its usual adult patrons.

She is eleven and all her friends from school are there, ready to watch a movie and eat popcorn. Dotty and Eric, her mum and dad, have strewn the bar with balloons and paper streamers, and there's a chocolate fountain, mountainous bowls of crisps and plates of sausage rolls and pastry cheese twists and a huge Victoria sponge cake with jam and buttercream filling, which is Tara's favourite.

She has been waiting to start the movie because Ramsay isn't there yet, and Ramsay is her best friend. Even though she has been distracted with everyone else being there and the stack of presents they've brought for her, the later it gets and Ramsay doesn't arrive, she wonders where he is and why he is so late to her birthday party. Surely, he wouldn't just not come, when he's been as excited as her about it? When they have been best friends since either of them can remember?

When she hears the knock, she dances to the door, knowing that it will be him. She is relieved that her movie can start and *that she can sit next to him and share popcorn like they always do. Relieved that Ramsay will hold her drink for her and that, at some point, she will comfortably nestle her head into his shoulder or lean against him, his body as familiar to her as her own. None of their friends make fun of them for the way they are together. Everyone knows that Tara and Ramsay are two halves of the same coin. They are the interlocking hearts of the pendant that is his gift to her, this birthday. She is not embarrassed when she opens it, later, because she knows that all her friends secretly want someone to share a locket with.*

When she opens the door, Ramsay stands with his hands in his pockets, looking down. There is a smear of blood under his nose and across his cheek, and his eye looks swollen. He is standing unsteadily, not putting weight on his right foot. Happy Birthday, Tara-boo, he says, smiling weakly and handing her a beautifully wrapped box. Sorry I'm late.

Tara runs to get Dotty, who takes one look at Ramsay propped up in the doorway and hauls him inside to the bathroom at the back of the bar. What happened to you? Dotty asks him, making him sit on one of the toilet seats and wetting a wad of balled up toilet paper under the cold tap and wiping his face clean. Tara, go to the freezer and get a bag of peas for his eye. That's goin' tae come up black and blue.

Tara doesn't want to leave Ramsay, but she does as her mother asks. She runs to the kitchen off the back of the bar where her mother usually makes food for customers and plunges her hands into the long chest freezer. The cold makes her hands numb. In the dream, she remembers that sensation so clearly. Her heart is as numb with fear as her hands are. Who would do this to Ramsay?

When she gets back to the bathroom, Dotty takes the frozen peas and makes Ramsay hold them over his eye. He'll be all right, hen, she reassures Tara. Go back to your friends an' we'll be there the now.

I want to stay, Tara says, feeling tears well up in her eyes. Who did this to you? she asks Ramsay, but he shakes his head. It was my fault, he says, avoiding her eyes. I was wrappin' up your pressie and the noise of the sticky tape and the paper was inter- ruptin' the football. I'm sorry I was late.

Tara and Dotty exchange glances, but there is something in Dotty's face that tells her that her mother already knows what this means. If Tara is honest, then she knows that Ramsay's dad isn't like her parents. There have been many times that she has called for Ramsay – never been invited in – and heard harsh words. She has never seen Ramsay's dad hug or kiss him or give him a kind word. His mum is long gone; she hardly remembers her at all, and Ramsay never mentions her.

Get away with ye, Dotty ruffles Tara's hair kindly. He'll be right as rain in a wee bit. Start the film an' I'll bring Ramsay in a couple of minutes.

Tara doesn't want to leave him, but she obeys her mum because Dotty has that look in her eye. When Ramsay slides into the seat next to her on the leather sofa in the TV room in the bar later, he doesn't say anything, but takes her hand and squeezes it.

Open your pressie, he whispers, and, as the film plays, she opens the carefully wrapped box and takes out the silver necklace with half a heart hanging on it. You've got half, I've got half, he whispers, helping her fasten it around her neck.

They never mention that night again, but after that, Dotty makes a point of asking Ramsay over for dinner and at the weekends and the school holidays. Eventually, Dotty and Eric put aside one of the guest rooms for Ramsay and he moves in.

As she wakes, Tara can still feel Ramsay's hand in hers, and him squeezing her fingers. She feels a hot tear roll down her cheek.

She hadn't thought about that night for years, but as she woke, Tara felt the pain of the memory wash over her like a wave. No doubt, it was because she had spent the night in her old room, in her childhood bed, surrounded by her old dancing trophies and outfits, her stuffies and the posters of her favourite teen bands that her parents hadn't taken down, and she'd never got around to changing when she'd visited. There was something in her that didn't want to get rid of those reminders of her childhood and her teenage years.

If Tara was completely honest, she knew where that reluctance came from. And the dream had put her right back in that emotion: it was Ramsay that she didn't want to forget, even if she didn't want to admit it to herself because he'd hurt her so badly when he'd disappeared.

They'd won those trophies together. She could remember each competition she'd worn her different kilts and socks to, in the various different colours: violet, blue, pink, red. In the Highland Dance competitions, girls wore tartan kilts and matching socks with a tailored, solid colour matching jacket to dance in. They were special dance costumes as opposed to the traditional kilts that featured clan tartans or tartans inspired by particular places or locations. Tara knew that there was still a box of laced dance shoes at the bottom of the dark wardrobe in the corner of the room, and a folder containing all the certificates she'd earned at dance class, at competitions and awards ceremonies and dance-offs.

Tara and Ramsay had loved dancing together. They'd started when they were small, with Dotty teaching them some of the jumps and the toe taps of the Reel and the Fling in the Inn's garden, and, then, at primary school, they'd all learned the Gay Gordons and the Pride of Erin Waltz. Even at a young age, they'd both showed an aptitude for it, and they'd started dancing in their spare time, just for fun.

When they were eight, Dotty and Eric had taken them to the Highland Gathering up in Dunoon, and both of them had spent the entire day watching the dancing competition. Eric had tried to take them around and show them the different attractions and activities – the caber toss, the pipers, the heavy bar – but Ramsay and Tara had only wanted to gawp at the colourful dancers, jumping and landing and twirling so precisely.

After that day, Tara had demanded that she and Ramsay go to a class. Eric had taken them both, every Monday night: there wasn't a teacher in Loch Cameron, so he'd driven them over to Loch Awe every week. Because she was a child, Tara had never stopped to think who had paid for Ramsay's classes, or why his parents had never driven them over. She hadn't questioned any of it, because she was a child who was loved, and whose parents had supported her in whatever she had wanted to do.

Part of the reason that Tara never let herself think about Ramsay, or even come back to Loch Cameron for very long, was because of that bank of joyful memories. It seemed odd to think that way, but she knew that if she opened the door to it, it would drown her.

She hadn't danced since Ramsay left Loch Cameron so unexpectedly. She could have continued – competed as an individual, or joined a group of other girls competing in the Highland Reel. But, she hadn't. She'd shut away all of her dancing, just like the dance shoes that were packed away carefully in that box at the bottom of the wardrobe. Because it was too painful without Ramsay. Yes, Tara loved dancing. But it was something she'd never done without him, and it had always just felt *wrong* to consider doing it on her own.

It wasn't just the dancing that she'd lost, though. It was *joy* that Tara had had taken away from her: it was the sense of home, of rightness, of completion, that she had always had with Ramsay. They truly *had* been the two hearts in the pendant that all her teenage friends had envied.

She had never even questioned it when they had been best friends for all those years, and when they had become lovers, and when Ramsay had proposed to her up on Queen's Point. It was just *right*. Tara had accepted and loved Ramsay and who they were together, without question. Her fingers went to the two halves of the pendant around her neck and fitted them together, tracing the interlocking edges with her fingers.

All my heart belongs to you now, he'd said, when he'd given his half to her: the night he'd proposed. She'd never taken it off, even after he'd left, disappeared, broken her heart.

Just as when Eric had driven them to dance classes in Loch Awe every Monday, and because both of her parents had been good to her and loved her, Tara had never known what it was not to have her needs met. But, now, with the tears streaming down her cheeks as she lay in her childhood bed, looking at her posters of bands she no longer listened to and the spines of books she had forgotten the story within, with her fist curled around the interlocking hearts, she knew that she had never known how lucky she was.

FIVE

'Get everything on the list, an' if the bakery stall's no' there, get the bread from the wee supermarket,' Dotty instructed, propped up in her bed like a queen. She wore a sage green velvet robe and a long, brushed cotton nightie underneath which was white with a pink flower pattern. Tara could see that the nightie featured long sleeves, because they poked out of the end of her mother's robe.

'Okay.' Tara took the list.

'There's shoppin' bags hangin' up by the door,' Dotty continued. 'If ye need tae make a few trips, it's no' far around the market. Just on the high street.'

'Right.' Tara nodded. She remembered the food market being around from when she'd visited her mum and dad last year. It hadn't been there when she'd lived at home, but it had been a good ten years since she'd called Loch Cameron home. 'So, what else do I need?' She scanned the list.

'Butter, loaf cakes – get about five o' those. Fruit or lemon drizzle. A big cake if there is one, like a carrot cake or a red velvet, aye. Jam needs toppin' up. Vegetables, salad, a few loaves o' bread. Milk and meat gets delivered, so that's a mercy.' Dotty ticked off the different requirements on her fingers. 'I usually do some bakin' fer the guests, so I have tablet or biscuits taē put on their tea trays. Are ye up tae that, d'you think, hen?' Dotty looked up at her daughter with a frown.

'I can follow a recipe, Mum.' Tara rolled her eyes.

'Fine. My recipe book's in the kitchen, ye can bring it up when ye get back wi' the shoppin' an' I'll show ye,' Dotty sighed. 'Ach, I hate bein' laid up.' She picked up a ball of wool and a square of crochet, then dropped it back on the eiderdown. 'How anyone fills their days wi' this kindae thing, I'll never know.'

'But you go to the crochet group every week usually, don't you?' Tara asked, with some amusement.

'Aye. But I can walk there, usually,' Dotty replied, snappishly. 'An' it's mostly just blether an' cake.'

'I see.' Tara smiled.

'Don't be cheeky.' Her mother gave her a sharp look.

'I wouldn't dream of it, Mum.'

Outside, it was a bright day in Loch Cameron, with the sun flashing intermittently from between white clouds. The loch glittered as the light hit it, flickering ever-changing shapes of gold over its surface, as if fairies had strewn a spell on its surface. Tara took in a deep breath of the fresh, clean air: that was something she always missed, living in the city. The air in Loch Cameron felt like pure oxygen: cold and glassy and so clean that you felt a year younger every time you went out for a walk. Tara swore that Loch Cameron was one of those places where the natural environment kept people young and healthy, like that Greek island where the residents all lived to be over a hundred because of their diet of local goat cheese and fish, the sea air and the local water which had some kind of superfood minerals in it.

In Loch Cameron it wasn't so much the food that was good for you, though it was delicious: Scottish cuisine had never been famous for lending longevity to its consumers. It was the air, the local water, perhaps, and something else. A vibe, a feeling, that Tara got when she came home. Yes, she had reasons for not wanting to be here, but she couldn't deny the *feel* of Loch Cameron. It had always been home, and despite what had happened, it had always had a feeling of comfort, steadiness, groundedness and community.

The food market came every couple of weeks now, Dotty had said, and after starting small with a few stalls, it had flourished into a sprawl that stretched the length of the high street. Tara, with Dotty's shopping bags tucked in her pocket, sauntered through the market, taking in the sights and smells. First, she stopped at The Loch Bakery, a stand whose logo she recognised from the high street, where they had a permanent shop.

'Morning, dear. What can I do for ye?' A friendly, middle-aged woman looked up from where she was arranging a basket of Belgian buns: Tara's mouth watered at the sight of their thick icing and the luscious shiny cherries on the top, even though she'd just had breakfast.

Fat loaves of bread lined the back of a wide table: wholemeal, white, tiger bread with its cracked, crusty exterior and soft inside, wide granary loaves thick with seeds. There was a stack of thick, gooey brownies – some with nuts, some without, some vegan, and a plate of white blondies next to them, dotted with white chocolate chips and macadamias. Tara looked at her shopping list: she'd dutifully scribbled down *bread, loaf cakes, big cake,* just as Dotty had dictated. Brownies weren't on the list, but she decided to get a few anyway. If nothing else, she knew her dad loved them.

Individually wrapped fruit loaves were stacked to one side, next to a sign that said PLEASE ASK, WE HAVE BUTTER TO GO WITH THESE.

'Hi. I've got a bit of a list, actually. My mum sent me over from the Inn,' Tara explained.

'Ah, Dotty sent ye? You're her daughter?' the woman asked, her face lighting up.

'Yes. I'm Tara,' she replied a little shyly.

'Ah, I've heard so much about ye!' the woman exclaimed. 'I'm Aggie. I run the stall wi' my husband Bill, but he's at the shop the now.'

'Right. Mum's mentioned you. Hi, Aggie.' Tara offered her hand, and Aggie shook it. She was perhaps in her early forties, wearing slouchy jeans and a cream sweatshirt emblazoned with the bakery's logo arranged in the shape of a loaf. She had long hair in a brown plait that reached all the way to her waist: Tara wondered how she managed to get it so long. Perhaps it was all the cake.

In truth, Dotty probably had mentioned Aggie and Bill to Tara at some point, along with a swathe of other local gossip that she unloaded on Tara whenever they spoke on the phone, but Tara had developed the ability to tune most of it out.

'You're a teacher, aren't you? Dotty's so proud,' Aggie continued. Tara was surprised; as far as she was aware, Dotty was still put out that she hadn't followed her dance career.

'I am. Primary 4' She nodded; she didn't see any need to involve Aggie in a years-long dispute between her and her mother – who she had always assumed wasn't a fan of her teaching.

'Ah, that's adorable,' Aggie cooed. 'Bill and I never had bairns but I do see the little ones comin' out of the school most days and I do think, aww,' she chuckled. 'Still, I also see the little hoons run their parents ragged when they come in the shop, so...' She shrugged. 'Anyway. What can I do ye for?'

Tara read out the list, and Aggie filled a couple of paper carrier bags for her with granary and white loaves, loaf cakes and a large Victoria sponge – it was Tara's favourite, and she couldn't help it when she saw it on the cake stand. Dotty had said, one big cake, after all. Tara resisted the cinnamon buns, hot cross buns, lemon Danish, chocolate pastry twists and all manner of savoury treats that Aggie also offered her.

'If I take it all, you won't have anything left for anyone else,' she joked, turning away, already laden with two large bags and the Victoria sponge in a box. The market was busier now, and Tara frowned, thinking that she still had the vegetables and salad to get. She decided to take the bakery haul home first and come back to get the rest and started to retrace her steps to the Inn, balancing the large cake box on one upturned hand as she took both bags in the other.

'Watch out!'

Tara had re-joined the crowd, but because she was concentrating on holding the cake box steady and because the weight from the two heavy bags was making her arm ache, she didn't see the man who walking briskly through the crowd until she collided with him.

The man swore. The impact of his body hitting hers – she wasn't sure if it was his elbow or his shoulder, or the whole side of his torso – was more of a sudden shock than being painful in any way, and it made her cry out. Worse, she felt the cake box falter in her hand. As if it was in slow motion, she reacted, adjusted her grip and trying to right it, but the box fell from her grip.

Tara lunged for it, but it was no use. She was too slow, too clumsy to get it. At the last minute, she screwed up her face in horrified anticipation, waiting for the moment that the cake in its box would hit the ground and be forever smushed. No, no, no! She'd literally just bought the cake and she'd already dropped it. She'd have to go back and get another one.

'Phew. That was close,' the same voice said.

Cautiously, Tara opened her eyes. A man stood before her, holding the cake box intact in his hands, and smiling at her.

'I almost didn't get it,' he said, smiling. 'It was just luck I caught it... oh.'

But when their eyes met, the smile left his face, to be replaced with a look of incredulous shock.

'Oh, my... Tara?' he stammered.

It was his voice that did it. He'd changed – grown a beard, filled out. His shoulders were broader, his arms were bigger. He looked like he'd been lifting weights and not dancing. He was ten years older, and there were light creases around his eyes and a few individual grey hairs at his temples. But his voice was the same, and it was the voice she'd known all of her life. It was the voice that had asked him to marry her up on Queen's Point, all those years ago. It was the voice she'd known before it had deepened into a man's voice, when he was still a boy. She would have known Ramsay Fraser's voice anywhere.

SIX

'Hi, Ramsay.' Tara gulped and tried to arrange a smile on her face in what she hoped looked like a natural way, though this felt anything but natural.

'Tara. It's so good to see you.' His face had lit up, and now she could see the Ramsay she knew. She knew those sparkling eyes and the sense of mischief that lay behind them. Mischievous, but never cruel. Ramsay was the most kind hearted boy – man, now – she had ever known. He wouldn't so much as squish a spider if there was one in the bath, or skittering along the kitchen floor. No, he was one of those people who would carefully scoop it up on a piece of paper or under a glass and shake it gently outside.

'I... yeah. Sorry, it's just a bit of a shock,' Tara replied. She was aware that she was staring at him and realised it must look rude, but she couldn't help it: here was a face that she never thought she'd see again. Ramsay had been such an important person to her for so long that it had taken her years to get used to the fact she *didn't* see his face anymore. Her brain and her heart were resistant to the loss: Ramsay's face was a pattern that they had incorporated within them, and, after he'd gone, Tara had spent months – years – looking for his face in vain. If she saw someone who looked vaguely like Ramsay, she would stare at that face, taking comfort from the temporary familiarity; feeling a sense of perhaps, maybe, an edge of possibility that it might actually be him. Ramsay was just *right*, as far as her brain and her heart were concerned. His was a pattern that she had missed so deeply.

'Here.' He handed her the cake box. 'You should check it's okay.'

'I'm sure it's fine.' She took it, and her fingers grazed his. As soon as their skin touched, Tara felt Ramsay's familiar energy. It wasn't ever something you could properly describe, that instinctive combination of smell and feel and taste and that indefinable *something* about a person. She'd forgotten how Ramsay felt. There was something warm and comfortable about him; manly and protective, now, especially that he seemed to have grown into himself as a man, more than the limber young dancer she remembered.

The touch of him made her remember another day. A time when he had held her close and told her that he would never let go.

Her hand went to her neck: to the necklace that she still wore every day. Luckily, it was hidden under her sweatshirt. She felt strangely protective of it, not wanting him to see that she still wore it.

It was New Year's Eve. She remembered how cold it had been on Queen's Point that night. They had gone to sit in one of their favourite places – an old wooden bench at the end of the Point, past all the cottages, on the stony pathway that led all the way over to Gyle Head. They'd watched the fireworks at midnight, cuddled up to each other for warmth under two blankets, exchanging hot chocolate from a flask. When she kissed him to welcome in the new year, Ramsay had tasted of cocoa and the toasted cheese sandwiches she'd made in the Inn's kitchen and brought up with them, wrapped in foil.

'Happy new year,' she'd breathed, after they kissed. 'Are you sure you didn't want to go to the Inn for Hogmanay? It would have been warmer.' She'd snuggled up to Ramsay's shoulder as he'd tightened his arm around her. Her parents were hosting their usual new year's party, and there was a bonfire planned, as well as a ceilidh and lots of delicious food. Tara had spent two days helping Dotty prepare it all. She was nineteen, that year.

'No way. It's nicer up here. I only want to be with you, anyway.' He'd kissed the top of her head. 'But, Tara? I had something I wanted to ask you.'

'What?' She'd sat up, noticing his serious tone. It was amazing how well she remembered everything about that night, still, ten years later. 'Is everything okay?'

'Very okay,' he'd chuckled. He'd untucked the blanket from around his own shoulders and knelt down in front of her on the cold ground. *Tara Ballantyne, will you be my wife?* He'd handed her his half of the necklace then. *You have my whole heart.*

Those words had never left her. The memory of his face as he'd said it. The cold air around them and the moonlight on the loch. Of course, she had said *yes*.

She was so full of love for him, and in love with the idea of their future together. They wanted the same things: to win the international Highland dance competition, travel, then get good jobs – structural engineering for him, teaching for her. Tara had fantasised about teaching at the same little primary school in the village that they had both gone to. Then, a home in Loch Cameron. Two children. All the simple happiness that anyone wants.

'Right. Okay. Wow, Tara! I can't believe it's you!' Ramsay laughed suddenly, and she couldn't help but smile with him. In that moment, the fact that he'd just disappeared from her life so many years ago was eclipsed by the rawness and sudden impact of being in his presence again. As if no time had passed. She blushed, realising that she had been remembering that moment so clearly: the moment when Ramsay proposed to her, and she'd said yes.

'It's me.' She made a *tah-dah* gesture with her hands, which was difficult as she was holding the bags and the box still. She set the bags down on the street carefully to rest her arm, and wrapped both arms protectively around the cake box.

'What are you doing here?' he asked. 'I mean. I can see you're shopping. But, you don't live here, right? I mean, since I've been back, I haven't seen you around...' He trailed off. 'Sorry. I just can't quite take it in. It's weird, right?'

'It is,' Tara agreed. She wanted to reach out and touch his face: his cheek, his beard, his lips. 'I'm here for the summer, helping Mum and Dad. Mum broke her leg – a fall. I'm helping at the Inn until she can get around. I'm a teacher, so I get the summers free,' she added.

'Right. Ah, I'm sorry to hear about your mum.' Ramsay frowned. 'I've wanted to go in and say hello since I've been back, but... I guess I didn't think I'd get a warm welcome.' He bit his lip.

'How long have you...?' she asked. Part of her wanted to berate him for what he'd done, but she was so pleased to see him again that she just couldn't. Not right now. It was all still too unreal.

'About a month. It's weird being back.' He looked around him. 'Like, in so many ways, it just hasn't changed, you know? Same people. Same gossip. I've had a few looks, some people have said hi, but I've been keeping myself to myself.'

'How come you're...' *how come you're back?* was the question that Tara wanted to ask, but Ramsay frowned and reached into his pocket, bringing out his phone, which was buzzing.

'Sorry. Got to get this,' he said, smiling apologetically. He turned away as he answered, stepping away from her. 'Hello, Ramsay Fraser.'

Tara took him in from behind. He had always been tall, and even though he had filled out now, he still had that athletic grace from the years of dancing. Highland dancing involved a lot of jumps and twirls, often on tiptoe, and it not only kept you very fit but made your legs incredibly strong. She and Ramsay had also done a lot of ballet together, and she thought about the times he had lifted her into the air; of his strong hands on her waist, supporting her. She shivered involuntarily.

'Okay. I'll be there shortly.' He finished the phone call, looking distracted. 'Sorry. I've got to go. But we should catch up.'

'Sure. You know where I am, I guess.' She shrugged.

'Okay. Great. Soon, then.' He waved and jogged off through the crowd. It seemed as though he was suddenly desperate to get away and Tara wondered if she had said something wrong. Or whether it was just the sudden realisation on his part of what they would have to say to each other: the truth that he owed her.

But, perhaps there was a truth that Tara also owed him. That was the thought that she really didn't want to face, and yet it was the one that had never stopped bothering her, since the day Ramsay had disappeared from Loch Cameron. Had it been her fault? And, if it had, what had happened to Ramsay, all those years ago? Had she been responsible for something so terrible that he had cut himself off from everything that was good in his life?

Tara didn't know. But he was here, which was completely unexpected. And she was in equal parts elated, guilty and angry.

She walked back to the Inn with the bags and the cake box, bewildered by her feelings. But, one thing was true: she was also relieved, because there was a part of her that had always wondered whether Ramsay had finally either lashed out at his father in a way that he couldn't recover from – or, his dad had finally hurt him badly. As a child of an abusive family, Ramsay had always been at risk, despite the fact that Dotty and Eric had tried their best to protect him. And when he had gone missing – despite the letter she'd had – Tara knew that her parents had thought the same dark thoughts as she had.

The fact that Ramsay was alive was a huge relief to Tara. Because, there had always been a possibility that he might not have been.

SEVEN

'Tea could be stronger. I'd have left the bag in.' Dotty opened the china teapot and peered inside it. 'How many did ye use?'

'One.' Tara opened the floral chintz curtains in her parents' bedroom and let in the morning sunlight. She'd helped Dotty sit up in bed and put a knitted bedjacket around her mother's shoulders after bringing her breakfast on a tray and setting it carefully over Dotty's legs. Then, she'd gone to the window. This was the order that her mother had specified the day before, because, in her words, *I dinnae want the whole o' Loch Cameron seein' me in me nightie, Tara.*

Tara had really wanted to point out to her mother that not only was her bedroom on the first floor, and so it was deeply unlikely that anyone would see her from a vantage point outside, but Dotty was also in bed under the covers, and wearing a long-sleeved nightdress. Quite what her mother imagined anyone could see of her, apart from brushed cotton and her hair slightly askew, Tara had no idea. Still, she knew that it wasn't best to argue with Dotty.

'I'd usually put two bags in,' Dotty instructed. 'Make sure ye do two tomorrow, hen.'

'Yes, Mum.' Tara returned to sit at the end of Dotty's bed. She'd been thinking about how to tell her mother the news about Ramsay, but she hadn't said anything the day before. She'd still been processing it herself. 'Errr... I have news.'

'Do you?' Dotty chewed a piece of toast. 'What?'

'When I was at the market yesterday, I saw Ramsay Fraser.' *Better just to say it in one go,* Tara thought. *Just get it out.*

'Oh, did ye?' Dotty pursed her lips. 'I thought that might happen, though perhaps no' on yer first trip out.' She sighed. 'I was goin' tae tell ye, darlin'.'

'You knew?' Tara asked, incredulously.

'Only just. A few days ago. I saw him on the high street. Didnae say hello, but it was him all right,' Dotty told her. 'I havenae spoken tae him. The day after I saw him, I had my fall, an' I forgot all aboot it. Are ye all right, poppet? It must've been a shock. I must say, it was a shock tae me too.'

'It was, yeah. We had a brief chat and then he had to run off.' Tara let out a long breath. 'Agh. It was weird. But I think there was a part of me that always thought he might be dead. I know it was stupid, but...' she trailed off.

'Aye, I thought the same, over the years. Ye never know. Your father an' I even filed a missing person's report at the time, hen. We were that worried that someone had done somethin' awful tae him.' Dotty shook her head. 'His family were terrible. I dinnae if ye ever really knew the Frasers. We kept Ramsay away from them as much as we could.'

'I do remember you asking him over all the time. And he had his own room here.' Tara nodded.

'Hmm. I'll tell ye about them one day. Make your hair turn white.' Dotty closed her eyes. 'Still. Now he's back, what'll you do?'

'I don't know, Mum. It's a lot to take in.'

'Aye. Ye could start dancin' together again,' Dotty suggested. 'It always made ye so happy.'

'Mum. I teach Primary 4. When am I going to find time for a Highland dancing career?' Tara snapped. She'd never felt that Dotty had taken her teaching seriously; she'd always wanted Tara to be a dancer.

'Listen, whit's fer ye won't go past ye.' Dotty raised an eyebrow. 'Maybe Ramsay bein' back, is a sign. That ye should start dancin' again. It made ye so happy. Up there, on the stage, free as a bird.' Her mother looked misty for a moment, deep in her memories.

'Mum. I'm way too old for that. I haven't even done any cardio in years,' Tara protested. 'And, anyway... it's not about that. Seeing Ramsay... it's really messing with my mind. I grieved him like he was dead, Mum. And now he turns up, back in my life, just like that.' She realised that she was choking back tears. 'It's a lot.'

'All's I'm sayin' is, think aboot it.' Dotty sighed again. 'Dancin' was such a happy time for ye. I used tae watch ye up on stage an' be so proud o' how free ye were, in yerself. Ye were always so bright, so happy. I'm not sayin' yer not now, but some o' that... *radiance*, it's no' there anymore.'

'Oh. Thanks a lot.' Tara felt immediately defensive.

'I dinnae mean it like that. It's just because I care.' Dotty looked uncomfortable.

Tara felt as though she couldn't ever make Dotty understand how heartbroken she was when Ramsay left. Perhaps that was just the way that her mother was: she'd always been brisk and kind, not one for showing deep emotion. Dotty and Eric had been supportive when Ramsay had disappeared, but Tara had never really felt that they'd understood just how deeply it had hurt her. It had taken years for Tara to recover from the loss, and she'd thrown herself into her teaching career to distract herself.

Teaching was consuming, needed focus and took up most of her free time with marking and planning and involving herself in various after school clubs and pastoral care for the children that needed it. After she'd finished university and her teaching qualifications and got her first job, Tara had put herself forward for as many extra responsibilities as she could. She wanted to fill her time so that she didn't have to think about Ramsay. And she'd got so used to pushing the memory of him into a corner of her mind – behind a locked door where all of her memories of him lurked – that when she'd seen him again, it was a shock. That door had been blown open, and all of her memories had been jolted free.

Yet, there was a truth in what Dotty was saying, too – once, Tara had been so carefree. In the days when she'd been a dancer, she'd had a freedom in her spirit and her soul that wasn't connected to Ramsay or anyone else. Dance had been her way to connect to that sense of being that she'd heard described on social media as a *flow state*. A sense of being completely in the moment, of feeling connected to something profound and just being in a state of joy.

She didn't experience joy anymore, not in that same way of complete freedom, complete abandonment to the moment. Teaching gave her plenty of heart-full moments with the children, who she genuinely loved, but it wasn't the same.

She didn't know how to explain that to her mother, who was looking at her concernedly.

'Aww, hen. I'm sorry.' Dotty handed her a tissue from a box by the bed. 'Come and give me a hug. Gentle, mind ye.'

Tara hugged her mum briefly around the shoulders and blew her nose, sitting back at the end of the bed. 'Ugh. Sorry.'

'No' a bit o' it, poppet. It's a shock,' Dotty sighed. 'Ye know, you've always put me in mind o' my aunt Agnes,' she added. 'She was independent. Bookish. Emotional, like ye. And a teacher, of course.'

'I know.' This was familiar ground for Tara. Her similarity to her spinster great-aunt was a common theme of conversation between her and Dotty, even though Dotty never seemed to remember the fact that they'd talked about Agnes before. 'She never married. Taught at the primary school all her life.'

'Aye, she did.' Dotty nodded sagely. 'Became a teacher after the war. She would only have been young while all that was happenin', I think, and then there were more jobs for women after the war, weren't there? Emancipation, an' all that. I'm not sure what qualifications she had. Not like you, probably. But she loved it. Never married.'

'Thanks, Mum.' Tara rolled her eyes. 'Are you saying I'm destined to be a spinster all my life?'

'No! Just, that she was happy wi' her life. That's no' a bad thing,' Dotty said, defensively. 'Loved books too. Ye know, we have some o' her books down in the bar. The poetry ones, leather bound. Ye'll have seen them.'

'I don't remember seeing them. But okay.' Tara shrugged. 'I'll check them out.' She still felt very glum, and the prospect of leafing through great-aunt Agnes' old poetry books wasn't particularly thrilling. Plus, she had a million chores to do.

'Hmm. Ye should take them back with ye, probably. Bein' the family bookworm,' Dotty said. 'Listen, hen. It'll be okay, with Ramsay. I know it's ootae the blue, him comin' back. But it's a good thing, isn't it? Ye might have a second chance at happiness. I've prayed fer it. I really did.'

'I don't know, Mum. It's been a long time.' Tara still felt utterly overwhelmed by the impact of seeing Ramsay. 'I'm not even thinking about that right now.'

'Well, perhaps ye should,' Dotty said, quietly.

But there was the thought in the back of her brain that she couldn't get over. What if, rather than a second chance at happiness, she'd done something terrible – something that had ruined her chances of reunion with Ramsay forever?

EIGHT

'You are *joking!*' Carla sounded like she was standing in the middle of a motorway. 'After all this time?'

'I know. It's crazy. We honestly thought he might have died or something. It was that abrupt of an end.' Tara was sitting on a bench on Queen's Point, a lovely promontory of rock that over-looked Loch Cameron, on the phone to Carla. There were several whitewashed cottages on the Point, all with their doors and window frames painted in blue or sometimes green. The cottages were generally looked after, and the cottage gardens were abundant with flowers of all kinds, it being the height of summer.

'Dear lord. Are you all right?' Carla asked, sounding concerned.

'I guess. It's weird. Do you mind if I don't talk about it right now?'

'Sure. Here if you need me, when you do want to,' her flat-mate said.

'Thanks. Tell me about Berlin.' Tara watched as a fishing boat chugged lazily across the loch below.

'Hotel's nice. Glad I booked it, otherwise we'd have been

staying in a hostel with no internal plumbing,' Carla began. 'It actually backs onto the Berlin Zoo, so you can have your breakfast and watch the giraffes. Quite trippy.'

'That sounds fun, although I don't really approve of zoos.' Tara smiled, glad to hear her friend's voice. She'd been feeling out of sorts since running into Ramsay, and it was good to talk to someone other than her mum and dad about it.

'No, well, you're right, of course. But, when in Rome.' Tara could practically hear Carla shrug. 'So, how did he look? Ramsay?'

'*Carla.*'

'Ah, come on. Otherwise I'll have to tell you all about me and Craig, and I really don't want to,' Carla said with a sigh.

'He looked... like a bigger, more buff and manly version of himself, if you must know. But, otherwise, exactly the same,' Tara said. 'What about you and Craig? I thought Craig only had eyes for me. That he was going to be horribly disappointed that I didn't come to Berlin.'

'Hmm. Well, it turns out that Craig and I got on quite well on the plane,' Carla said. 'The flight was just long enough for me to get just tipsy enough to...'

'To what?'

'Fancy him a bit,' Carla muttered. 'Sorry, if it's noisy here it's because I'm standing by Checkpoint Charlie, and there are all these bloody tourists everywhere.'

'You're a tourist.'

'Fair point. So, Ramsay looks good, does he?' Carla asked, innocently.

'I don't know. Yes. Maybe. I wasn't really looking. It was all a bit of a shock.'

'You should get it on with him again. He's the love of your life.'

'Carla. I am not going to *get it on* with Ramsay Fraser. He broke my heart.'

'Eh. You're always going to get your heart broken at some point anyway. Might as well get some nookie while you're at it.'

'What a way to look at it.' Tara suppressed a laugh. 'And don't think I've forgotten what you just said about Craig. What did you do?'

'Oh, what haven't I done, at this point? Those PE boys have a lot of stamina, it turns out.'

'Carla!'

'What? Look, if you were here, then you'd have taken me to all the museums and we'd have found the most darling little restaurants and, I don't know, probably gone boating on a lake or something innocent and lovely. But, you're not here, and you've left me in Berlin for a week with a group of unhinged, alcoholic Drama and French teachers, and one actually quite hot PE bod. What else am I going to do?'

'Well, I'm glad you're enjoying yourself.' Tara sighed, looking over the loch. 'It's weird being back. I keep coming to places like where I am now, and reliving the past. And my mum's driving me mad. I mean, I love her, but she's hard work, as a patient. She hates not being able to run around and do all her jobs, and be in charge. Mind you, she's still bossing us around from her bed.'

'She sounds brilliant. Props to your mum,' Carla said. 'Listen, I've got to go. But try not to be too hard on yourself, okay? You're back in your home town and living with your parents for six weeks, so it's basically going to be like visiting for Christmas, but on crack. Plus, you've run into the love of your life that you thought was dead or disappeared or whatever, and that's playing games with your mind. So, basically, just take it a day at a time, okay?'

'Okay. Thanks. I'm sorry I'm not in Berlin.'

'I'm sorry too, babe. But, to be fair, I am now having a lot of sex. So, swings and roundabouts. Speak soon. Love you.'

'Love you too.' Tara ended the call, and put her phone in her pocket.

She gazed out over the loch, and took in a deep breath of fresh, cool air. She'd forgotten how good the air was here; Dotty had always said that the air in Loch Cameron was *a tonic*.

Talking to Carla had been *a tonic*; it had been good to hear her friend's voice. Since arriving in Loch Cameron, rather than feeling that she was reconnecting to her roots, Tara had felt unmoored from the normality she knew. What she knew was her school, her flat, Carla, the nights out at the pub with the St Clare's Massive. She wasn't part of Loch Cameron anymore, and hadn't been for a long time. Meeting Ramsay again had just made her feel even stranger, as if the last ten years hadn't happened at all. And, it had brought back the guilt she'd felt every day for the past ten years. That she had been the reason he had disappeared in the first place. She still didn't know if what she'd done had caused it, and the thought weighed heavily on her.

Still, there was something about the land here that she had forgotten. There were her special places – out of the way nooks and crannies where she had used to come, alone, with a book, when she had wanted some time alone. The oak trees on Queen's Point; the little beach at the edge of the loch.

Yes, it felt strange and disconnected to be back in Loch Cameron and transported away suddenly from her ordinary life. Yet, the land itself was familiar, and she was grateful for the comfort that she found in its quiet shade, in its clean air and the soft trees that sighed in the breeze. This was what felt like home, and it was a peace she'd forgotten for a very long time.

NINE

'The thing is, I booked a king size, ensuite room. But the ensuite has a bath and not a shower.' The woman – Tara estimated she was in her late thirties – stood at the reception desk with her hands on her hips. She was petite, perhaps five feet one or two, wearing high heels with a platform sole and leather-look leggings and a fluffy white T shirt. Tara thought she looked very pretty, but she did wonder at the practicality of those heels on Loch Cameron High Street's cobbles.

'Right... okay.' Tara frowned. 'You're in room six, aren't you? That's got the roll-top bath.'

'Yes. It's huge. I can hardly get in and out of it.' The woman sniffed while her boyfriend stood behind her, looking awkward.

'Oh. But you would have seen pictures of the room when you booked online?' Tara said, looking at Dotty's laptop and the online booking system she used, which was open on it. 'Ms ... Hemsley?' she added, checking the booking name on her computer.

Dotty had explained that most bookings came in online these days, though some people still called by phone and asked for availability. Occasionally, her mum had said, they still had more elderly guests who would write a letter to enquire about availability, and expect a handwritten letter back to confirm. In fact, Dotty had directed Tara to a pad of special Loch Cameron Inn notepaper and envelopes in the reception desk drawer that were to be used for just such a purpose, though had expressly told Tara that if she did receive any letters asking to make bookings, Tara should bring the writing pad up to her and she would reply, because, in Dotty's words, she had *by far the nicer handwriting, dear*.

'Emma. Emma Hemsley. Yes, I did. But it had a shower when I looked online,' the woman argued. 'How am I supposed to wash my hair?'

Tara opened the Loch Cameron Inn's website, clicked on 'Rooms' and went to the pictures of room six, which very definitely showcased the room's beautiful, large, white cast iron roll-top bath with its black cast iron claw-footed base, and no shower.

'There's not a shower there, I'm afraid,' Tara said, carefully, knowing that the customer was always right, even when, on occasions like this, they were absolutely, one hundred per cent wrong. 'There is a shower attachment for the taps, and I've used it to wash my hair. It's pretty good, actually. Good pressure,' she added.

'Well, that's not good enough,' Emma argued. 'I have a very particular hair washing and conditioning routine. I need a power shower.'

'Well, I'm afraid I can't help you there. All the rest of the rooms are booked.' Tara frowned, checking the booking diary. She was reminded of the demanding parents at Lomond Primary, many of whom also seemed to think that they were owed perfection, and that their children were all special geniuses, cruelly under-appreciated by a dysfunctional school system. Whereas, in fact, Lomond Primary was far and away the most responsive, well-resourced and child-focused school Tara had ever worked at.

'Well, that's not good enough!' Emma raised her voice and actually stamped her foot. 'This is our holiday and you're not making any attempt to correct your error! You're going to ruin our lovely time away!' Her voice rose and she looked on the verge of tears.

Tara exchanged a brief glance with the boyfriend, who put a gentle hand on Emma's arm.

'Maybe you should try the shower attachment, love,' he suggested, querulously. 'It might be fine. And you look lovely anyway.'

'Shut up, Colin,' Emma snapped, and shook his hand off. Tara raised her eyebrows, and wondered what her mum would do with a difficult customer. Tara was inclined to give this little madam a piece of her mind, but she knew she couldn't.

'Okay,' she said, in her most placating voice. The voice she used on the head of the PTA at Lomond Primary, and on the most troubled children at the school when they got into a tantrum and needed to be taken into the quiet room for a bit. 'Let's think about what we can do. What about if you use the shower in my room? And, as an extra way to make up for the... confusion,' Tara said, diplomatically, 'I can gift you dinner on the house one night this week. I recommend tomorrow, if you're available, as we have some lovely salmon coming in. From the Laird's own fish farm.'

'Oh. Well, that's very nice of you,' Emma said, haltingly. 'I'd probably need to use the shower twice. Or three times. Every other day,' she said.

'That will be fine. Just let me know when you need to use it. I'm working most of the time anyway.' Tara smiled.

'The offer of dinner's really kind, thank you.' Colin gave her a grateful smile that said *thank you, I know she's a bit much.* 'Salmon sounds lovely tomorrow, doesn't it, darling?'

'It does sound quite nice,' Emma admitted, begrudgingly. Tara wondered what it would take to make her actually enthusiastic about anything. The roll-top bath was a real feature, usually: room six got booked all the time, and people even shared pictures of it on social media because of the amazing view over the loch that you got, lying in it and looking out of the big window beyond. It was a lovely room: really, the best at the Inn.

'Great. Happy to help.' Tara smiled until she thought her face was going to stretch permanently. The couple made their way out, and Tara watched them go, waiting for them to leave the Inn completely until she relaxed her face, stuck her tongue out and let out a long sigh. How did Dotty do this every day? Being a primary school teacher was one thing, but customer service was something else completely.

Tara was starting to realise that though she'd felt for a long time that her mother hadn't understood her feelings or her life, it was possible that she'd also had a certain idea about who Dotty was, that wasn't all that accurate. Tara had never considered what it took to keep the Inn running and for it to be as successful as it was – she was starting to realise that Dotty had to be far more sensitive to other people than she'd ever given her mother credit for.

Tara was happy to help, but this had never been her dream – and, customers like Demanding Emma weren't doing anything to change her mind.

And, the dreams she'd once had... well, she didn't think about them anymore. She couldn't. It was too painful.

TEN

'You're so kind to help me with this.' The woman took a paperclip from between her lips with a frown and slid it onto a stack of handouts, then picked up a new sheaf of papers to do the same. 'I can imagine your mum's keeping you pretty busy at the Inn.'

'She is, but it's nice to have a bit of a break, to be honest.' Tara stapled a stack of paper together into a booklet and reached for the next one.

'I love that *this* is your break. Stapling handouts.'

Tara had been walking past Loch Cameron Primary school, on her way back from posting some letters for her mum, when she had stopped to watch some building work which was happening in the grounds. It was strange to see her old primary school, and she'd stood there for a moment, taking it all in: the little concrete playground and square stretch of green grass behind it, with the small building itself squat in the middle. It wasn't anything fancy, but it held good memories.

It was funny, how when you were a kid, school seemed so big. Yet, in reality, it was a tiny little place, with a school hall no bigger than a large dining room, and the classrooms really only big enough for ten or fifteen children at a time. Luckily, the class sizes at Loch Cameron Primary had always been small, as there weren't that many children in the village. Or, there hadn't been, once upon a time. Clearly, things were changing.

As she'd stood there, lost in her memories, a woman with a shoulder length black bob and white denim dungarees had come out of the building and walked over. She'd introduced herself as the Headmistress, Emily Cargyle, and when Tara had explained that she was an ex-pupil, Emily had invited her in for a cup of tea.

'You aren't any good with making posters, are you? I'm trying to design one for our Variety Show event but I'm absolutely rubbish.' Emily led Tara into her office and busied herself with a kettle and some mugs in the corner.

'I'm not bad. D'you want me to take a look?' Tara offered.

'Goodness, yes. You're a lifesaver.' Emily placed a mug of tea in front of Tara and spun the screen of a laptop around to show Tara what she was working on.

LOCH CAMERON'S GOT TALENT
PRIMARY SCHOOL FUNDRAISER
HELP US FUND A NEW CLASSROOM
SINGER, DANCER, COMEDIAN? WE WANT YOU!!

There was an image of the old-timey World War One man from the recruitment poster at the bottom of the poster, and some fairly cringeworthy clip art graphics under that, showing people dancing and holding a microphone.

'What do you think?' Emily asked, frowning. 'It's a work in progress.'

'Errr... It's good!' Tara said, brightly, like she would to one of the kids in her class. 'Maybe the World War thing is a bit strong for a talent contest? Just a thought.'

'You don't have to be kind. I don't know what I was thinking.' Emily sighed. 'Since I've been a headteacher, I don't really do this kind of thing anymore. Not that I was brilliant at it before.'

'I teach Primary. In Glasgow, though. I'm just here for the holidays,' Tara said.

'Oh, what a coincidence! I feel like this is fated.' Emily winked at her. 'Do you want a job? There's one going. Two, actually.'

'Ha. No, but do you want me to have a go at the poster? I quite like doing stuff like that.'

'Please. I need all the help I can get.'

Tara sat down, tilting the laptop towards her.

'The thing is,' Emily sipped her tea, 'if we can't recruit two new teachers by the start of next term, we may have to close.'

'Close the school? Surely not!' Tara changed the font of the poster to something that looked fun and readable, instead of Emily's boring block font in black, and swapped out the aggressive image for a friendly rainbow background.

She looked up, appalled.

'It's the last thing we want to do,' Emily told her with a sigh. 'But, Miss Bly is leaving at the end of term, and we're also having to accept a double form entry for the first time this year, because of the increased demand. Hence the new classroom. It's one thing for the powers that be to build new houses, but the community has to shift to accommodate the needs of all those new people.'

'The new houses on Gyle Head?'

'Yeah. I'm not against having more people in the village, but when you build new homes, you have to allow for the local infrastructure to support it,' Emily said. 'The laird and the developer have been great, overall, but I don't think they thought about the school. Just sort of expected us to cope.'

'That's always what people do with schools. And hospitals.' Tara replaced the clip art images with some more sophisticated ones, and reordered the text a little. 'Progressively take away our resources and just expect us to continue doing everything to a high standard, out of the love in our hearts. Thing is, we do.' She shook her head. 'In a way I wish all teachers and nurses would just give up overperforming so that the powers that be would realise just how much of society is being run on good will and kind hearts.'

'Oh. Agree, one thousand per cent. Are you sure you don't want the job?' Emily made prayer hands.

Tara laughed. 'I've got a school in Glasgow to go back to. I'm just here for the summer helping my parents out.'

Not that I'm not tempted. Tara thought of the icy atmosphere in the staff room back at Lomond Primary with a shiver.

'Of course.' Emily nodded. 'Well, if you change your mind, I need two of you. So...'

'I'll think about it. And keep my ear to the ground if any teacher friends need something,' Tara offered. 'There. How's that?' She turned the screen around to Emily.

'Oh, my sainted aunt. That looks a thousand per cent nicer! Thank you, Tara!' Emily cooed. 'You are a lifesaver. I can tell you're a primary teacher. I just threw that at you and you ran with it.'

'It's all right. Happy to help. So, the fundraiser is for the new classroom? Can you get one built in that time?' Tara asked. In fact, it was nice to do something school-oriented. She didn't mind helping out at the Inn, but even though she disliked the politics and the pushy parents at Lomond Primary, she was missing her pupils. The children were lovely, and she'd always liked all the crafty class prep you had to do as a primary teacher. Teaching wasn't the problem: it had always been a joy.

'Not in time for September. We're having to bring in a temporary classroom for a year, or until we can get it built. The laird can cover that, he says, but ideally, if we can help out with the costs for a new classroom it would help him out. The developer can contribute, but he says he didn't have money in the budget for that.' She rolled her eyes. 'Tell me something I haven't heard before.'

'I'm happy to help more, if I can,' Tara said.

'That would be great. We'd asked your mum if we could do the Variety Show at the Inn and she said it was okay.' Emily nodded. 'I can see from your face that she hadn't mentioned that to you yet, though.'

'No, but I'll ask her about it when I get home,' Tara chuckled. 'I expect she'd love to have something to think about. Take her mind off the leg.'

'Hm. How is the leg?'

'Fine, really. I mean, she's in pain of course, bless her, but she's being brave, overall.' Tara sighed. 'Mind you, I do love my mum, but she is an absolute nightmare as a patient. Last night she had me folding napkins into swans just in case anyone ordered room service. I'm not sure why swans were vital.'

'That's mothers for you.' Emily grinned. 'Mine keeps telling me that my biological clock is ticking. *Only a few years left for me to be a grandmother, Emily Sue.*' Emily rolled her eyes. 'I've told her a million times, I don't want kids. I have enough of them at work.'

Tara laughed softly, nodding. What she didn't say was that Dotty and her didn't have that conversation, because Dotty – as much of a gossip as she was – knew how much Tara had wanted a family of her own. And how deeply it had hurt her to have lost Ramsay.

'Mums,' she agreed, noncommittally.

Tara felt a sense of strangeness: the ghosts of the past had returned, and being back at her old school certainly wasn't helping. It was weird to be there: she felt like she could turn a corner and see her child self – skipping, dancing, laughing. She felt a pang of homesickness for that little girl.

Though it felt odd to be at the school, it also felt nice to be there: a way for her to be with that little girl part of her, and to be with her memories of Ramsay, too. Their childhood together had been so pure. Being in the school again, Tara found that she was able to separate those memories from what came after. It wasn't little Tara and little Ramsay who were at fault now, or who had created difficulties by deserting each other. Their love was as pure and innocent as it had ever been, and Tara realised that it was good for her to know that.

'I'm sorry for the noise.' Emily nodded to the window of the classroom, where a group of builders were digging the foundations for the new classroom with a big yellow machine.

'How long are they going to be at it?' Tara asked.

'Ugh. Months. We need them to get as much as they can get done in the summer holidays, but they're going to need to be on site in term time too.' Emily rolled her eyes. 'Still, we can't use the temporary classroom that long. Those things aren't built for long term use, though I remember going all the way through primary school in one when I was a kid.'

'I can believe it.' Tara peered out of the window at the builders. 'With schools, it's always a question of *how long can we make this work?* not *what's the ideal situation here?*'

'Hmm. You get it.' Emily finished pinning together her papers and stood up, going to the window. 'Sure you don't want to come and work here? I'd love to have you.'

'I don't think I can,' Tara replied apologetically. 'I'd miss my kids. And... there's some personal stuff going on that might make it a bit difficult to be here.'

'Oh?' Emily turned to her. 'Spill the beans. I could do with some intrigue in my life, even if it's secondhand.'

'Oh, it's kind of complicated.' Tara didn't want to talk about everything she was feeling just yet. 'Maybe another time.'

'Of course. I'll butt out. Always happy to lend an ear, though.' Emily returned her gaze to the window, frowning. 'What on earth are they doing out there? They've all stopped and are staring at the ground. Hey!' she knocked on the windowpane and held up her hands questioningly. 'What are they up to? The classroom's never going to get built if they keep taking extended coffee breaks.'

'I think that guy's waving us over.' Tara looked out to the excavation site outside. 'Shall we go and see what he wants?'

'Oh, for goodness' sake,' Emily tutted, irritated. 'Fine. But, really, are they not capable of doing anything without supervision? Come on.'

Tara followed Emily outside onto the playground and towards the field, which she remembered so well from her own childhood at the little primary school.

'What seems to be the problem?' Emily approached the group of builders, who were looking down into a large hole. 'I don't want to play the bossy headmistress card here, fellas, but we are on a bit of a deadline. You know we want to get as much of the new classroom done by the time term starts, which is in...' she consulted her phone 'Three and a half weeks. Ah, Ramsay. Can *you* explain what's going on?'

Ramsay?

Tara looked up.

Surely, it couldn't be.

It wasn't that common a name, but there could be another Ramsay in Loch Cameron. It didn't have to be him.

It didn't have to be the man who had broken her heart so finally and completely, ten years ago, and left her a husk of a woman.

It didn't have to be the only man that she still compared all other men to. The one that they failed to measure up to in every way.

But, it was.

Ramsay Fraser was approaching the building crew, wearing a hard hat and carrying a clip board. Tara looked around her frantically, but there was nowhere to go.

'Oh. Tara,' he said, as he saw her, his expression unreadable. 'Hello.'

If she could have jumped in the hole in the ground in front of her right then, and, somehow, magically disappeared, then she definitely would have.

'Hello, Ramsay.' She nodded, politely, feeling a blush creep up her neck.

ELEVEN

'We found something,' one of the men said, pointing at the hole in the ground. 'Looks like a metal canister of some description. It's not piping, or anything attached to the building.'

'What d'you mean, a canister?' Emily walked to the edge of the hole and looked down.

'That's my guess. Something metal that sounds semi-hollow when you tap it with a spade.' The man shrugged. 'We have to dig it out, anyway, to get down further. So, you might as well look at it now.'

'Fair enough. Dig it up.' Emily tucked her hands under her armpits and exchanged a look with Tara. 'Do you know each other, then?' she whispered as Ramsay turned away. 'I sense an atmosphere.'

Tara nodded. 'I'll tell you later,' she murmured.

'Intriguing.' Emily raised an eyebrow.

'Nice to see you, Tara.' Ramsay appeared at Tara's elbow as the machine brought up a small metal box.

'Hi,' she replied, not knowing what to say. 'So, you're... you work on the building site?'

'No. I'm involved with the planning. Just popped in to see

how they were getting on. Looks like I chose the right moment,' he said.

'I guess it's not every day that there's an exciting discovery in the grounds of a school.' Tara tried to think of something neutral to say.

'I mean seeing you, actually. But, sure.' He shot her an unreadable look.

'Oh. Right.' Tara desperately wanted the earth to swallow her up, and thought for a moment at the sheer irony of life with the actual hole in the ground right in front of her that had opened up, like some kind of living metaphor. When Ramsay looked away, Emily made a face at her and mouthed *what is going on between you two?*

'Oh! You know, I think I might remember what this is,' Tara said, as the tin canister was dug out and handed up to them. It was a large coffee urn, and a memory sparked in her mind as she looked at it. 'When we were kids, we made time capsules and buried them. I think this is one of them. Don't you remember?' She looked up at Ramsay, her excitement temporarily chasing away her awkwardness at seeing him again.

'No. We did this?' Ramsay frowned. 'I don't remember. But I don't remember a lot of stuff, I guess.'

'You went to school together? Here?' Emily looked from Ramsay to Tara. 'So, you're old friends, then?'

'Kind of.' Tara really didn't want to explain it; Ramsay looked away, also looking uncomfortable.

'No way! I didn't know that had happened. Let's look inside.' Emily took the coffee tin from the builder and tried the lid. 'Hmmm. It's a bit stuck. Let's take it over to one of the tables.'

The three of them went to one of the brightly painted picnic tables that were dotted around the playground and sat down. This table was labelled FRIENDSHIP BENCH. It felt surreal being there with Ramsay, and more than a little cringe-

worthy standing around a brightly painted FRIENDSHIP
BENCH with Ramsay Fraser, of all people.

Emily placed the tin on the table and, this time, managed to
wedge the lid open.

'Oh, my,' she breathed. 'Look! All the little letters.' She
pulled out a handful and passed a collection of folded pieces of
paper to Tara, taking out more for herself. 'You're right. These
are all dated 2003. Twenty odd years ago.'

'This might be our class,' Tara marvelled, opening the first
letter. 'My wishes for the future,' she read aloud. 'Ben Travis,
age 7. I wish for world peace, and a tortoise.'

'Awww. I hope he got the tortoise,' Emily chuckled. 'How
old are you? Would this boy have been in your class, then?'

'Twenty-nine. I think so, or maybe the year below? I don't
specifically remember a Ben Travis, but I think there was a Ben,
somewhere,' Tara mused. 'In fact. I'm almost sure of it. I mean,
there were only ten kids in our class. Probably sixty or seventy
kids in the whole school at that time.'

'That's about the number of letters, looking at this.' Emily
counted a handful of papers and reached into the tin for more.
'You must have known each other pretty well, then.' She raised
an eyebrow, obviously keen for more details, but Tara shrugged.

'Reasonably well. It's been a long time, though,' she added,
pointedly. Ramsay coughed and looked away, clearly feeling
uncomfortable.

Good, Tara thought. *I'm glad you're uncomfortable. I've
been uncomfortable for the last ten years.*

'Listen to this, this is cute. Tinkerbell McCallister, age 6. I
wish for fairies to be real. Don't we all,' Emily continued.

'Tinkerbell. That's adventurous.' Tara was more or less
ignoring Ramsay and she wondered if it was obvious that she
couldn't get it into her head that he was there at all. It was still
so weird, seeing him, in person. When she'd spent so long
thinking she was never going to see him again.

'I've got a Dante at the moment in Primary 4. No Beatrice, unfortunately. Or, fortunately, depending on how you look at it,' Emily mused as she looked at the letters.

'I guess you didn't get the perfect combination of parents who are fans of renaissance Italian literature,' Ramsay commented.

'Indeed not. Goodness knows why not. It's all I can talk about, most days.'

'Haha. Some parents don't seem to care about the play-ground test, do they?' Ramsay grinned. 'You know. Like naming a dog. If you're not happy shouting the name across a play-ground, don't name your kid that.'

'Well, I guess Tinkerbell's parents were okay with it.' Emily chuckled, again. 'Takes all sorts. She likely shortened it to Tink, or Bella. It's quite cute really.'

Tara felt an unreasonable, sudden jealousy at the easy back-and-forth between Emily and Ramsay. They seemed to know each other fairly well, and Tara wondered why. Was it just because of the building project, or was there more going on here?

And would it be any of your business if it was? She stopped herself.

No, it wouldn't.

'Oh.' Tara had looked back at the piece of paper in her hand, and it made her stop in her tracks. The handwriting was so eerily familiar. She swallowed, hard.

'What is it? Emily asked, leaning over.

'I... I think this is... mine,' Tara said, in a low voice.

'No way! That's crazy. Let me see?' Emily leaned over to look. 'Tara Ballantyne, aged 8. I wish to inspire and help others. Awww. That's so sweet,' she read aloud.

'I don't remember writing that. I would have thought I'd write something about dancing, or travelling to other countries or something.' Tara gazed at the small piece of paper in disbelief that something she had made, touched, marked in such a way, was back in her hands. It was odd. Disquieting, in a way.

'Wow. Can I see?' Ramsay asked, softly. Tara met his eyes. There was a terrible sadness there, and her heart clenched in response to it. She handed him the note.

He held it for a moment, lowering his eyes, then handed it back to her.

'Yeah. That's weird to see,' he said, looking away.

'I think we'd all be surprised if we could meet our childhood selves,' Emily replied, thoughtfully. 'I wonder what I would have written. Probably something about Sylvanian Families, but, maybe I'm doing myself a disservice by saying that.'

'I must have been feeling very socially conscious that day.' Tara set her eight-year-old-self's letter to one side. 'It's strange to see my handwriting. The thought that I put that ink on the page, twenty-odd years ago, and here it is now.' She was prattling on, following Emily's lead, but she was doing it to mask the sheer awkwardness of the situation.

'Absolutely. It's crazy,' Emily agreed. 'Oh. Listen to this one. This is heartbreaking. He's only written *have a happy family*. That's all he wanted.'

'Whose was that?' Tara asked. But, she knew.

She knew from Ramsay's expression as he turned his head with a look of dawning horror on his face.

Tara's heart felt like it stopped for a moment: a clench of tension in her chest.

'Let's see. Where's the name. Ah. Ram–' Emily broke off and looked right at Ramsay. 'Ramsay Fraser,' she finished, weakly.

TWELVE

'It was a long time ago.' Ramsay shoved his hands into his pockets and stepped away from the table. 'Anyway, I should get back to the lads.'

He turned and walked away. Tara and Emily exchanged glances.

'Ramsay,' Tara called after him, but he waved a hand dismissively at them both.

'Have to get on,' he called, over his shoulder.

'Oh dear.' Emily made a face at Tara. 'I wouldn't have read it aloud if I'd known. I'm so sorry if I made that awkward. I could sense some weird vibes between you, but I thought it was just maybe because you used to go to school together. I mean, that can be strange, can't it?'

'We did go to school together. Grew up together. We were engaged at one point.' Tara sighed, and shook her head. 'It's a long story.'

'Oh, my goodness!' Emily whispered. 'I had no idea! I'm so sorry!'

'It's okay. You weren't to know.' Tara let out a long breath.

'He was my best friend,' Tara continued, emotion making her hoarse. 'We were... very close.'

Her hand went to her neck – the instinct guiding it there, to find the heart pendant necklace. Tara blinked back the tears that had sprung to her eyes. 'Oh, wow. Sorry. It's just really hard, seeing what he wrote.'

'Love, I'm so sorry!' Emily squeezed her hand. 'Do you want to talk about it?'

Tara glanced up at the building crew who were busying themselves back with the digger at the edge of the playground. She didn't want to cry in front of them, or Ramsay, or Emily.

'No. It's okay. It's just a bit weird, seeing him.' Tara wiped at the corners of her eyes. 'It's been nice being back here, if I'm honest, sort of reconnecting to those nice memories of us as children. But I guess that just brought it home to me. All the pain of what happened. And I didn't expect to see him. I met him out of the blue the other day, in the street. I haven't worked out how to be around him yet.'

'I can see that.' Emily looked concerned.

'He... Ramsay... he had a hard life at home. I don't think I really understood, when we were kids. You know? I knew that he'd come to school with bruises sometimes, and that I never went to his house to play. But, you know how kids are. That was just sort of normal.' She let out a long breath. Emily frowned, looking over at Ramsay at the other side of the playground. 'Poor thing. Well, I suppose he's a man, now. I wonder whether, in small communities like Loch Cameron, there's something that happens where, on one hand, people care and are in each other's business, like the crochet coven. And then on the other hand, there's sometimes this kind of... unspoken agreement to look the other way about some things. It's strange.'

'I think you're right. My parents always had him over as much as they could. They must have known. But nothing was ever said. Not to me, anyway. I mean, maybe it was spoken about in the village, among the community. I was too young to have known either way.'

'You should ask your mum about it.' Emily folded up the letters that she'd looked through and returned them to the canister. 'It's not like you're a kid anymore.'

'Yeah. I should.' Tara let out a long sigh. 'It's just all a bit... raw still, seeing him again. I thought I would never see him again. It's a long story.'

'I can see that,' Emily said, sympathetically. 'I'm here if you want an ear, at any point, by the way. I know we've just met, but, you know. Teacher pinky promise, or something.'

'Thanks.' Tara allowed herself a small laugh. 'That's really nice of you, Emily.'

'Of course. You're going to do a stack of laminating in a minute, so I most definitely owe you.' Emily winked.

'Well, I still appreciate it. Can I keep these two? The letters?' Tara asked: she didn't want to let them go.

'Of course.' Emily let go of her hand and stood up. 'Come on. Let's go inside and have a cuppa and a biscuit. I feel like we earned it.'

'All right. I'll be there in a minute.'

Tara stood up, and looked back at the small, red brick building. At some point, she and Ramsay would have played on the spot where she currently stood. She knew – though she didn't specifically remember the event – that she and Ramsay would have stood at the edge of the playground and watched their wishes being lowered into the ground.

She wondered what she had thought and felt at the time, but her mind was a blank. Clearly, at the time, the time capsule hadn't felt like such a big deal.

Now, though, it seemed deeply symbolic. The fact that it had been unearthed just as she had come back to Loch Cameron, and right at the same time as Ramsay had reappeared in her life, was not lost on her. Tara wasn't one to believe in signs from the universe, but this seemed over-whelming.

She had ended up fulfilling her wish: as a teacher, she at least hoped that she sometimes inspired and helped children. Had Ramsay gotten what he wanted too?

Tara swallowed the lump in her throat. That was a question that she didn't know the answer to, and, if she was honest, she wasn't ready to know.

THIRTEEN

Later in the day, there was a knock on the door of the classroom that Tara was working in. Emily had offered to finish up the preparation on her own, but Tara wanted to stay. She'd messaged her mum and dad so they didn't think she'd just disappeared; as long as she was back for dinner prep, she thought it was okay to have an afternoon off.

She felt awkward, being in the same space as Ramsay, but she also couldn't stop watching him through the classroom window. All these years, she'd thought she would never see him again, and here he was. There was a kind of solace for her soul in watching him walk around, talking to the builders. He seemed so sure of himself as an adult. His body, his posture and the way he held his head: she couldn't stop looking at him. She had thirsted, hungered for him, and here he was, finally.

Was it sort of stalker-y to feel like this? Maybe. But it was just so intense seeing him again that she couldn't quite bring herself to walk away.

She also wanted to stay near the memory of Ramsay; the Ramsay that she had loved, and who had loved her. The Ramsay who had existed before the day that he had betrayed her. The Ramsay who had existed in a time when both she and he were innocent children, hopeful for their future. She hated that feeling of being untethered to 'normal' that she'd had since being in Loch Cameron, and connecting to their past had helped to push it aside, albeit temporarily.

But, she reminded herself that she also needed to remember her own carefree self: the young Tara that had felt in a state of flow when she danced. In those moments, she could have done anything and been anyone; she had felt free, wild, and totally herself. If she felt a pang of nostalgia – or, more than a pang, it was an ache of deep loss – connected to Ramsay, then she had to realise that it was also her own, younger, freer self that she was also mourning.

After about half an hour of being back inside, Tara saw Ramsay walk to the car park, get into an SUV and drive off. As he got into the car, he sat in the driver's seat for a moment, staring at the school building. Tara wondered whether he was looking for her. What he was thinking.

When he drove away, she felt an illogical pang of loss.

There was a tap at the door.

'Come in.' Tara looked up to see one of the builders who had been working outside. 'Oh, hi. Can I help?'

'Sorry tae disturb ye,' the man apologised: he was stocky, her dad's age, and Tara thought for a moment that he was too old to be doing such a physical job, out in the elements all day. However, she was hardly in a position to be giving life advice to anyone, and if this man was anything like her dad, he'd nod politely and even give her a kind smile, and then do exactly what he'd intended to do in the first place. 'We just thought we should let ye have this one, since you wanted the other one.'

'The other what? The time capsule?' She watched as the man set down a different container on the wooden desk at the front of the room. It was also made of metal, but where the other was a large coffee container with a tightly fitting round lid, this was some kind of metal toolbox, with rusty hinges. She got up and went over to look at it.

'Aye. This was buried a bit further out, and lower down. But, maybe it's the same kindae thing, eh?' The man tapped its metal carapace. 'Looks like it's been down there a lot longer. I remember this kindae toolbox from when I was a bairn – my faither had one not too different. They made these tae last.' He paused, took out a rag from his pocket and rubbed at a spot on the box. 'Hmm. See, ye can see the maker's name and the date there. 1938.' He nodded. 'That's definitely been down there a wee while, eh?'

'Wow. I guess so.' Tara peered at the date on the raised iron-work of the box. 'Thanks. I'm not sure if I can get it open, though.'

'Hmm. Okay, let me try.' The man reached into his pocket and brought out a large screwdriver. He stuck it into the metal fastenings of the box and jimmied them for a minute or two before they popped open. 'Aha. There y'are,' he said, with satis-faction. 'Must admit we were curious as to what's in it.' He looked on as Tara raised the lid.

'Well, in the other one, there were a lot of letters from former pupils at the school,' Tara explained. 'I wonder whether there was some kind of tradition at the school for making time capsules. Perhaps the later one was inspired by the earlier one.' She shrugged and opened the lid, which squeaked.

'No mice inside, then,' the builder joked as Emily popped her head around the door.

'Hey. What's going on here? Having a party without me?'

'Come in! The builders – sorry, I don't know your name?' Tara said, apologetically, looking at the man.

'Jack.' The man nodded politely to them both.

'Jack found this buried outside,' Tara added. 'We were just about to look at it.'

'Ooooh! What a day!' Emily strode into the classroom and bounced on her toes as she stood next to Tara. 'Let's see, then!'

'All right... here we go!' Tara said, opening the metal lid fully.

Inside, there were more letters, and what looked like children's toys. 'Look at these!' Tara breathed, handing Emily a metal toy horse, which still had its paint fairly intact.

'Awww. This is lovely!' Emily took it and showed it to Jack, who touched its head gently.

'That's bonny,' he said. 'Tae think it's been down there all these years.'

'What do the letters say?' Emily asked Tara. Tara handed her a couple and opened one. Again, they were letters from the children, but, this time, the wishes were a little different.

'I wish for dad to get home safe,' Tara read aloud. She opened another. 'I wish for dad to come home soon. I wish for Uncle Benny to stay safe on the front line. I wish for Mum not to have to work so hard. I wish for all the children in London to be safe. Dear me.'

'World War Two, then.' Emily read hers out loud. 'I wish for peace. I wish for an end to the bombing. I wish that the people of Poland would be safe. These are all dated 1941.'

'Sad that likely none of those wishes came true, aye,' Jack sighed. 'This is heartbreakin'.'

'It is, isn't it?' Tara reached into the box and pulled out some more toy animals and set them gently on the top of the desk. 'Ah, goodness. Look at this.'

She drew out a painting which was labelled *Vision of Hope for the Future* in a careful, adult hand. Tara read the text on the back of the painting aloud.

'This is the winner of our school competition for a painting that best portrays our hopes for the future. The winner was Molly Taggart, aged 9.'

'Bless her,' Emily said, as they all stared at the painting. 'I wonder what she'd think of life now.'

Molly had painted a picture of a lush green field, thick with wildflowers and surrounded by trees. In the foreground, a group of boys and girls danced in a circle, holding hands, with the flags for their countries emblazoned on their vests. Everyone smiled, the sun shone yellow in a blue sky, and Molly had painted a swirly title for the painting which just said HARMONY.

'It's not all that different to something a child now would paint,' Tara observed. 'They're all utopian at that age. Real life hasn't got to them yet. They still believe in peace and love.'

'Ouch. I still believe in peace and love, sometimes,' Emily chuckled. 'But I know what you mean. However, you can understand how appealing but also evasive peace and harmony must have felt to those children.'

'Aye. So sad,' Jack repeated. 'Ye should frame that. Put it up for the wee bairns tae see.'

'That's a lovely idea. We will.' Emily nodded. 'Oh. What's this? There's a longer letter here too. It looks like this is written by an adult. This is turning out to be the most interesting day!' She took it out and frowned as her mobile phone started ringing. 'Oh, I need to get this. Tara, you take it.' She handed the letter, written in a beautiful copperplate hand on thick, cream writing paper, to Tara and walked off to the back of the classroom to take the call.

'Well, I best be off.' Jack waved through the window and nodded politely to Tara. 'We'd love tae know if ye find anythin' else interestin'. What do people say, now? "We're invested".' He gave her a warm smile.

'Thanks, Jack. Really appreciate your help with this.' Tara opened the letter and started to read it. 'Of course. We'll keep you updated.'

'All right then.' He left, and Tara looked back at the beautifully written words on the page.

At the top, there was a name and a date. *Agnes Smith, 1941*, and then the school's address.

Agnes Smith. Dotty had told her about Aunt Agnes many times, who was a schoolteacher in Loch Cameron. Dotty had always compared them, saying that she and Aunt Agnes were so similar. *So bookish*, Dotty would say, with apparent dismay that she could have given birth to a child that loved books so much.

Was this the same Agnes? She read on:

To whoever may open this capsule,

We, as the current staff and pupils of Loch Cameron Primary School, are burying this time capsule in 1941 as the Second World War rages on around us and in Europe. We are fortunate to live in a small, rural Scottish community, and, as such, have been relatively untouched by the bombing, though we have lost many of our young men to the war effort.

In a bid for hope for the future, I decided that the children would benefit from doing some kind of material activity to focus their hopes and dreams, and help them feel positive about the future, as the war drags on. As time goes by, our expectations that this would be a few months' skirmish, easily ended by the superior mettle of the Allied troops, have well and truly been dashed. Now, two years in, many of us adults neither hope for nor believe in peace.

Yet, the children do, and I'm glad of that. When this capsule is opened, we hope that there is peace throughout the world, and an end to the terrible fighting. This war must be the final war. Humanity cannot face horror like this again.

Since this box will be locked away under the earth for many years, I also feel compelled to use the opportunity to write down some of the things that are torturing me, in the hope that, writing this, I may exorcise some of the ghosts that haunt me.

Hopefully, I will be dead by the time any human eyes read these words.

As a child, I lost both parents to pneumonia, within a month of each other. In the two months between January and March 1919, I went from a happy child with both parents alive – Father was in a protected occupation and never enlisted in the war – to an orphan. I write this to partially explain the reasons why, perhaps, I am the kind of injured person who seeks comfort wherever it is offered.

Teaching has always given me a sense of family. I have loved each child I have taught – even the naughty ones – like my own children.

I desperately wanted a family of my own. This is perhaps understandable when one considers the fact that my own family were taken away from me so dramatically. My care was given up to my spinster aunt, Poppy, who packed me off to boarding school as a solution. It was as a result of this that I became so dedicated to books, for they provided me with solace and comfort, and a way to escape my new life of loneliness.

Hence, perhaps it was a foregone conclusion that I would become involved with the first man that paid me any attention. Unfortunately, I fell in love – or, what I thought was love – with the headmaster of this school, Mr Paul McLeish.

I will not sully the pages of this fine notepaper with what passed between us, but, as a very naïve young woman, I thought that the soft words and sweet entreaties meant something.

I was wrong.

Mr McLeish – Paul, though I have very seldom addressed him as such – will not leave his wife for me. He says that our time together was a mere dalliance, and that I should expect the attentions of married men, as a spinster, working in his school. He considered congress with me his right. That he has some kind of paternal oversight of me. That I, in a way, belong to him, as a single woman in his care, at the school.

There was a time when I greatly desired Mr McLeish's attentions. I do not desire them any longer. I have made it clear that if it happens again, then I will leave the school.

I do not want to leave the children. I do not want to leave Loch Cameron, because it is my home. This is all that I know. So, I will endure seeing Mr McLeish every day and knowing what happened between us, because of the children. And because I will be damned if I let him win this battle of wills.

I will stay at the school. I will outlast him. And I will never, ever, make myself vulnerable to a man again.

Agnes Smith

Tara put the letter down and looked out of the window. It had to be the same Agnes: her own great-aunt, who might once have stood in the same spot as she stood now. Who had taught so many children here, and loved them all. Agnes Smith, who had endured the indignity of Mr McLeish, and, Tara was fairly sure, had taught at Loch Cameron Primary until she retired.

Tara was immediately sad and angry on Agnes' behalf. Angry that her great-aunt had had to endure sexual harassment, and had no way to counter it, except to write this letter for her own catharsis. What must it have been like, to walk into work every day and have to see the man who had taken advantage of you in that way? Who had used you for sex and then cast you aside, not even thinking that he had done anything wrong? Worse, he thought that Agnes was his *property* in some way. That he was entitled to her body, because he was her boss.

What a world it was then, Tara thought. *People think things are bad nowadays, but at least we have laws protecting us from this kind of thing. At least most people now agree that manipulating your employees for sex isn't acceptable.*

Suddenly, she remembered seeing some old black and white photos in the long hallway that linked the classrooms. Was McLeish there? Was Agnes?

On a whim, Tara went to look at them.

The school had organised a display of photos of the current members of staff in the hallway: Tara's school had a similar display in the school reception. But, underneath the modern pictures of Emily and her fellow teachers, there was a row of older, black and white photos, leading to some that were sepia tinted. Tara followed them along, noting the way they had been painstakingly labelled with class years and names of teachers. Mrs Strong, Mr Irvine, Miss Hay.

The oldest photo was of a Miss Peabody, who taught at the school from 1794 to 1833. Tara's eyebrows raised at that: she hadn't known that the school was that old, and she read the caption to the picture, which was longer than the rest.

Muriel Peabody, schoolteacher at Loch Cameron Primary School from 1794 to 1833, when it was a "Dame School" – run by a local woman, who the locals paid a small fee to educate their children. Muriel eventually retired from ill health. She never married or had children of her own, but taught generations of local children in this village. She was greatly loved, and recently immortalised by Loch Cameron Distillery in their Old Maids range of whiskies, named after important women in the village's history.

Wow, Tara thought. The picture must have been a new addition to the school wall, or perhaps it had always been there, but she had no memory of knowing about Muriel Peabody from when she'd been a pupil at the school. It was good to know that Muriel had achieved some posthumous fame for her dedication to Loch Cameron: Tara thought that she should remember to ask her mother about the whisky.

Her gaze moved along the line of photos. Finally, there he was. *Mr McLeish, Headmaster, 1938–1943*, the caption read.

She stared at Paul McLeish's face intently for a few moments. The trimmed beard, the small, mean eyes. She shivered involuntarily. He'd only stayed as Headmaster for another two years after Agnes had written the letter she still held in her hands.

And, then, there she was. Tara's eyes alighted on a sepia tone picture of a stern-faced woman with her hair in a bun, wearing a sensible skirt and blouse, with a brooch at the neck, just like Dotty still often wore. *Miss Smith, Headmistress, 1943–1980, with Class 4*, the caption read.

1943–1980. A lifetime. Or, at least, a long time, Tara thought. She had got her wish: Agnes had outlasted Mr McLeish.

She stared at Agnes' face. There was a definite resemblance to Dotty: the same eyes, though her mother's face had more laughter lines. The same chin.

I'm so glad you stayed, Tara thought, touching her great-aunt's face in the picture frame. *I'm so glad you endured. But, at what cost?*

It seemed that there was a history of spinsters that had taught at Loch Cameron Primary for most of their lives: Muriel Peabody, Agnes Smith. Both had been loved; both had loved the children in their care. Both had worked, all their lives. Both were dedicated to Loch Cameron, despite the difficulties they might have found living here as single women.

Yet, it seemed that Aunt Agnes had had to sacrifice herself as a woman – as a person worthy of love – to keep her job as headmistress. She had said at the end of her letter that she was determined to win against Mr McLeish, but she had also said *I will never, ever, make myself vulnerable to a man again.*

Tara wondered if Aunt Agnes had ever found love. Dotty had always referred to Agnes as a spinster, so Tara was fairly sure that her aunt had never married. Like the Old Maids popularised by Loch Cameron Distillery in their range of whiskies, the village clearly had its share of single women who had, for whatever reason, stayed unmarried. But did that mean that Agnes was unhappy? Or that she hadn't still had relationships? Tara didn't know, but she desperately wanted to find out now.

She was proud of Agnes: proud to be related to a woman like her, who had resisted powerlessness. Despite the setbacks in her life, Agnes had pursued what she loved, and that was inspiring.

Would Agnes have let heartbreak stop her living her life? No. She hadn't. Not according to that letter, anyway.

The impact of seeing Ramsay again was hard. Finding his letter in the time capsule – and watching him read it – was heartbreaking.

But, she had to get over Ramsay Fraser. And maybe, as the phrase went, the only way out was through. Agnes had waited out Mr McLeish. She hadn't run away. She had faced her demons, and stayed.

Then, I can do the same, Tara thought. *I can at least not crumble next time I see him. And, at the end of the summer, I can go back to my life and leave him here.* The thought of leaving Ramsay made her heart tug with grief, but, she rationalised, she didn't *have* Ramsay now any more than she had a month ago, when she hadn't seen him for ten years. She could return to her real life and leave behind this feeling of being lost. She needed to find herself again, reclaim the person she once was.

She took out her phone and snapped a picture of the photo to show Dotty later. Dotty would like to see it; she'd always compared Tara to Agnes. They were bookish, she'd always said. But, perhaps, Tara thought, there was another similarity between her and her great-aunt. If she had even a little of Agnes' steely determination and resilience, then she would be proud.

And, I think I do, she said to herself, looking into Agnes' eyes. *I'm proud of you, Great-Aunt Agnes*, she thought. *I'll do my best to make you proud of me.*

FOURTEEN

'Did ye find the books yet?' Dotty called from the stairs, and Tara swore under her breath, dropping the duster and polish and running to help her mother, who was stubbornly descending the Inn's carpeted staircase with her new walking stick.

'Mum! You shouldn't be up!' Tara scolded Dotty, but Dotty ignored her and continued making her way down the stairs.

'If I have tae stay in that room another minute, I'm goin' tae go batty,' she complained. 'Look at me! I'm so peely-wally, the walls're jealous.'

Peely-wally was a favourite phrase of Dotty's that meant pale or looking ill. She used *peaky* interchangeably.

'Take my arm at least, then.' Tara fought the urge to roll her eyes and guided Dotty to a chair. 'Do you want tea? There's some cake, as well.'

Tara had realised, since being home and looking after her mother, just how much tea Dotty drank in a day. If she didn't have a pot on the go, then she wanted one.

'Aye, but only if yer makin' one.' Dotty smiled tiredly at her daughter. *She did look pale*, Tara thought.

'I will in a minute. I'm just polishing the bar.'

'Aye, good.' Dotty pointed to a shelf of old leather-bound books over the fireplace. 'Those are the books I was tellin' ye aboot. Belonged tae Aunt Agnes.'

Tara hadn't been putting the fire on most evenings, because it was the summer. Her dad had said that was fine, but as soon as September began, they'd start burning logs again. People liked the cosy warmth of a fire on an evening, he said. She looked over, frowning.

'Aye. I told ye. Those were her books,' Dotty repeated, waving regally at the volumes from her chair. 'Poetry, some novels. This an' that. I always meant for ye tae have them, but they do look nice over the fireplace.'

'I always just thought they were ornamental. I didn't know they belonged to her.' Tara went over to the fireplace, curious, and ran her finger along the bottle green, dark blue and tan leather spines of the books.

'Aye. I did tell ye, but ye weren't listenin'.' Dotty tutted affectionately. 'I always said, Agnes was bookish, like ye.'

'Right, but I don't remember you saying these were her books.' Tara frowned.

'I did! The other day when we were talkin' upstairs.'

'Oh. Right. Hmm. You know, we found a letter from Agnes at the primary school the other day. In a time capsule. I've been meaning to show you.' Tara reached for her phone and opened the photos, showing Dotty the picture she'd taken.

'Oh, my!' Dotty said as she read it, putting on her glasses from where they hung around her neck on a chain. 'And this was in a memory capsule?' She handed the phone back to Tara.

'Yeah. At the school. From 1941. Even weirder, we also found one from when I was at the school. Ramsay and I had both put little letters in there,' Tara continued. She didn't tell her mother that Ramsay had been there at the school, when the time capsules had been discovered. She was still processing it herself: seeing Ramsay Fraser twice in such a short period of time, when she thought she'd never see him again – well, she didn't know what to think. Part of her was relieved, part of her wanted to scream at him, part of her wanted to hug him and not let go.

'Really! Isnae that strange!' Dotty marvelled. 'What a scandal, aboot Agnes and the headmaster, though! I had nae idea.' She passed Tara's phone back to her. 'Poor darlin'.'

'So she was single all her life? Encouraging.' Tara rolled her eyes.

'A spinster, that's what they used tae call it.' Dotty ignored her daughter's eyeroll. 'Single. Yes. Why is that encouragin'?'

'It's not. I was being sarcastic. Because you always say I'm like her. So that means I'm destined to be alone,' Tara explained.

'Oh. Silly lass. We had this conversation before. You'll never be alone. Agnes was a bit of an odd duck. She may have had a personal life, but she just never talked aboot it.'

'So there was never a guy – or a woman – around? A partner?' Tara probed. 'Apart from Mr McLeish, as it turns out.'

'No' that I can remember, hen. She liked her own company. Or, she didnae like it, but was stuck wi' it.' Dotty shrugged. 'Have a look at the books, you might like tae have somethin' that was hers.'

'I thought I was making you a tea?' Tara raised a playful eyebrow.

'Aye, right enough. In a minute.'

'Fine. Let's see these books then.' Tara went to have a look at the shelf again. Dotty was right: there was a variety of poetry titles: Robert Browning, Christina Rossetti, Rupert Brooke, Siegfried Sassoon. Then there was a set of the Brontë sisters: *Jane Eyre*, *The Tenant of Wildfell Hall*, *Wuthering Heights*, *Villette*. Tara took down the dark blue leather-bound copy of

Jane Eyre and flicked through the opening pages. 'Oh, look. There're notes here.'

She took the book over to Dotty and showed her some of the pages. In a meticulously neat copperplate hand, Agnes had written her name on the top right-hand corner of the title page. Tara frowned as she looked at the date the book was published: 1921.

'These were already quite old when she got them,' she said. 'Agnes was in her twenties in 1941. That was when that letter was dated.'

'Hmm. She may've inherited them, bear in mind.' Dotty rested her head on the back of the chair. 'I dinnae know much aboot Agnes' parents, but I do remember my mum sayin' Agnes' dad was a doctor. They were keen on education, I think, even for Agnes, an' that wasnae that common at the time.'

'I guess that's why she became a teacher.' Tara looked back at the book, flicking through the pages. Further into the book, Agnes had written tiny, crabbed notes at the margins of the tissue-thin pages of the aged paper. 'Hmm. Listen to this. She's underlined some things. *I am no bird; and no net ensnares me; I am a free human being with an independent will.*'

'That's Agnes, all right,' Dotty chuckled. 'Ye can tell from that letter she wasnae aboot tae take any funny business from anyone.'

'Right.' Tara nodded, flicking through more pages. She read some more underlined passages aloud. They were all about finding a soulmate, it seemed: Charlotte Brontë called it a *good angel*.

'That's romantic,' Dotty sighed. 'Yer father's never said anythin' half as romantic as that tae me.'

'*Mum.* You love Dad, and he adores you.'

'Aye, I know,' Dotty admitted. 'He's a good man. Still, a girl likes a bit o' romance, every so often.'

'Hmm. Here's another one. *It is madness in all women to let a secret love kindle within them, which, if unreturned and unknown, must devour the life that feeds it.'*

'Maybe that was about the headmaster, Mr McLeish. She mightae felt like that aboot him at first,' Dotty said, thoughtfully. 'She was just a young girl, inexperienced. He was older, married. He took advantage of her, poor thing.'

'Yeah. It does look that way.' Tara continued turning the pages. 'It would be nice if Agnes had found love, you know? To make up for her terrible time with Mr McLeish.'

Tara thought about what it must have been like to teach at the tiny Loch Cameron primary school. She wondered how many pupils there had been in Agnes' time. She could imagine class sizes of around eight, or maybe, then, there hadn't been year groups in the same way as there were now. Tara had the sudden vision of Agnes reading to a group of children of different ages, spellbinding them with her own passion for books.

'Aye. She was clearly a romantic soul.' Dotty shifted uncomfortably in her chair.

'It's like she was taking strength from this book, though. She's underlined this: *I can live alone, if self-respect and circumstances require me to do so. I need not sell my soul to buy bliss. I have an inward treasure born within me, which can keep me alive if all extraneous delights should be withheld or offered only at a price I cannot afford to give.'*

'Good advice fer anyone. What's this book again?'

'*Jane Eyre.* Charlotte Brontë.'

'Well, that Charlotte Brontë was a bit o' a feminist, I'd say. Good for her.' Dotty nodded. 'I might read it.'

'I guess she was a feminist, in her own way. It's a book about love, but it's also about an independent woman who refuses love if it isn't on her terms. Are you a feminist, Mum?' Tara didn't think she'd ever heard Dotty use the word before.

'O' course I am. Silly question,' her mother scoffed. 'You

girls now think ye've got it hard. Think about what it was like in Agnes' day. An' in my day. Let me tell ye, it wasnae easy, bein' a woman in Scotland wi' the likes o' Paul bloody McLeish around every corner, an' men tellin' ye yer place was at home, mindin' the bairns. I've never let a man get the better o' me an' I never will. Part o' the reason I fell fer yer father was that he always treated me like a queen. If yer no' the queen, lassie, then forget it, because he's no' the king ye're lookin' fer.'

'All right, I only asked.' Tara held up her hands in a mock defence. 'I know, I know. It's not as easy as all that to find a king, though. Believe me.'

'Ye havenae tried, as far as I can tell, poppet. No' since Ramsay,' Dotty said, her tone softening. 'Listen. All I want is fer ye tae find someone who'll treat ye like a queen. I want ye tae stand upright an' have the gumption that Jane Eyre had. That I had to have in my life, hen. I know ye've got it in ye.'

Tara was touched. She was so used to thinking that Dotty wasn't really in her corner that she hadn't stopped to think that her mother really might be.

'I have tried to find someone. You don't know what it's like out there,' Tara argued, but she knew it was a lie. She'd hardly dated at all in the past ten years. She'd told herself that she was concentrating on her career, but she knew, deep down, that wasn't true.

'Have ye? Ye havenae brought anyone home.' Dotty pointed to a teal velvet pouffe next to the chair she was sitting in. 'Move that fer me, there's a love. Help me put ma feet up.'

Tara moved the pouffe and knelt down to gently raise her mother's ankles onto it.

'I haven't met anyone that I wanted to bring home.' That was, at least, honest. She hadn't, but she also hadn't been looking for anyone.

'Well, Agnes mightae been a spinster, but there's no need

fer ye to be, Tara.' Dotty put her hand on Tara's, on the armrest of the chair. 'Listen tae yer mother. I raised ye tae be a strong woman. Like Agnes, like me. Ye've got that in ye: like that passage in the book says, yer strong in yerself. But I also raised ye tae enjoy life, hen.' Dotty looked uncharacteristically reflective for a moment.

'I do enjoy my life,' Tara protested.

'Aye, but it's in a reserved kindae way, now. When ye were dancin' – wi' or wi'out Ramsay – ye were so free, so happy. I used tae love watchin' ye, up on stage. An' it wasnae aboot the prizes an' the trophies. Or even aboot winnin'. It was aboot takin' joy in life.' Dotty shifted, a grimace of pain crossing her expression. 'All I want fer ye is tae have that joy again.'

'I want that, too,' Tara said, quietly. 'But I don't know how. It's like I lost it and I've never been able to find it again.' Unexpectedly, tears welled up in her eyes. 'Sorry, Mum.' She wiped them away. 'I don't know where that came from.'

'Don't ye ever be sorry, poppet. Not ever, not to me.' Dotty gathered her daughter into a fierce, tight hug. 'I just want ye tae be happy. That's all a mother ever wants fer her daughter.' Dotty took the book from Tara's hands and flicked through it, thoughtfully. 'Ye know, I always told ye, ye were like Agnes. Because ye always loved tae read. But it's different times now, ye have tae remember. An' just because Agnes may have had her heart broken, an lived like a spinster forever after that, ye dinnae have tae. We all make our own destiny. Yours can be full o' joy again, if ye want it tae be. Okay?'

'Okay, Mum.' Tara, still kneeling, rested her head on Dotty's lap. It was something she hadn't done since she was a little girl, and the memory of her childhood self rose within her. Dotty was right: she had been full of joy, once. She longed for that feeling again.

'Awww. Bless your heart,' Dotty said, and stroked Tara's

hair. 'My little one. You'll always be my little girl, Tara. But you're a woman now, too. Ye can find yer joy again if ye look fer it.'

'But I don't know where to look,' Tara replied. Her hand went to the two hearts around her neck and clutched them.

'What's that?' Dotty reached for Tara's hand. 'Oh, my goodness. I didn't know you were still wearin' that.' Her eyes widened.

'Yeah. I just forget it's there.' Tara tried to make nothing of the fact that she was still wearing the pendants.

'Aww. Ramsay and you used tae wear them. And... that's right. He gave ye his half.' Dotty's eyes misted. 'Darlin'...'

'Mum. It's okay. It's just habit. I should take them off.' Tara tried to deflect her mother, but Dotty just gave her a look that said, *you can't fool me.*

'Well, ye could *try* dancin' again,' Dotty said. 'I never saw ye so happy as when ye were in yer little dance outfit, jumpin' away on the stage.'

'Maybe. It was so long ago, though. I'm so out of shape,' she replied.

'Nonsense. Ye look great, an' it wouldnae take long fer ye tae remember it all.' Dotty patted Tara's head, and Tara sat up, back on her heels. 'Now. Off ye go an' make me a cuppa, an' then when yer finished fer the day, go an' look up some dance videos on the internet an' get back intae movin' yer body. God knows, darlin', one o' these days, ye'll be in yer sixties an' broken yer leg an' sittin' in a chair, an' it willnae be so easy.'

'I guess I could,' Tara said, reluctantly.

'That's the spirit! I think ye definitely could,' Dotty said, her tone brisk. 'Okay. Tea! Off ye go, poppet. Ma little twinkle toes.'

It didn't do to argue with Dotty Ballantyne, and so Tara got up and went to the kitchen. But, though it pained her to think it, maybe her mother was right. Tara hummed one of the old Scottish tunes that she had used to dance to, and stepped through the familiar foot positions. Dotty was right: it was all still there, in muscle memory. It felt good to dance. All of a sudden, she wondered why she had taken so long to remember that.

FIFTEEN

'Here you are, then.' The elderly woman pushed open a door off the short corridor that led into the community centre, and flicked a switch. A long, harsh overhead LED light flickered on in a somewhat airless room, long ago painted in that light green that seemed reserved for public buildings and hospitals. 'Hasn't been used for a while, but you're welcome to it.'

'Thank you.' Tara followed the woman into the room, noting the fact that its scuffed wooden floor was sprung underneath, and the wooden piano that stood in the corner. Across one wall, a tarnished mirror stretched the width of the room, with a wooden barre across the middle.

'Used to be used for a kids' ballet class, but it hasn't run for many a year now,' the woman continued, giving Tara a friendly smile. She was dressed elegantly in loose lilac-coloured linen trousers and a matching linen shirt, the sleeves rolled up and a scarf knotted around her head. 'You're Dotty's daughter, aren't you? I recognise you from your photos. I'm June, a friend of Dotty's.' She held out a lined hand, and Tara shook it.

'Hello, June. Thanks for this. It's perfect, actually. I've been wanting to get back into dancing a bit, and there's no room to do it at the Inn.'

Tara had taken her mother's advice and started to refresh her dance skills in her old bedroom, but there was no real room to move, and Dotty complained that the noise was keeping her awake. So, she'd suggested the community centre.

'Ah, that's right. You used to dance, didn't you? Dotty told us all about it. I didn't live in the village then, but I hear you were amazing.'

'Ah, well. We won a lot of trophies.' Tara nodded.

'And you haven't danced for a while?'

'No. I sort of got involved in my career, and it... took a backseat,' Tara said, which wasn't a lie exactly, but she had no inclination to tell this June the whole story.

'These things happen, dear.' June shook her head. 'Well, I'll let you know when I'm going to close up, but I'll be an hour or two, so no hurry.' She nodded, and held the door open. 'Enjoy!'

'Thanks.' Tara waited until June had left before getting out her phone and the portable speaker she'd brought with her, and putting on some warmup music. She laid down a yoga mat and began with a hatha yoga workout on an app, moving from gentle stretches into the different poses she remembered from a class she'd taken about a year ago. She could feel her body waking up, and it felt good.

When she'd warmed up, she found one of the dance class videos she'd been watching online and played it. The hip hop music filled the room, and Tara started to follow the instructor. It was a basic street dance routine, and after a while, her concentration paid off, and the movements started to flow. Tara started having fun with it and relaxing into the beat; watching herself in the mirror, she realised that she was grinning. Enjoying herself in the moment.

The next video by the same dance teacher followed on automatically; Tara thought that she might as well try and follow it. It was a salsa class, which she'd danced before.

As she followed the steps and relaxed into the salsa rhythm, Ramsay popped into her mind, and the memory of them doing dances like this. The connection of their bodies together had been electric.

Her phone buzzed: it was an unknown number. Tara answered, expecting it to be a sales call of some kind, or Carla, on her travels.

'Hi, Tara. It's Ramsay.' Ramsay Fraser's voice boomed across the room: she still had the phone connected to the speaker. *Speak of the devil.* She had a moment, wondering if she had somehow conjured him by thinking about their dancing past.

'Oh. Hello.' She was slightly out of breath, and hoped that he didn't think it sounded strange.

'Your mum gave me your number,' he continued. 'I hope that's okay.'

'Did she? Right,' Tara replied, knowing that she sounded like an idiot but unable to think of anything clever or witty to say.

'Yeah. I just popped into the Inn to see you, but she said you were out,' he said, sounding awkward. 'I hope that was okay.'

'Oh. I see. Yeah, I guess so.'

'How are you finding working at the Inn? Your mum said she's so relieved to have you there,' he continued, striving to make conversation. Tara wasn't trying to be obstructive or dull, but she was a little lost for things to say. What did it mean, that he was calling her?

'It's okay. Busy,' Tara replied, wondering what else Dotty and Ramsay had said in this cosy little chat of theirs.

'I bet.' There was another silence. 'What are you doing? You sound out of breath,' he asked.

'Dancing, actually. There's a fairly decent rehearsal room at the community centre: Mum mentioned that she thought they had somewhere I could practice, and it's not bad. What about you?'

'Just walking home from the Inn. You're at the community centre? I'm literally walking past right now.'

'Oh,' she replied, not knowing how to respond.

'I'll come in,' he said. She could hear him walking, on the phone: the sounds of the high street in the background. 'I'm right here anyway.'

'Oh, but I... right. Okay.' Tara ended the call and looked wildly around her for her hoodie; she'd stripped off to a sports bra and a pair of yoga leggings to dance in, but she felt exposed just wearing that in front of Ramsay. She pulled it on just as he walked through the door.

'Hi.' Ramsay grinned at her. 'We meet again.'

'Well, you found out where I was and sort of invaded, but sure.' Tara took down her ponytail and tied it up again firmly, then stood with her hands on her hips. She was cross at being interrupted, and confused by Ramsay's sudden appearance. He threw her off balance when he appeared like this, out of the blue, and she didn't like it.

'Sorry. I was literally just passing, though. Fate.' His tone was breezy, and that annoyed her even more. It was like he was deliberately ignoring the elephant in the room, which was her broken heart.

'I'm not sure that's what I'd call asking my mum where to find me,' Tara countered, tersely.

'Well, I'm here.' He pulled a face that she remembered; it was Ramsay's face for when he thought she was being unnecessarily difficult, but he was going to take it on the chin because it was Tara, and he loved her. She blinked. It was a subtlety she had forgotten, that expression. An intimate thing that existed between them. It was strange to see it again, just as it would have been strange for them to say the words they used to say to each other in the dead of night as they lay in each other's arms.

Tara felt herself blushing and looked away. She didn't want to blush; she wanted to stay angry, because angry was infinitely easier to feel and act from than longing, love and loss.

'I was just doing the salsa,' she said, flatly, and hoping that this was enough of a hint to make him leave.

'Cool. Challenging. I used to enjoy it,' he replied, instead, showing no sign of wanting to leave or indeed any sense of awkwardness.

'I know.' Tara remembered how his hand on her waist had felt. How his body had felt: long-limbed and strong. When he'd dipped her, he'd stare deep into her eyes, and a glow of heat would erupt in her belly.

'So, it was weird seeing you at the school the other day,' she said, fiddling with her speaker and changing the subject.

'Yeah. Small world. But that's Loch Cameron for you.'

'Hmm. How come you were at the school? You seemed to be working with the building site?'

'I'm a quantity surveyor. I got roped in to that little project, less as a surveyor and more just because I'm a friend of Emily's and she wanted someone who understands building projects to keep an eye on things.' He looked out of the little window.

'I thought you studied engineering at uni.' She pulled at the edge of her sweater.

'I didn't finish uni. I trained later on, in the evenings, when I could. Got fully qualified a couple of years ago. That's actually the reason I came back to Loch Cameron. The firm I was working for was working on the development up at Gyle Head. When I saw it all come together up there, I thought, this seems like a good place to put down roots. So, here I am.'

'Right. It's nice up there,' Tara replied. She wondered if they were going to get beyond exchanging pleasantries anytime soon.

'It is.'

'So, quantity surveyor. It sounds like a grown-up job,' Tara said.

'You can talk. A teacher! Dotty told me all about it. That's what you wanted, right? Good on you.'

'Thanks. I do enjoy it.' Tara shrugged. 'Although the school I work at is kind of awful. The kids are great, but the PTA are... Sorry. Parent-Teacher Association. It's like, the club for the very engaged parents. You have to give them some sense of being involved. Fundraising, that kind of thing. The *parent voice.*' *Look at us, pretending like nothing happened,* she thought.

'I know what a PTA is.' He smiled.

'Oh. Right.' She gave him a thin-lipped smile. 'Well, I should get on... I've only got the room for a little longer,' she said, pointedly.

'It's nice that you're dancing.' He looked around the rehearsal room. 'Not quite what we were used to, but not bad, eh? Sprung floor.'

'Thanks. I haven't actually danced in years. Not since...' she trailed off. There was an awkward pause.

'The time capsule was freaky,' he said, suddenly. 'I didn't know how to deal with it.'

'You seemed upset,' she said, carefully. 'It was emotional for me too.'

'I was. It brought a lot of memories back. I'm sorry for leaving quite abruptly. I just wasn't sure how to act around you,' he confessed.

'I know. I wasn't prepared to see you. Then or when I bumped into you on the high street.'

'Listen, Tara,' Ramsay said, haltingly. 'I know it's been weird, seeing each other around the village. I know you must have a lot of questions for me. About what happened.'

'Yes,' she said, quietly.

'I know,' he said, softly. 'It's weird for me too, seeing you.

But it's nice, right? I missed you so much. I saw... you were wearing the necklace...'

Something about him mentioning the heart pendants hit too close to home, and Tara felt her heart thrum with a deep pain. It was too much. She'd been holding that pain for so long and seeing him brought up feelings she wasn't prepared for.

'I missed you too. Obviously,' she snapped, without meaning to. Did he think that she'd just blithely carried on with her life when he disappeared? That she didn't care at all? 'I'm sorry, Ramsay. This isn't something I actually want to talk about right now.'

'Sorry, it's a bad time.' He sounded contrite, and looked down at his shoes, which somehow made her more annoyed.

'Yes. Look, I didn't expect to see you. But that's not why I don't want to talk about this now.'

'Why, then?' he sounded confused. 'I just thought...'

'No. You didn't think at all,' Tara cut in. 'Do you think that you can just pick up where you left off with me?' her hand went to the heart pendants, protectively. The pain in her chest was as raw as it had been all those years ago, like the fragile scar that held her heart together had burst open.

'No! I just...'

'Just what? Thought we could pick up again, just like old times, as if nothing had happened? You DISAPPEARED, Ramsay. For ten years! I didn't even know if you were alive or dead! Can you imagine what that did to me? Do you have ANY idea?' Tara was shouting now but she didn't care. The anger had welled up within her quickly, as if it had been waiting just under the surface of her heart to be let out. Well, there was no "as if" about it – it *had* been there, waiting, for so long. At least it was better to be angry than to cry.

'I know it was bad. I... that was why I wanted to talk to you. After we met on the street... I didn't know what to say to you then...'

'So, talk,' she said. 'Tell me what could have possibly happened, because unless you were abducted by aliens and you just came back last week, then I think you could have got in touch before now to explain.'

'Tara. Please. This isn't easy.' He sounded tortured, but Tara's pain had resurfaced, and it hurt too much for her to be able to feel sympathy for Ramsay.

'I'm listening. Tell me what you need to tell me,' she demanded.

'Umm... it's difficult,' he repeated.

'Try,' she said, frustrated. What was so difficult? 'I've waited for ten years. You owe me an explanation.'

'You're right. I do. But... this was a mistake. I thought I could talk to you, but not like this.' He turned away.

'Not like what? You don't think it's understandable for me to be angry?' she shouted. 'For god's sake, Ramsay! All I had was that vague little note you sent to know that you weren't dead! Do you know how that feels? For the person you love most in the world to just disappear? Do you?'

'No,' he said, dully. Tara knew his face and his expressions so well; being in his presence and talking to him was like re-reading a familiar book. A story, a novel that she knew by heart. She had hardly ever seen him so devastated, so vulnerable and open to hurt.

Part of Tara wanted to retract her words; she could feel the hurt in his voice and she hated hearing it. She knew him so well; even after all these years, there was a part of her that instinctively wanted to comfort him. That was what she'd always done.

And, there was something else in her: she felt guilty. There had been a worry in her mind, all these years, that she'd been to blame for Ramsay disappearing.

But, there was a bigger part of her that knew it was more important to protect herself. To protect her own heart from being broken again. And, she was allowed to be angry. Anyone would be, in the same situation.

So, instead of trying to talk him around – to heal the pain in his voice – Tara held herself back.

'I think you should go,' she said, keeping her voice level.

'Is that what you really want?' His eyes met hers, and she almost wavered at the sight of the raw emotion there. 'It must mean something that you've kept the necklace.'

'Yes,' she said, lowering her eyes. 'I want you to go. And the necklace has nothing to do with you.'

'Tara...' Ramsay reached for her.

Just at that moment, June popped her head around the doorframe.

'Just wanted to let you know I'm going to close up soon, Tara,' she said. 'Oh. Sorry, I didn't realise you had company.'

'Ramsay is just leaving,' Tara said, smiling politely.

'Oh – I can give you ten minutes or so, it's no trouble,' June said, smiling maternally at them both. Clearly, she thought that something was going on.

'No, it's fine, thank you, June.' Tara turned away from him, deliberately hiding her expression. She felt like she was on the verge of tears.

'Yeah. I'll get out of your way,' Ramsay said. 'Sorry to have bothered you, Tara.'

'No trouble,' she called after him, turning to watch him go. *No trouble.* The most inaccurate thing, the most nonsensical politeness she could have said, in that moment.

There was trouble, and there was hurt. Ramsay's visit – out of the blue, again – had troubled her.

She didn't want to say goodbye. She wanted to hear his voice. She wanted to talk to him and see him. Yes, some of her did want to go back into their old dynamic, as if nothing had changed. All of that was true.

And, there was still that spectre of panic and horror that

never went away: the night that she'd done something she would never forget, just a couple of days before she'd got the letter from Ramsay, telling her that he was leaving. That she'd never see him again.

That night that she'd done the thing she would always regret – because, how could it be unconnected to him disappearing? She'd regretted it every time she thought about it. No. Not just regret. She had dreaded the thought that she had somehow been instrumental in his disappearance. Or, worse. That she had caused him pain.

Yet, despite the hurt, Tara was also far too angry just to slip back into their old ways and not express her feelings.

'Are you all right, dear?' June stood aside for Ramsay to leave, giving him a polite nod as he did so. She walked into the room and looked at Tara with a concerned expression.

'Yes. I'm fine. Thank you, June. I'll get out of your hair.' Tara snatched up her speaker and her phone. 'Thanks so much for letting me use the room.'

'You're welcome, dear.' June beamed at her. 'I wonder, would you be interested in doing some dance training for some of us ladies at the Thursday group? We have this fundraiser coming up, and we'd intended to have a ceilidh as part of it. I know we all sort of muddle along in one of those but if we had someone to teach us a few advanced steps, that would be fun. Or even help us prepare a special routine.'

'Umm. Yeah, sure. No problem.' Tara was reminded of the pushy PTA parents at Lomond Primary; June had a similarly confident way of asking a favour in a way that was difficult to refuse. At this point, she just wanted to go home and bury her face in a pillow; she felt like she would agree to pretty much anything if it meant she could leave and be on her own right now.

'All right, then. I'll be in touch. Just pop in when you're ready, or I'll get your number from your mum.' June gave Tara a little tap on the arm. 'You're sure you're all right, dear? Things seemed a little strained with your young man just now.'

'He's not my young man,' she said. 'I'm fine, really.'

'If you say so. But there did seem to be a certain frisson there.' June raised an eyebrow.

'I better be off. Stuff to do at the Inn,' Tara said, desperate to get away.

'Right you are, dear.' June stepped aside as Tara passed, and turned off the light. 'Least said, soonest mended, as they say.'

Tara nodded and made her escape onto the high street. For a moment, she worried that Ramsay would be there, waiting for her, but the cobbled street was empty.

She ran to the loch and took off her trainers, rolling her yoga pants to her knees and wading in to the water; it was always cold, regardless of the time of year, but there was also something gloriously clean and smooth about it too. She'd always loved the loch, and spent time wading in it or just being next to it when she was young, especially when she was stressed.

She took in a deep breath and released it. *Calm and clarity. Calm and clarity.* It had become her mantra when she was a teenager, spending time with her thoughts at the loch. It was a way she self-soothed, and she felt instantly relieved by doing it now.

With her back to the high street, she let the tears come. She didn't feel calm, but she knew it would be better if she could let her feelings out safely.

She was so angry, but she was also so sad. Why had everything with Ramsay gone so wrong?

SIXTEEN

The Wee Dram had been part of Loch Cameron's high street since Tara was little. She remembered coming in with her dad on the weekends to pick up supplies for the Inn, and having to wait patiently while Eric chatted with the owner, Grenville McNulty, who still ran the shop.

In the window, faded posters for Cinzano and Martini Rosso competed with a classic globe-style cocktail cabinet. There was a large display for Loch Cameron Distillery single malt whisky, and a sign outside that said:

LOCAL STOCKIST, OLD MAIDS
SINGLE MALT
BOOK YOUR DISTILLERY TOUR HERE
FREE SAMPLES

Of course, Grenville was a good deal older now, although he'd always seemed old to Tara. He wore a white, neatly trimmed beard and was dressed smartly in dark slacks, a cream-coloured shirt with a pointed collar that Tara assumed had been fashionable in the 1970s. It was open at the neck, and Grenville wore a wine-coloured cravat with it.

He sat in a black leather armchair behind an impressive green baize-topped table, greeting Tara as she pushed open the heavy glass-panelled door to the shop. As soon as she opened the door, a fusty aroma of leather, cigars, dust and whisky hit her: it had never changed, as far as she could remember.

'Afternoon, Miss Ballantyne,' Grenville sang out as she walked in. 'How are you, my dear? It's been a while.'

'Fine, thanks, Grenville.' Tara approached the desk, smiling, even though she felt that now-familiar sense of unreality in coming back to somewhere she hadn't stepped inside since childhood. There had been no reason to come here as an adult on her infrequent trips to Loch Cameron. But, now, she could almost see herself, aged eight, holding her mother's hand as Dotty gossiped with Grenville. It was slightly surreal. 'Mum's sent me over for the drinks order.' The shop was lit by gold-hued lamps, and Tara thought that added to the feeling of being transported back in time. It always seemed to be sometime in the past in Grenville's shop.

'Aha. I have it just here for you, dear.' Grenville got up and went into the back room behind the counter, returning with a box containing a number of bottles of whisky and two of gin. 'All Loch Cameron Distillery, as usual, and the botanical gin your mother likes.' He put the box on the counter. 'On the tab, I assume?'

'Please. I think Dad said he'll come in and settle up.'

'Right you are, dear. So, how are you enjoying being home? And how's poor Dotty? I expect she's being the world's absolute worst patient,' Grenville chuckled. 'And I say that with love, of course. Never let it be said that I don't appreciate your dear mother.'

'Oh, well, she's okay. But, yes. A terrible patient.' Tara

smiled. 'Yesterday she called me from the bedroom to remind me how to make tea properly for the guests. I'm twenty-nine.'

'Ah. Mothers.' Grenville clucked his tongue. 'We do love them so.' He gave her a cheeky grin. 'Well, please do give Dotty my regards, and let me know if I can be of any help. I was thinking that I should pop over and entertain her with a cross-word or something of that type. What can you suggest, dear?'

'Actually, I expect she'd just really appreciate a chat. You know that she, err... likes to keep up to date with what's happening in the village.' Tara knew that both she and Grenville understood what that was code for: Dotty was a huge gossip and was probably missing her usual opportunities to glean all the new goings-on from her friends. That said, Tara had noticed that her mum had been on the phone an awful lot, so obviously the rumour mill wasn't quite exhausted as yet.

'I can certainly do that.' Grenville nodded decisively. 'Poor dear. Don't worry, Miss Ballantyne. I've got plenty of salacious titbits to entertain Dotty with, from the distillery tours. There have been some unbelievable happenings of late.' He lowered his voice conspiratorially. 'You know that I've taken over the tours of the distillery, I take it? It started a couple of years ago, and I rather enjoy it. Gives me an opportunity to stretch my talents for amateur dramatics.'

'I didn't know, but that sounds fun.' Tara wondered if Grenville was lonely; the shop didn't seem like somewhere that was always packed full of people, although it had been open for years and so Grenville must be doing okay for custom. She realised that she didn't know much about him: he was single, as far as she knew, and though he was a friend of her parents – all the shopkeepers and businesses on the high street knew each other – she'd never really spoken to him, just one to one.

'Oh, it is, dear. Of course, you used to perform yourself.' Grenville sat back down in his leather chair with a sigh. 'My dancing days are probably behind me, but I used to love a foxtrot.'

'Well, it's never too late to get back into it,' Tara said. 'If it was something you enjoyed.'

'Well, I'm not doing anything now.' Grenville twinkled at her, standing up and appearing at her side rather suddenly. He held out an arm and bowed. 'Would you do me the honour, Miss Ballantyne?'

'What, now? Oh, my... all right.' Tara was thrown by the sudden action, but acquiesced as Grenville put one hand on her waist and clasped her other hand in his. 'Alexa. Foxtrot,' he called out, and after a couple of seconds, some big band, jazzy dancing music came on.

'Goodness. You'll have to bear with me, it's been a long time since my ballroom classes.' Tara giggled, despite the unexpectedness of it. Being a teacher had made her a little more used to a certain level of unpredictability; at school, she could often end up dancing with children in the hallways or talking about gerbil names without warning. A sudden foxtrot with someone she'd known all of her life was just one of those things: she could roll with it. And, since she'd started dancing again, it seemed as though the universe was going to put opportunities to dance in front of her.

'Nonsense, dear. You're doing fine. Just follow my lead,' he said, gently guiding her in the steps. 'Right foot back, now step to the right... that's it. Just follow me, dear.'

They danced around the circumference of the shop, and Tara tried to concentrate on remembering the steps.

'It's like a waltz, isn't it? The foxtrot?' she said, frowning.

'Yes, not dissimilar. Though the waltz is 3/4, and the foxtrot is 4/4. Time signature,' Grenville explained, spinning her under his upheld arm. 'That was just for fun. And, forward.' He hummed along with the music.

'Looks like I'm interrupting something.'

Ramsay's voice was so familiar that Tara didn't need to turn around to know it was him standing behind her in the whisky shop. She tensed immediately, her heart going from a pleasant rhythm to racing in a matter of seconds.

Grenville turned her around so that she was facing Ramsay: Tara found herself smiling, reflexively.

She felt the old joy at seeing his face; the familiar energy of him, the rightness of his body.

It was weird seeing him again. Her body reacted to him just like it had in the rehearsal room, the other day. But her memory still knew how many days of grief had passed in the time he was away. Her heart was a raw wound again, and it was almost impossible to stand there with him in the same room and not want to either cry and run away, or leap into his arms and never let go.

That was the thing that was messing with her, and she didn't know how to deal with it.

'Ah, Mr Fraser, isn't it?' Grenville halted for a moment and smiled politely.

'Aye. Hello, Grenville,' Ramsay replied.

'It's been a while, eh?' Grenville let go of Tara and took both of Ramsay's hands in his. 'How are you, lad?'

'I'm okay, thanks.' Ramsay shot Tara a shy look out of the corner of his eye. Neither one of them had acknowledged the other, yet. 'Hi, Tara.'

'Hello again,' she replied, self-consciously rearranging her ponytail, which was a little awry. She felt as though it must be obvious to absolutely anyone that there was an awkward tension between them, but Grenville hadn't seemed to notice.

As children, sometimes they'd stared into the dim windows of The Wee Dram and speculated on what whisky tasted like. As teenagers, they'd tried their luck once, aiming to buy a bottle of Loch Cameron single malt, even though they were underage. Looking back, Tara had no idea how they thought they would get away with it: Grenville was her mother's friend, after all. Everyone knew how old they were.

But, that day, Ramsay had really wanted to get drunk.

Grenville had turned them away with a chuckle, and that had been that. *Away with you*, he'd shooed them out of the shop.

Ramsay hadn't said why he'd wanted that bottle of whisky, but Tara could guess. They had snuck a bottle of wine out of the Inn's bar a couple of times as teenagers and taken it up to a hidden spot, up on Queen's Point, and, sometimes, he'd cried. He never wanted to talk about it, but she knew it was about his dad.

Let's get out of here, Ramsay had pulled at her hand, that afternoon, so many years ago. She could still feel his hand in hers. The shadow of his fingers in her palm, the pressure of his anxiety. It was rare for him to be like that, but there was a darkness in him, under the sweetness. Not that it had ever been directed at her. Ramsay's demons punished him, and him only. Tara may not have known the details of what went on in Ramsay's home life – despite asking him frequently – but she knew enough about Ramsay's dad to guess.

'You were Miss Ballantyne's original dance partner. Please, do cut in.' Grenville held Tara's hand out to Ramsay, smiling paternally. 'I remember you two. You were the pride of Loch Cameron! Come on, do a little turn for me now. Alexa – Tango!'

'Oh, I don't think...' Tara protested, a crashing feeling of grief mixed with joy at seeing Ramsay, filling her. She wanted to pull her hand back, but she also wanted to bury her face in Ramsay's chest. Grenville didn't know what had happened between them, and the emotional inferno that was raging inside Tara's heart.

Grenville wasn't privy to her feelings, and neither was Ramsay, although he must be aware that they were intense and difficult. He had always been the one that had known her best, after all. That didn't just disappear.

'Better do as we're told.' Ramsay surprised her by taking her hand. His hand found her waist, just as it had done a thousand times before. They had danced so many times; it was familiar, easy, natural. She was aware that the tango was a very particular choice, and if Dotty hadn't schooled her so rigorously as a child about being polite to her elders, she would have protested. But, it seemed easier just to comply.

'Hey,' Ramsay breathed, his eyes finding hers.

'Hey,' she replied, quietly. They stood there awkwardly for a moment. 'Grenville, I don't think...' Tara began, but then the music began, and Ramsay started to lead her in the tango, a smile at the edge of his lips.

How can he smile? she wondered. *Doesn't he know how difficult this is for me?*

And, yet, as soon as he touched her, Tara felt pleasure and *rightness* erupt in her. It was excruciating, but it was also the feeling she'd craved for so long.

She found that she was concentrating on remembering the steps: her body had kicked in to its old habit of following Ramsay's body as he led her in the dance. Without really saying anything to each other, the chemistry was flowing between them effortlessly.

She made an involuntary moaning sound as Ramsay dipped her; thankfully, she'd remembered to place her feet correctly so that she didn't fall over, but she felt unsteady.

'You never know when you'll be called upon to tango.' Ramsay shot her a shy grin as they moved together. They'd mentioned the tango when he'd intruded on her dance practice at the community centre; now that they were actually dancing it again, she could tell that he was slightly awkward. But he was also an ex-dancer, and Tara knew that he wouldn't deliver less than a professional performance.

Tara tried desperately not to think about how sexual the tango was: how intimate its movements were, how good it felt to be pressed against Ramsay. How good it felt to be led by him in this deeply sensual way.

They turned, Tara tossing her hair instinctively at the well-known about-turn move at the edge of the shop floor, where the dance changed direction and her and Ramsay's hands swapped, re-joined and powered forward, arms outstretched. Ramsay led her back to the counter, his hand in the small of her back. There was a passion in his eyes as they held hers that made her swallow hard. But, she returned his fiery gaze.

Grenville clapped approvingly. Tara almost didn't hear him: she was so caught up in Ramsay and the dance – the propulsive, sexy beat of the tango and the heat between them – that real life felt as though it had faded into a background, distant hum.

'I didn't expect to be dancing today,' Ramsay murmured. 'Or to have you in my arms.'

'I... I didn't either.' Tara blushed hard.

Ramsay held Tara in a deep dip, staring into her eyes.

His gaze flickered to her neck: the heart necklace had come free and was dangling on top of her T shirt. He didn't say anything, but his eyes returned to hers.

He had seen that she was still wearing it when she'd seen him at the community centre. But, having that secret exposed made her feel vulnerable. She didn't want Ramsay to know that he still mattered so much to her.

'Wonderful! Excellent! What a treat!' Grenville cried, clapping them both, his hands making a delicate prayer shape. 'Little did I know when I opened the shop this morning that I'd be getting a personal performance from Loch Cameron's dance champions! You've brightened by day, my dear ones. My week!'

'You're welcome.' Ramsay let go of Tara, and she felt the loss of his touch immediately.

'Um. Yeah. Sure.' Tara adjusted her t-shirt, and tried to look unruffled. She took her hair down and tied it back up in a ponytail.

'I actually just came in for a bottle of wine. I'm cooking beef bourguignon and I realised I didn't have anything. I don't tend to keep alcohol in the house,' he added, clearing his throat. She knew what that meant. *I'm not like my dad.*

'Ah, good, good. I do have some lovely red wines.' Grenville held up a finger and went over to a shelf to the left of the shop, and brought back a couple of different choices. 'These are robust, not too expensive, tasty. I'd say they'd cook well.' He handed them both to Ramsay.

So, let's pretend that nothing just happened, Tara thought. *Let's pretend that we didn't just connect deeply, out of the blue, here in a little whisky shop. That we didn't just feel what we felt.*

'Thanks. This one will be fine.' Ramsay held out one of the bottles to Grenville, who nodded appreciatively and turned away to the counter.

'I'll wrap it for you,' he said, pulling out some brown paper with a flourish.

'So,' Ramsay jammed his hands into his pockets and met Tara's eyes, tilting his head to one side. 'We meet again.'

'Yeah. Here we are,' she replied, feeling her heart pounding in her chest. It wasn't from the exercise.

'Sorry for the tango,' he said, his awkwardness belying the confident, controlled way that he had just steered her around Grenville's shop floor. 'He put on the music... I guess it was muscle memory that kicked in.'

'That's okay. Same here, I guess. You don't forget.'

'I certainly haven't,' he said, his expression unreadable. 'You still wear it.'

She knew he meant the necklace. He'd mentioned it before, at the community centre.

'Yes,' she replied, softly. There was a silence between them;

Tara realised that she was biting her lip. 'It's a nice memory. Just because something's in the past doesn't mean that you can't still take pleasure from it.' She'd said it before thinking, and as soon as the words were out of her mouth, she regretted them.

His eyebrows hiked in surprise.

'Oh. I...' he began, awkwardly.

'I should be getting back,' she said, interrupting him.

There were a million things Tara wanted to say to him, but she couldn't: not with Grenville right there, and not even then, perhaps. Those things were too difficult. She'd inadvertently said more than she intended to, already.

'Oh... Okay.' He frowned, and reached out his hand towards her; awkwardly, he gripped the cuff of her cardigan for a moment and then let it go. 'Ummm... sure.'

Grenville said something, and Ramsay turned to the counter to pay. Tara didn't know what to say; she didn't know how to *be* around Ramsay Fraser. Not now. Being in his arms just now had made it all the more confusing.

To quell the rising feeling of panic in her stomach, she stepped up to the counter and gestured to Grenville that she was taking the box of bottles for the Inn.

'Good to see you,' she murmured, ostensibly to both of them.

'Bye, dear! See you soon.' Grenville looked up and smiled, halfway through operating the shop's antiquated till. Ramsay looked like he wanted to say something, but she just nodded to him, and left.

Once outside, Tara strode down the high street, keen to put distance between her and The Wee Dram. Her heart was still raw; it still felt as though its tender healing had been ripped open again. Was she going to keep bumping into Ramsay? Was that how it was going to be, now that she was back in Loch Cameron? If so, she had to come up with a better strategy than getting spooked and running away.

But, the truth was that Tara really didn't know how to be around her lost love. Because, when the love of your life reappeared unexpectedly in your life, it felt as though you had had your heart cut out, all over again. That you were standing on top of a tower that was falling, and you could do nothing but fall with it.

And, worst of all, she had the terrible feeling that she'd been the one to push the tower over in the first place. And the guilt and the worry over that washed over her whenever she dared to think about what she'd done.

SEVENTEEN

'Hello?' Tara called as she walked into the community centre. It was a Thursday morning, and her dad had reminded her that she needed to go and pick up some brownies and other baked goods from someone called Sheila, who ran a drop-in coffee morning there today. Her mum had told her to send her regards and apologise for the fact she couldn't attend. Tara was also mindful that she'd promised June she'd help the ladies with some dancing, and felt guilty that she hadn't followed it up yet.

'What yer mother means is,' Eric had said as he'd handed her some cash and a carrier bag for the cakes, 'Tell everyone at her crochet coven she misses them. An' she misses the gossip.'

'Good mornin'.' A woman standing at a trestle table looked up and smiled. 'Can I help ye, lassie?'

'Morning. My mum sent me over to pick up some cakes for the Inn? I'm Dotty's daughter, Tara. And I'm supposed to teach you some country dancing... I chatted to June the other day...' She looked around for the woman she'd seen before.

'Ach, Tara, of course!' The woman jogged around from the other side of the table and enveloped Tara in an unexpected hug. 'I've heard so much about ye!'

'All good, I hope?' Tara replied, smiling politely.

'Ach, o' course. Dotty's so proud o' ye, bein' a teacher, an' all. I'm Sheila. Welcome,' the woman said, pulling away and disentangling her bright yellow jumper from Tara's heart pendant necklace. 'Sorry, hen. I made this thing with big stitches, and it gets caught on everythin'.'

'No trouble.' Tara's hand went instinctively to the pendants around her neck; she'd worn them for so long now that she hardly remembered they were there, most of the time.

'That's pretty. Aren't ye supposed tae wear the one, though?' Sheila nodded to the half heart pendants.

'Oh. Yeah. Long story.' Tara frowned. 'So, this is the crochet coven?' She changed the subject.

'Indeed it is. Welcome to our not-so-secret circle of crochet and cake.' Sheila nodded and gestured to the trestle table of mouthwatering-looking cakes in various open Tupperware containers.

'Wow. That truly is a magical combination. I mean the cakes, really.'

'Aye. All hand baked. I made the cookies, Mina made the brownies an' the blondies. June, over there –' Sheila pointed to a black woman with grey hair, dressed in a long purple kaftan type dress with an elegant long line cream jumper over the top, like a robe – 'She made the carrot cake an' the lemon drizzle. I'd recommend those, but they're all good.'

'Yes, I met June the other day. She persuaded me to come and teach you all some country dancing moves. For an event you're having, I think?' Tara tried not to think about seeing Ramsay that day, and then after, at The Wee Dram. She hadn't heard from him since: he hadn't tried to find her again, or call her. She was grateful for the silence, but it also weighed heavy on her.

'Oh, she did say! Ah, that's marvellous. Now...' Sheila turned away, holding up her index finger, then turned back to

Tara, holding a white cardboard box. 'These are for the Inn. Twenty-four brownies, an' the same blondies. That's what Dotty asked fer.'

'Amazing. Thank you.' Tara took them, and gave Sheila the cash her dad had pressed into her hand. 'Mum says hi, and Dad says that she misses the gossip. So I guess if you've got any in particular, you can give it to me and I'll take it back for her.'

'Haha. Indeed, indeed. I expect there is some; this is Loch Cameron, after all. But I'll give Dotty a call later, or pop in,' Sheila chuckled. 'Give her my love, won't you?'

'I will. So, what are you raising money for?'

'The primary school fundraiser. You must've heard aboot this by now.'

'Ah. Right. I was up at the primary school the other day and Emily mentioned it.'

'Ah, Emily. She's a good sort, aye. She's over there. You'll say hello an' stay for a cuppa?' Sheila looked at her expectantly.

'Okay. Sure.' Tara looked across the room and waved at Emily, who was chatting to another woman and holding a ball of wool on her lap.

Tara chose a large oatmeal cookie and poured herself a cup of coffee, heading over to where Emily was sitting. She sat down in a free chair next to her.

When Ramsay had first left, Tara had spent a year trying to fill the hole he had left in her heart with food. It hadn't worked, and she'd put on two stone. After a lifetime of dance, her body relaxed and changed, losing its rigid muscle and toned middle. She didn't entirely mind being softer, now that she was older, and had stopped comfort eating quite as much. But, now that she was dancing again, she could feel her old body re-emerging, and it was good. She felt more like herself, even after a short while.

Still, she thought it was definitely okay to have a cookie. A cookie was hardly comfort eating. She was just being sociable.

'Hey.' Emily looked up as she sat down. 'So, you've discovered the crochet coven? What do you think? This is the beating heart of Loch Cameron, if you haven't realised it already. Where all the power-broking happens.' Emily grinned at her. 'Joking. But only kind of.'

'Hiya. Yeah. So, is this what you do here? Crochet and cake?' Tara took a bite of the cookie. 'Damn. That's good.'

'Pretty much. Gossip. We're working on the fundraiser for the school as well. I tend to just come along in the holidays,' Emily said. 'Hey. I'm glad I saw you, by the way. I wanted to check in and see if you were okay. It was all a bit fraught up at the school the other day, with Ramsay Fraser?' She lowered her voice. 'I didn't have your number otherwise I would have called you to check in. You seemed pretty upset at one point.'

'Aww. Thanks, that's kind.' Tara let out a deep breath. 'I have been kind of in a state about it. Also, I'm surprised that my mother hasn't just put my phone number on a community pin board somewhere. She seems to be giving it out to all and sundry.' Tara rolled her eyes.

'So, what's going on?' Emily leaned in towards her. 'It's fine if you don't want to say, by the way. But, as I said, I'm here if you want a friend.'

'Thank you. I appreciate it, really. And you're welcome to have my number, by the way.' Tara got out her phone. 'Tell me yours. This thing with Ramsay is just doing my head in, though. The other day I ran into him at the whisky shop, The Wee Dram? We ended up doing the tango. It was mortifying.'

'The tango? Why?' Emily looked mystified.

'We used to dance together professionally. From when we were kids. It's a long story. Grenville, the owner?' Tara paused, and Emily nodded.

'I know Grenville. He's a character.'

'Yeah. Well, he suggested it and it just... sort of happened.'

'Wow. I feel like there's a lot more to this story between

you.' Emily sipped her tea and looked at Tara over the top of her glasses.

'There is,' Tara sighed. 'There's a reason I haven't come back to Loch Cameron much in the past ten years.'

'Because he's been here?' Emily frowned.

'No. I don't think he was, until fairly recently. My mum would have told me. But it was just too much to come back. Too many bad memories.'

'There's definitely a bigger story there. I'm so sorry it's all a bit much to be back.'

'Thanks. It's okay.' It wasn't okay, but that was what people said.

'Hallo, Tara, dear.' June tapped her on the shoulder. 'I see you've met Emily.'

'Hello, June. How are you? Yes. Fellow teacher.' Tara smiled up at the older woman. As before, she was elegantly dressed and possessed an air of no-nonsense calm. Tara was glad of the distraction. She didn't really want to tell Emily the whole story in front of the crochet coven: even though they'd been speaking in low voices, she'd noticed that a few women were keeping a not-so-subtle ear open. She reminded herself that this group of women were her mum's friends, and, as Emily had wryly observed, this was the beating heart of the Loch Cameron gossip mill.

'Ah, I'm fine, thank you. I'm the same when I meet a nurse. Always a good gossip.'

'You're a nurse?' Tara asked.

'I was. Retired many years now. I miss it, but it takes a toll on your body after a while. I'm too old for the long shifts, but I still visit up at the local hospital. I used to train nurses until relatively recently, but I had to give that up too. Nowadays, I content myself with playing piano, crochet and baking.'

'That still seems like a lot of things.'

'Ah, well, I like to be busy. I just wanted to say thanks again for offering to help us with the dancing, and to see if you'd mind coming in again next Thursday lunchtime?' June pushed up the sleeves of her long, stylish cardigan.

'That should be all right.' Tara made a note on the calendar on her phone. 'I'll be here.'

'Thank you! And, I hope you and your young man made it up, from the other day,' June said.

'Oh... he's not my young man,' Tara said, a flush rising to her cheeks. 'He's just an old friend. Everything's fine.'

Emily shot her a look: it was clear that she suspected June was talking about Ramsay from the way that Tara reacted.

'Well, I should hope so,' June said, her tone teasing. 'Lovely looking boy, too. Man, I should say. Comes a time, dear, when everyone looks like a boy to you.'

Thinking about Ramsay made Tara uncomfortable. She stood up, suddenly, and scraped back her chair.

'Well, I should be going,' she said, abruptly. 'Thanks for the coffee and the cookie.'

'Oh. Are you going, already?' Emily looked up at her, in consternation.

'Yes. I should get back.' Tara felt silly, knowing that she was overreacting to a throwaway conversation, but Emily and June didn't know everything that had been going on in her mind recently. Emily and June didn't know how painful and confusing it had been, seeing Ramsay again. How much hurt she had locked away behind that door in her mind, in her heart.

'Okay. Take care, Tara. Give me a call, okay? We'll go out for a glass of wine or something,' Emily called after her.

'See you soon, dear,' June called.

'You're welcome. Yes, see you,' Tara replied hastily, suddenly desperate to be gone. She picked up the box of cakes, waved a quick goodbye to everyone, and headed back out onto the high street.

Loch Cameron was nice when she could find a quiet

moment in nature. The air was clean, the glittering loch was beautiful and there were so many tranquil spots where you could go and re-centre yourself.

But when it came to being in the community, it was difficult to navigate. There was a big part of her that found Loch Cameron soothing, but what she definitely didn't find calming at all was the presence of her old, lost love. There were memories around every corner. Like the vision she'd had of herself, holding her mother's hand, in The Wee Dram. Now, as well as those old shadows from the past that just felt strange, Ramsay's presence was an extra layer of emotional bleariness.

June mentioning him just now had made her feel confused all over again.

What did he want? It had seemed as though he wanted to see her. And there was a connection between them: a heat, a deep love that couldn't be denied. But they always seemed to speak at cross purposes, and there was an ocean of misunderstanding between them.

I don't know if I'm ready for whatever drama comes with being around Ramsay Fraser again, Tara thought, standing still for a moment and staring out at the loch. The loch had always been the place she had gone to re-centre herself: if she hadn't been holding a box of cakes right then, she would have waded in and let the cold water still her jangled nerves. Instead, she took in a deep breath of that clean, cool air and let it out again, slowly.

I don't have to get involved in any drama that I don't want, she told herself, firmly. *All I have to do is get through another few weeks of helping out mum and dad, then I'll be out of here and I never have to see Ramsay Fraser again.*

Did she never want to see him again? In her heart of hearts, she knew that she'd be sad if she didn't. But it seemed that every time she saw him, something happened to make her feel disjointed, disconnected and wrong. It wasn't as easy as picking up where they'd left off. There was a valley between them: a depth of wrongs that need to be bridged before either one of them could cross to the other side.

Maybe that bridge would never be built. Tara didn't know if she had it in her to build it, and she wasn't sure if Ramsay wanted to try. *I guess I'll see,* she thought, feeling calmer as the lochside air loosened the knots of anxiety in her muscles. *One way or the other.*

EIGHTEEN

Tara looked at her phone as she changed the sheets in one of the Inn's bedrooms: a lovely Canadian couple in their fifties had just checked out, and she had to get the room ready for two friends who were checking in that afternoon. They'd requested that the room be made up as a twin, and so Tara had spent a good ten minutes pushing the two large divans that had been sandwiched together to make a king size bed, into two beds with a good sized gap in the middle. She'd built up quite a sweat doing it and, not for the first time, wondered how her mum was doing it every day and not becoming totally exhausted. The more that she worked at the Inn, the more she realised that Dotty probably needed some help – and, characteristically of her mother – wasn't asking for it.

She'd been texting Carla on and off, and thought it might be her, texting from somewhere on her travels. Apparently, Carla and Craig had decided to spend another couple of weeks touring Europe together. The last text Tara had received said that Carla was in Paris.

Hi Tara, good to see you in The Wee Dram the other day. I'm not stalking you, honest! It would be good to have a chat.

It was Ramsay.

Tara stared at her phone for a moment. She didn't want to reply. She wished Dotty hadn't given Ramsay her number.

Another text popped up.

I've missed you so much. There are things we have to talk about.

Leave me alone, she thought, desperately.

I'd love to talk to you soon, Tara another message flashed up.

Tara felt suddenly overwhelmed.

She stared at her phone for several minutes before striding into her mother's bedroom. She was angry that her mother – who knew exactly how she felt about Ramsay, and, she hoped, remembered how hurt she'd been when he disappeared – would betray her trust and just give him her phone number, willy-nilly. She'd been cross about it the other day, when Ramsay had turned up in the rehearsal room, but she hadn't said anything to Dotty then.

Had Dotty told Ramsay how much Tara had missed him? *Ye know*, Dotty might have said, leaning in towards him, her voice dropping to a confidential tone, *she was never the same after losing ye. Ruined her for all other men. Lived like a nun for the last ten years.*

God, I hope she didn't say that, Tara thought. She knew her mum probably wouldn't have gone that far, but Dotty was an oversharer by nature.

She picked up her phone and stormed into her mum's room, where she found Dotty lying on her bed, watching TV.

'Thanks for this,' she said, holding her phone up so that her mum could see the messages. 'He won't leave me alone, now that you've given him my number.'

'I hope yer no' havin' a go at me, hen.' Dotty looked up from her bed, where she was crocheting what looked like a cardigan for a baby. 'Because it sounds suspiciously like ye are.' She fixed Tara with a steely gaze. 'May I remind ye that I'm yer mother.'

'As if I could forget!' Tara blurted, and then saw the look in her mother's eye. 'Sorry, Mum. But I just don't know why you gave Ramsay my number.'

'Why not? It's no' like yer just never goin' tae speak tae each other again.' Dotty poked her crochet hook in and out of the cardigan, with a skein of wool stretched expertly between the fingers on her other hand. Tara had watched her mother crochet so many times that she knew Dotty didn't need to look at what she was doing. Tara took a deep breath and tried to control her temper: it didn't do to shout at Dotty Ballantyne. She'd learnt that many years ago. 'You and Ramsay were joined at the hip. Peas in a pod.'

'But, I don't know what to say to him. And he keeps texting me, and the other day – after you gave him my number, which I didn't give you permission to do – he came and found me at the community centre, and we had a really uncomfortable conversation. And then, when I was at The Wee Dram, he found me there – accidentally? Maybe not? And we ended up doing a bloody *tango* because Grenville asked us to.'

'I know. Grenville told me.' Dotty's eyes flicked back to the cardigan for a moment as she turned it and began a row in the opposite direction. Tara wondered if she was counting stitches or whether she just knew, instinctively, how many to do.

'You knew, and you didn't tell me?'

'Ye didnae seem tae want tae talk aboot it.' Dotty gave a world-weary sigh. 'I learnt a long time ago that I cannae make ye talk tae me unless yer ready.'

'Hm. Well, he blindsided me at the community centre,

thanks to you. When I'd gone there to spend some quality time alone, dancing. He just bowled in like I owed him something. And then, at Grenville's shop, we ended up doing the tango. And it was really awkward, actually,' Tara continued, angrily.

'What did you and he talk aboot? When he came to the community centre?' Dotty asked, in a level tone. 'And I'm sorry if ye feel I crossed a boundary. I was just doin' what I thought was best.'

'Well, it wasn't *best.* I would have preferred it if he just left me alone,' Tara snapped.

'You'd prefer it if the world left you alone.' Dotty raised an eyebrow. 'But, I'm sorry tae say, lassie, that's no' how the world works. Ye have tae face up tae things. And people.'

Tara stared at her mother for a few moments, knowing that if she argued, Dotty would probably tell her off. *Is she right?* she thought. *Do I have to face up to the past at some point?*

She gave Dotty the outline of Ramsay's impromptu visit. Dotty sighed, and put her crochet in her lap.

'I'm sorry, hen. I shouldnae have given him your number without askin'. I didnae think you'd mind.'

'Well, I do mind.' Tara was trying not to disrespect her mum – *but I'm still allowed to have boundaries,* she thought. *I am a grown up.*

'Right enough. Sometimes I forget yer a grown woman,' Dotty sighed. 'I know I can be bossy. But it's because I love ye.'

'I know, Mum.'

'I wanted the two o' ye tae talk,' Dotty said. 'Clear the air. I know it's bothered ye so much. All these years.'

'I know, Mum,' Tara repeated, patiently.

'He was the son we never had,' Dotty said, wistfully.

'I know.' Tara knew she needed to curb her impatience in talking to Dotty, but sometimes it could be hard. 'But I want to know what to do about him now.' She sat on the edge of the bed, pushing a pile of sudoku books to one side.

'He had a hard time, ye know.' Dotty nodded, as if Tara hadn't said anything. 'At home.'

'I know,' Tara said, remembering the bruises, the day that Ramsay had wanted to steal the whisky from The Wee Dram. The times they had made off with a bottle of wine from the Inn's bar when they were older and drunk it together under the stars. 'His dad.'

'Aye. He was a right so-and-so.' Dotty shook her head. 'Turn your hair white if I told ye what he did tae that poor lad.'

'You've never told me. You just always say that. That it'd turn my hair white.'

'Aye, well, what's the point now? All in the past.' Dotty's hands started crocheting again, as if the action was soothing to her, or a helpful distraction.

'Mum. Tell me.' Tara reached for her mother's hands and held them gently until they stilled.

'Tara. Ye dinnae want tae know,' her mother said, in a warning tone. 'It'll just upset ye.'

'I'm already upset. I want to know,' Tara insisted. Dotty sighed.

'I dinnae see the point, darlin',' she prevaricated, but Tara met her eyes with a level stare.

'Mum. Please.'

'Fine.' Dotty put her crochet down and let out another long sigh.

'Jack Fraser. That was his name. Ye probably dinnae remember him.' Dotty's voice was low. 'God knows we kept ye away from that hoose. Poor Ramsay. We kept him here as much as we could,' her mother began.

'I know that,' Tara said.

'Aye. Well, when he was younger, Jack was a nice enough fella. Used tae come tae the Inn, have a few drams, nae bother. Then, long story short, after his wife left – Stella, nice girl – he got nasty. We started hearin' from Jack's neighbours there was noise at night. Crashin'. Yellin'. Course, ye wonder what Stella was puttin' up with that made her leave.' Dotty raised an eyebrow. 'To this day I dinnae why she didnae take Ramsay with her. I can only think that he wouldnae let her take him.'

'He never talked about his mum leaving,' Tara said. 'I knew she did, kind of, but I was a kid. I mean, I remember her a bit, but we were hardly at his house. It all sort of passed me by.'

'Aye. Some of us girls in the village tried tae find her when she left, but she'd gone wi'out a trace.' Dotty looked sad.

'I wish he would have talked to me about it,' Tara said, sadly.

'I think, when he was with ye, darlin', ye made him so happy that he didnae want tae think aboot his home life. We gave him a little oasis away from all that. See it as a compliment.' Dotty smiled affectionately at her daughter.

'So, what then?'

'Well, Jack started showin' up to the bar already drunk, an' he just got worse after a few drinks. Yer Dad had tae bar him in the end. He didnae like it.' Dotty raised an imperious eyebrow. 'Let's just say that he made Ramsay's life hell after that. There's a reason they call it *the demon drink*, hen.' She shook her head sadly.

'In what way?' Tara wanted to know more, but Dotty shook her head and pursed her lips.

'Least said, soonest mended,' she said. 'He wants tae talk to ye. So, talk. You owe each other that,' Dotty said, gently. 'He loved ye so much, Tara. An' I know how much ye loved him. All I'm sayin' is, there's a lot o' pain on both sides, eh? At the very least, ye can communicate. He's obviously got somethin' he wants tae say. Maybe be friends again, aye? I miss the lad. I'm glad he's back. Aren't you?'

Dotty met Tara's gaze with such a kind and yet direct look that Tara felt it penetrate her soul.

'Yes. I am,' she breathed. She could never lie to Dotty. 'I missed him so much.'

'Come here, hen,' Dotty said, her voice full of love, and Tara sat on the bed next to her mother, taking care not to disturb her injured leg. She rested her head on her mother's shoulder, and Dotty stroked her hair, just like she'd done when she was a child. 'It'll be all right,' she said, and she put her arm around Tara. 'You and Ramsay are meant tae be together. I believe that,' she said.

'It's too late for that, Mum,' Tara said, her heart breaking. She thought of the text message on her phone. Ramsay wanted to build bridges. But how could she?

'Maybe. Maybe not, eh,' her mother said. 'If not together, then make an old woman happy and at least be friends, aye? It's been a long time since I had ye both around the dinner table. I'd like that again, if I could.'

'I'll talk to him,' Tara sighed. 'That's all I can promise. Okay?'

'Okay.' Dotty continued to stroke her hair. 'You know best, darlin'. But I want ye to know that I love you. Okay? And I love him. I told ye, he was the son we never had. Regardless of what happened between you two. An' I will love ye both, always, whatever happens.'

'I love you too, Mum,' Tara whispered.

They sat there in companionable silence for a while.

Looking back, Tara could see that she had closed herself off from her mother after Ramsay had left: it was too raw, too much to deal with, and even though Dotty had felt Ramsay's loss keenly, Tara hadn't been able to share it with her.

'I'm sorry, Mum,' she said, hugging Dotty a little tighter. 'I'm sorry I didn't talk to you about it.' A sob burst from her chest as she finally said what she needed to say. 'I'm sorry, Mum. You lost him too.'

'Ah, Tara.' Dotty's voice broke a little, and she hugged her daughter back just as tightly. 'It wasnae yer fault. It wasnae anyone's fault. We were just both heartbroken. But maybe now, we can move on. Eh? Give your old mother a smile.' Dotty kissed Tara's forehead and sat back, studying her face. 'Come on. I know ye've got a beltin' smile. Remember all those dance judges that ye melted with it.'

'That was Ramsay.' Tara chuckled, wiping her eyes. 'He was the beauty.'

'Oh, no, Tara.' Dotty stroked her daughter's cheek. 'It was always you, darlin'. Don't ye know that? Ye were always the most beautiful lassie in the room. Still are. An' wi' the kindest heart.'

'Aww. Mum.' Tara didn't know what to say.

'Aww, Mum, nothin'.' Dotty patted Tara's hand. 'Use that good heart, my girl. It'll never lead ye wrong.'

'Okay.' Tara nodded.

'Good girl.' Dotty sighed and leaned back on her pillows. 'Now. It's comin' up fer lunch, an' I suspect ye've still got the rooms tae finish. I'm here if ye want tae chat later. All right?'

'Yes, Mum.' Tara stood up, picking up the tea tray. 'Thanks.'

'Always here fer ye, sweetie. Me an' yer Dad. Ye know that.' Dotty nodded.

'I know.' Tara smiled.

In the kitchen, she set the tray on the side and took out her phone from her pocket. Ramsay had texted again.

Tara, I'm sorry to pester you. Would really love to talk.

I'm sorry not to reply. Let's meet for a chat. Lots to catch up on! Tara x she replied to Ramsay, and found herself smiling as she watched the three little dots as he wrote an immediate response.

Would love that. Meet me for a coffee on Gyle Head on Thursday morning? he replied.

Sure x she replied. Her heart lifted, despite all of her doubts. Perhaps Dotty was right, after all. She was following her heart, and it felt good.

On impulse, she slipped out of the Inn for a moment and jogged over to the loch. She needed a moment of calm. It was a clear day outside, and the high street was quiet.

She knelt down and trailed her fingers in the silky, cold water of the loch. She took in a deep breath and released it.

Calm and clarity. Calm and clarity.

It was scary, following her heart, but she had to believe she was doing the right thing. Perhaps she hadn't ruined everything, after all, though the worry niggled at her, still. She had the thought again of the tower, falling, and the same brief sense of vertigo, but pushed it away. She had worried about whether she'd caused Ramsay's disappearance for years.

But she couldn't think about that now. What was done, was done.

Wasn't it?

NINETEEN

'No, it's okay, you're getting it... step, close, step, hop... okay.'
Tara laughed good-naturedly as the women of the crochet coven
rehearsed some basic Scottish country dancing moves.

Kathy, who was perhaps somewhere in her early thirties,
with a striking two-tone black and cerise hairdo, tattoos up her
arms and wearing black jeans and a baby pink T shirt with a
Japanese cartoon cat on it, raised her hand.

'Tara. Can ye show us the foot positions again, like, in super
slow motion?' she called out. 'My body just isnae gettin' it.'

'I can't get it either,' Mina chuckled, who was her partner –
a woman of Indian origin with her hair in a neat black bob and
dressed smartly in tan jodhpurs and a white sweatshirt with a
prominent designer logo in diamante across the front. Tara
guessed Mina was in her forties. She had liked Mina's aura of
firmness with a sparkle of mischief straight away. 'I keep
wanting to go right when I should be going left.'

'Right. Okay, watch me again. June, would you mind?' Tara
had been standing in the middle of the women as they prome-
naded around her, two by two, in a makeshift circle. June, the
matriarch of the group, who Sheila had pointed out to her

before, was playing traditional Scottish tunes on the piano for them to dance to. 'Can someone walk through it with me?'

Teaching the crochet coven the basics of Highland dancing was another one of those experiences that plummeted Tara right back to her childhood. If she closed her eyes, she could remember her first ever lesson in a hall with a wooden floor very similar to this one: the squeak of her feet as she moved slowly through her first ever steps, the cabbagey, jumble sale smell of that first rehearsal room. What was missing was Ramsay, next to her, a studious expression on his face as he copied the teacher.

'Aye, I'll be your guinea pig,' a short-haired woman in jeans, worn trainers and a plain grey T-shirt volunteered herself. 'Bess Black. We havenae met so far. Thanks fer givin' up yer time tae transform a lot o' middle aged women intae fleet-footed goddesses,' she said with a twinkle in her eye. 'No' that I've got much faith in my dancin' skills, but at least the rest o' you lot stand half a chance of not showin' yerselves up at the fundraiser.'

'You're welcome. Least I can do to help the school,' Tara replied.

'Fleet-footed goddesses, my arse.' Sheila laughed uproariously. 'Middle-aged menopausal gossips, more like.'

'Can't we be both?' Bess raised a playful eyebrow. 'You're all goddesses tae me.'

'Awww. Haha. All right then. I suppose a lot o' those Greek and Roman goddesses had ample thighs an' bosoms.' Sheila shrugged.

'How many of you have done traditional dance before?' Tara asked. 'Just out of interest?'

'It's been years since I learned country dancin' at school. Done my share of ceilidhs, obviously,' Kathy said. 'Probably like most o' us. Like, ye can manage, but no' necessarily an expert.'

'Okay. Just so I know where we are.' Tara took Bess' hand. 'So. Very slowly, if everyone can see?' She demonstrated a

Strathspey setting step, which was a simple travelling step that went from right to left and then left to right, back and forth.

'Step, close, step, hop,' she said, as she demonstrated the move. 'Bess? With me. June, nice and slowly, if you don't mind?'

'Step, close, step, hop,' Bess repeated, brow furrowed, as they executed the steps slowly to June's patient piano.

'Now, everyone,' Tara said, and watched them. 'Just take it slowly. It's an easy step. Step, close, step, hop. That's it! You're getting it!' She stood by Mina and went through the step with her again, so that she could sense the rhythm.

'Ahh!' Mina grinned as she did the step. Tara could see it *click* in her, in the same way as sometimes when she was in the classroom and she saw understanding dawn on the face of a child. That was part of why she loved teaching.

'You've got it! Well done!' Tara clapped. 'Keep going! Step, close, step, hop!' She joined them in a line, as all the women coordinated their steps to the music. She'd never specifically taught dance before, apart from now and again with the children at her school when it was PE on a rainy day, but she realised that she was really enjoying it.

'Right, let's have a break,' Sheila called out. 'Tara, I'm sweatin' like a horse. Can we have tea an' cake an' then go back tae it in a bit?'

'Of course.' Tara nodded. Bess groaned and flexed her shin.

'All that jumpin'. I'm goin' tae feel it tomorrow.' She rubbed her leg.

'Well, it's not *much* of a jump, in that step.' Tara grinned, following her to the trestle table where the women had laid out a number of tupperware containers of cakes as before. 'It's more of a hop.'

'You say hop, I say cardiac arrest waiting tae happen,' Bess chuckled. 'Ah, I'm jokin', I'm jokin'. Do us all good tae get a bit o' exercise fer a change instead o' sittin' around, doin' crochet an' eatin' cake.'

'To be fair, we are eating cake now,' Emily said. 'Thanks for this, Tara. I really do appreciate your help, prepping us for the fundraiser. People love a dance, and it's so nice of you to help us out like this.'

'It's a pleasure,' Tara said, selecting a large, soft oatmeal cookie studded with raisins from a Tupperware box and accepting a cup of tea from June, who had left the piano and was sorting out the drinks for everyone. 'How much do I owe you?' she asked, but June frowned and waved her away.

'On the house, darlin'. You're here doin' us a favour,' she demurred.

'It's really no trouble. I'd like to contribute,' Tara said, but June gave her a sharp look.

'Absolutely not. I have spoken.'

'Don't argue,' Emily advised her, smiling at June, who gave her a twinkly grin that utterly dispelled her sternness. 'If June says no, she means no.'

'Okay. Thank you, then.' Tara accepted the tea and cookie gracefully. 'So, are you all planning to perform something in particular, or is it more that you just want to upskill yourselves?'

'We thought it would be nice to do a sort of performance, yes,' Emily said, cutting a slice of a large red velvet cake and putting it on a plate. 'Nothing too complicated or energetic, something that we can all do. A ladies' dance.'

'Right.' Tara nodded. 'Do you want me to choreograph something? We could start on it now. Nothing fancy, just something you can all do.'

'That would be amazing. Yes!' Emily waved her arms at the group of women, who were milling around and chatting. 'Everyone! Tara said she'd choreograph a piece for us to learn for the fundraiser! Isn't that nice of her?' she called out.

'Fantastic!' Mina clapped. 'Three cheers for Tara! Hip, hip!'

The women cheered, and though Tara blushed – and part of her wanted to fall into the ground – her heart was warmed.

Since she had been back in Loch Cameron, she had felt distanced from her real life back in Glasgow: adrift and unmoored. Yet, she could see now that her life with Carla, tolerating life at Lomond Primary had been a half-life. She'd refused to open herself up. She was grieving, all that time.

But, now, it was lovely to be accepted by this group of women, and to feel a part of something new and wholesome. All of her memories of Loch Cameron had always been entwined with Ramsay or her parents; she'd had friends, but no one really close. She and Ramsay had been inseparable; there just hadn't been any room for anyone else.

Tara thought back to the promise she'd made in front of the picture of Aunt Agnes. That she would face her demons, and be resilient, just like her great-aunt had been.

At that point, she had known that she needed to find herself again and reclaim the person that she once was.

Tara had thought then, looking at her aunt's picture, that if she had even a little of Agnes' steely determination and resilience, then she would be proud. And that she would do her best to make Aunt Agnes proud of her.

Now, she could look at her life and start to see the old Tara coming back. The one that was joyful and carefree. And, with the crochet coven, she felt part of something. And it felt good.

TWENTY

Gyle Head had changed a lot.

When Tara had been a teenager, this had been one of her favourite places to get away from her mum and dad, from dance practice or school, and enjoy some quiet time with a book. She vividly remembered reading one of her favourite novels, *Wuthering Heights*, sitting on one of the deep windowsills of the old folly, a mini mock-castle that one of the old Lairds of Loch Cameron had built once upon a time. It was strange that Agnes Smith, her great-aunt, had also been a fan of the Brontës.

Tara had been carrying Agnes' copy of *Jane Eyre* around with her and had started reading it; she'd read the novel before, while she was at high school, but it had been years since she'd looked at it. As well as loving the story and the writing – it was so romantic, so heartbreaking – Tara was really enjoying reading Agnes' carefully written annotations in the margins. So far, Agnes' thoughts were stream-of-consciousness. Sometimes, Tara didn't know what they meant; on one page, next to a description of Rochester, Agnes had written:

Just like J. Hot-headed

On another, she had written:

I will never understand him.

Who was J? He was mentioned a few times in Agnes' hand, but her notes were unclear as to what relationship J had had with Agnes. Still, it added an extra element of intrigue to Tara's reading experience, and made her feel as though she was almost talking to Agnes. As if the book provided her with some kind of direct line to her great-aunt's heart. She wondered if Agnes had ever thought that, one day, one of her descendants would be reading her words and puzzling over them.

No one had really come up to Gyle Head when Tara was younger. It was mostly overgrown, and there was a plaintive, melancholy feel to the place that Tara had never been able to fully understand. However, even though she'd felt that, it hadn't stopped her going there. In fact, reading about doomed love and gothic romance while overlooking the loch, nestled in the stone windowsill of an aged folly, had always made her feel like a romantic heroine. In her secret spot, she could pretend that she was Catherine Earnshaw, stalking the moors, heartbroken at the loss of her love.

Tara had agreed to meet Ramsay at Gyle Head that morning: since her chat with Dotty, she and Ramsay had been texting back and forward almost nonstop. It was just like old times; after some polite getting-to-know-you messages – *so looking forward to chatting!* – and *can't believe it's been ten years!* – they had lapsed back into their shared memories and jokes as if no time had passed.

Tara was still wary of Ramsay a little: she knew there were still difficult conversations to be had. But the seductiveness of their messaging had pulled her in. She found herself looking at her phone at every chance she got in between tasks at the Inn, smiling at his funny little jokes and sending pictures of what she was doing – lunches, making beds, serving at the bar. The night before, she'd finally gotten to sleep in the early hours because they'd been messaging so relentlessly. It was like a dam being removed from a river. All the conversations they'd missed. All the moments of connection.

She had time before her dad needed her back at the Inn. She'd already prepared a huge shepherd's pie, made sure there was enough salad ingredients in the large fridge in the Inn's kitchen and taken delivery of a bread order, including dinner rolls. For the vegetarian option, she'd made a vegetable chilli according to Dotty's personal recipe, which was handwritten in a food-stained notebook with RECIPES in flowery cursive text on the cover. As well as that, she'd already made up the Inn's six bedrooms, helped a new couple check in and given them local restaurant recommendations, cleaned the bathrooms and hoovered the bar area.

It was good to get some fresh air.

However, Gyle Head was now something completely different to what she remembered. Tara knew that there had been construction happening up here – Dotty had been telling her about it for months, although she hadn't been paying much attention. However, now, instead of an old folly that had been largely overgrown with holly bushes and the rest of it a wilderness, Gyle Head was the site of a smart new housing development with townhouses and flats, all of which featured sedge roofs and other ecological innovations.

Nicest of all, there was a large playground at the centre of the development, with a cosy-looking café, toilets, a shiny row of bike racks and a climbing wall next to it. Around the circumference of the flats and houses, a stream flowed, with a wooden walkway over the top of it that was signposted with information about the local wildlife.

She looked for him, but couldn't see him anywhere. She realised she was nervous: there were butterflies in her stomach and a tightness in her throat, so she went to the café, bought a bacon roll and a coffee and sat down on one of the wooden benches outside. She texted Carla.

Are you home yet? I'm meeting Ramsay for a coffee. Wish me luck.

It was bright and sunny, and though there were some children playing, she didn't mind the sound. As a primary school teacher, in fact, she was so used to the sound of children that she realised she'd been missing it since school had broken up for the holidays.

She didn't mind helping out at the Inn – even though she was still disappointed about missing out on the trip to Berlin with Carla – but it was a very different kind of work to teaching, and she missed little voices calling out *Miss!* and asking unexpected questions; the chatter and the giggles and the silliness. Still, it was revealing, getting a glimpse into her parents' world, now that she was an adult. It was a very different thing, seeing Dotty and Eric as colleagues at the Inn and not just her parents. She was able to see not just how patient her dad was – she'd always known that – but how sweet and thoughtful Dotty was. Her mother had given her a handwritten note every morning, full of what she called "extras" for the guests in all the different rooms on that day. The list comprised of things like putting freshly picked flowers in the rooms, taking up snacks according to the individual guest's preferences, booking them appointments and making recommendations for activities and restaurants Dotty thought they'd like, after she'd chatted to them.

It was a huge amount of extra work, but when her mother had handed her the "extras" list on her first day and Tara had made a comment along the lines of wondering when she would be able to get it all done, Dotty had said, *these're the things that keep people comin' back, hen. An' if I can make someone happy, I will. It's their holidays, don't forget that. We're here tae make it special.*

It was things like that that clued Tara in to how hard her

parents worked to make the Inn a success, and how thoughtful Dotty was.

Tara shaded her eyes from the sun, watching a father cheer his little girl as she came down a very tall slide. *Cute.*

'I wouldnae say no.' Two women with babies in prams passed by where Tara was sitting: Tara looked up to see one of them edge her elbow towards the man in the playground. 'He's fit.'

'Ach. You'd better no' let yer man hear ye say that,' the other one tutted, smiling at her friend.

'Aye, well, I willnae. No harm in appreciatin' a hot dad,' the first one giggled.

Tara looked away, not wanting to look as though she was eavesdropping on their conversation, but she had to agree. Whoever he was, he had that air of sexiness about him.

She frowned, returning her gaze to the man and the little girl, because she realised that there was something about the father that looked familiar. He had a baseball cap pulled down over his eyes, and the hood of his navy blue sweatshirt covered his neck from behind. But, Tara would have recognised Ramsay Fraser's body anywhere, even now. They way he moved. The way he stood. The way he held his head.

She had felt unmoored, untethered, being away from her normal life in Glasgow. But, her life there hadn't made her feel whole.

Back in Loch Cameron, she had constantly felt as though she was seeing apparitions of her past; of her child self, of the echoes of what had once been. And, all of those echoes and shadows were intimately connected with Ramsay Fraser. Now, seeing him again, she felt something in her click into place. Was *he* what she had needed to stop feeling lost?

Ramsay had been the man she loved for so long that, even though they had been apart for ten years, her body reacted instinctively to him being there. She wanted to run to him.

Jump into his arms. Wrap her legs around his body. Bury her head in his neck and breathe him in. She had missed his smell, the feel of his skin, the taste of him when she kissed him.

Tara had specifically locked those thoughts away in her brain a long time ago, but, now, they all came rushing out, making her heart pound, her breath quicken, her cheeks flush.

Yet, the thing was, these sensations weren't even *thoughts*. They were feelings: a deeply primal response to someone who had felt like home to her for as long as she could remember. The *rightness* of one person that couldn't be explained in words – it was something cellular, organic, some wisdom of the body or maybe some kind of spiritual connection, she didn't know. Something that made Tara feel like she could breathe a little easier, feel more centred in the world.

It was primal: it was her body's remembrance, as well as her heart's. All the feelings of being lost, unmoored, of living in a slightly unreal relationship with the past, dissipated like the morning haar over the loch when the sun came out.

And there was something else too. There was a tug at her heart because this was a glimpse in to the future she always wished they'd have together. *That could have been my child*, she thought. *That could have been me, playing with our child on the playground*. The thought made her throat close up in grief. Oh, she had wanted that. She had wanted it so badly.

And, as much as joy filled her on seeing Ramsay again – and it truly did, she felt like she was suddenly aloft in a hot air balloon – it also hurt to feel those things again. It was akin to all the feeling suddenly returning to a numb arm or leg. Life returning, so suddenly, was intense.

She took out her phone and started to compose a message to surprise him. *Hey. I'm here. Look to your right.*

Yet, something stopped her. In those first few moments seeing Ramsay again, it had been all she could do to process his proximity. The primal reaction of her body and her heart, knowing he was near, still in shock that he was even here at all.

But, now, she saw that he was with a little girl, perhaps nine years old. They were laughing, and Ramsay was handing her a juice box from his bag. She was slightly too old to be on the playground at all, but Tara knew kids that age still liked to play on swings and slides. It was an age when some children started to want to be grown up, but some hung onto childhood.

He had a daughter? It was either that, or he was looking after a little girl for some reason, but how likely was that, in the middle of the day?

Tara let the realisation hit her, and it felt like a punch.

Now, Tara started to process what she was actually seeing.

Ramsay Fraser helping his daughter on the slide.

Ramsay Fraser pushing his daughter on a swing.

Ramsay Fraser laughing and running after his daughter, playing chase.

Ramsay Fraser was a *father*.

Of course, it wasn't like he was forbidden to have had a life and a child and whatever else had happened in the past ten years. Yet, Tara felt betrayed.

And, he'd arranged to meet her here, after their relentless messaging after the last couple of days, and never once mentioned it.

She looked at the little girl for a long moment. She reached for the heart necklace at her throat.

Tara blinked: another realisation breaking over her. Before, she'd felt buoyed up by joy at seeing Ramsay again, as if she'd been floating in a hot air balloon. Now, she felt a jolt in her whole being, as if the balloon had suddenly dropped in mid-air.

The last time she'd seen Ramsay was ten years ago, when he'd mysteriously disappeared. This little girl looked about that age; a little younger. She was a tall eight, or she was nine, nine and a half maybe.

Tara knew that the little girl was Ramsay's daughter. She could see the resemblance in her face, the colour of her hair. Her eyes were Ramsay's dark, soft eyes. Tara could see that even from where she sat. She looked dumbly at the message she'd been about to send on her phone. *Hey. I'm here. Look to your right.*

She deleted it, her hand shaking.

If that girl was Ramsay's daughter – and it was clear that she was – then that meant that she had been born shortly after Ramsay had ended things with her. And, that meant that after breaking up with Tara, he had gone straight out and met someone else, and got her pregnant.

Why? Why would he ever have done such a thing? Tara couldn't process all this new information. It was too much, all in one go.

As she watched, Ramsay looked over to another bench near the playground, where a woman about Tara's age was sitting. Tara had noticed her when she'd sat down: she was about the same age as Tara, pretty, with a blonde bob, jeans, those flat sheepskin boots with the furry lining that everyone seemed to have. Tara's fist closed around the two halves of the heart; one slipped behind the other in her hand. Like it had been lost.

Ramsay pointed to the woman and said something to the little girl: then, they both waved to her, and she waved back.

Now, Tara's heart felt as though it had dropped out of her body.

Was that her? The woman that Ramsay had secretly left her for?

Oh, no. No. No.

Tara couldn't be here. She couldn't face whatever this was. Her heart was too tender, too raw. She got up, hurriedly, knocking over her cup of coffee and turning away, suddenly paranoid that Ramsay would see her and call her over, or come over and talk to her, and what would she say?

She would have to act normally about being introduced to his wife and his daughter. She'd have to say *pleased to meet you* and ask about them and their lives, and not do what she wanted to do, which was cry. She wanted to ask Ramsay, *what was wrong with me? I know you wanted children. I would have given them to you. I was ready. Why not me? Why her? And why leave me, saying absolutely nothing?*

Yes, she wanted to grab Ramsay and hold him, be close to his skin, be a part of him again. That thought was the thing that made her feel home, made her feel whole and grounded.

That was her primal reaction. But she was also furious. How dare he let her think that he might have died, that anything might have happened to him, with no word at all for all those years? And then, turn up here as if nothing had happened? To talk to her mum, get her number, message her for days just like old times, and never say anything about his wife and child? How *dare* he?

How dare you ruin my heart? she wanted to scream at him, but she bit her lip, hard, picking up her coffee cup and turning away to throw it in a rubbish bin before he could see her, and before she'd have to confront a situation that she wasn't ready for. She put her hands in the pockets of her jacket, hunching unconsciously, not wanting to be seen.

Ramsay definitely hadn't mentioned his wife or his daughter when they'd bumped into each other over the past few weeks. In fact, he'd been a little flirtatious with her. Had she imagined that? No, she didn't think she had. He *had* flirted. He had flirted with her and he hadn't thought to mention that while Tara had been breaking her heart over him for ten years, he'd been happily living a new life with his wife and his daughter and never thinking about her at all.

I can't believe it.

She turned back to look at him, one last time.

I can't believe you would do that to me. After everything we had. I was your family.

But now, Ramsay had another family, and it seemed as though he had never really wanted Tara at all. Maybe, he'd seen her in the street and thought that she'd be a good opportunity for some harmless, flirtatious texting.

Tara started to run, feeling tears building up in her throat. It felt as though they were coming direct from her heart: she fought back a sudden, tumultuous wail of disbelief and sadness that tasted of copper and bitter grief. As she turned away, she pulled hard at the necklace, and it came free in her hand, pulling painfully at the skin on her neck. She couldn't have it on her for another minute.

She hadn't thought it was possible, but Ramsay Fraser had broken her heart for a second time.

TWENTY-ONE

Ramsay: *Where are you? We said Gyle Head at 11? I'm on the playground by the coffee stand.*

Tara: *Sorry, I had to work. Catch up another time.*

Ramsay: *Oh. Okay, that's a shame. Let me know when is good for you.*

Tara was frying bacon when Carla called.

'I'm back. What the hell's been happening between you and this Ramsay, then?' She launched straight into the conversation with no preamble.

'Hello, Tara, how are you? Oh, I'm fine thanks. And you?' Tara replied, grumpily, putting the phone on speaker.

'Don't be like that. You texted me that you were meeting for coffee and then nothing. What happened?'

'Ugh. I'm sorry. I've been like a bear with a sore head.' Tara flipped the bacon with a spatula and cracked ten eggs into a huge cast iron frying pan. She was standing in the Inn's kitchen, making breakfast for the guests, all of whom were taking their meal in the bar this morning.

Every morning, she had to get up at seven and put the half-baked bread rolls in the oven, make toast, tea and coffee, put out the cereals, croissants and jugs of juice on the bar. The system for cooked breakfasts was that guests made their order the night before on a little notepad that they left hanging on the doorknob of their room. It was Tara's last task of the day to collect up all the orders and make a note for herself in the kitchen in the morning.

The options for breakfast were full Scottish, vegetarian Scottish, poached eggs on toast or the vegan option, which was smashed avocado on toast. This morning, everyone had opted for a full Scottish, which made Tara's life easier.

'Oh, no. What's that noise, babe? It sounds like you're standing in the middle of a raging inferno.'

'I'm frying bacon.'

'Nice. God, I could do with some of that right now. So? Spill the beans.'

'He's married, Car.' Tara lowered her voice. 'I went up to the place we'd arranged to meet, and I saw him with a kid and a woman. He never said anything about it. Still hasn't.' Her voice caught; she'd been trying to stay busy since seeing Ramsay, but she could feel the tears threatening.

'Oh, Christ. I'm sorry.' Carla's voice softened. 'How do you feel?'

'Awful. I mean, I know we're not involved, or anything. But I just wish I hadn't had to find out that way, you know? It's still hard, seeing him around the village. And now I have to risk running into him and his little family. I just think it would have been the decent thing to let me know.'

'Maybe that was what he was going to talk to you about,' Carla said, gently.

'Maybe. But it would have been nice for him to tell me without me having to find out for myself. They were such a perfect little family, Car. Playing on the slides and swings and waving to each other, being cute.'

'He's allowed to have moved on, Tara. I'm just putting that out there,' Carla said, still gently.

'I know that! But that was our dream. A family. That's what he always said he wanted with me.'

'And then he suddenly disappeared out of your life and reappears ten years later with exactly that, with someone else. Yeah, that sucks.' Her friend sighed. 'I'm sorry, babe.'

'Yeah. Thanks.' Tara sighed too. 'So, you're home now?'

'Yeah. Just got back.' There was the indistinct sound of a man's voice in the background. 'Oh. Craig says hi.'

'Hi, Craig.' Tara chuckled, despite her mood. 'That's still happening, then, is it?'

'Eh. I guess so.' Tara could sense that Carla was trying to sound casual, probably to spare her feelings. 'Whatever.'

'Come on. Spill. You don't need to hold back on my account.' Tara spooned baked beans from a saucepan onto the plates that she'd laid out and added bacon, two fried eggs, two sausages, two potato rosti and a couple of slices per plate of black pudding and a spoon of fried mushrooms to every plate.

'Oh, well, yeah. You know. It's been okay,' Carla said, lightly.

'He's right there, isn't he?'

'Yeah.'

'Text me later then. I assume things are going well,' Tara chuckled. 'It's okay, Car. You don't have to pretend you're not happy. I want you to be happy. Even with Craig from PE.'

'Oh my GOD!' Carla hissed. 'I can't talk right now but he's just gone in the bathroom. He is amazing. Just this morning he pushed me up against the–'

'Okay, okay.' Tara laughed. 'I get it. Listen, babe, I have to serve the breakfasts. But message me the details. Well. The overview,' she corrected herself. At least Carla was having a happy love life.

'I will. You take care. I love you,' her flatmate replied. 'Remember you're awesome. If he's shacked up with someone else, then it's his loss. Okay?'

'Okay.' Tara ended the call and picked up two of the breakfast plates. As ever, it helped talking to Carla, but she was still upset about what had happened.

If she was so awesome, then why had Ramsay Fraser dumped her so unceremoniously, all those years ago? If he had loved her, like he'd said in his letter.

I love you, but I can't be with you anymore.

How could he ever be with anyone else? How could he have severed all contact from her for ten years? In that letter – which she'd memorised, she'd read it so many times – he'd said that he didn't want her to be angry with him. But how could she avoid being angry and hurt and dismayed at what he'd done?

She couldn't.

Tara made herself wear a cheery expression as she took the breakfasts into the bar and served them to the guests. She was fast learning that it was part of the landlady's job to smile, chat and laugh with the people that were staying at the Inn, regardless of how she might be feeling. It was what Dotty did every day; surely there were days when her mother probably didn't feel up to being cheery and sharing a laugh and a joke with total strangers. Yet, she did it every day. In fact, Tara couldn't think of a time when Dotty hadn't been the model of hospitality at the Inn. This was probably the first time she ever even remembered Dotty having any time off. Even if she was ill, she tended to work, brushing off her symptoms as "just a sniffle".

Tara thought wryly about the television soap opera that she and Carla watched every week, and how they made fun of the characters, including the pub landlady. She thought about how both she and Carla mimicked their mothers. Obviously, it was all just in fun, but for the first time, Tara felt that she understood some of what Dotty really did on a daily basis, just to keep everything going. And, it was a lot.

As she went back out to the kitchen for more plates, Tara wondered if her mother would ever have asked for help if she hadn't had to. In a strange way, she was glad that Dotty had been put in the position to have to ask for her help.

After making sure all the guests were happy, Tara popped upstairs to take Dotty her breakfast. She pushed her parents' bedroom door open with her foot and leaned back with her bottom to push the heavy oak door open.

'Breakfast!' she trilled; usually, her mother was awake by now and was sitting up in bed reading a romance novel or crocheting. Yet, as Tara walked in, balancing the tray carefully, her eyes widened at the sight of Dotty lying back against her pillows, sobbing quietly.

'Mum! What's the matter?' Tara put the tray down carefully on a side table and went to her mother.

'Oh, love. I'm sorry,' Dotty sniffed. 'I didnae want ye tae see me like this.'

'But what's wrong?' Tara took her mother's hand. She didn't think she'd ever seen her mother cry, and it was a terrible feeling. Dotty was always so strong, so together. Nothing was too much effort for the guests, and she was always cheerful, always practical and strong.

'I'm just sad aboot ye and Ramsay,' Dotty said in a strangled voice. 'I wish we'd done more tae help him when he was younger, an' I'm sorry, about him bein' with someone else now. I really thought ye could get back together, an' be happy. I prayed for it. I just feel like it's such a shame, hen. An' I'm yer mum. I just want ye tae be happy.' Dotty started crying again. 'Ach. Don't take any notice o' me. I think bein' stuck in bed's getting' the better o' me.' She wiped her eyes.

'Of course you're going to feel low. It must be really hard being up here all the time,' Tara agreed, handing her mum a tissue. 'But as far as me and Ramsay goes, you shouldn't feel bad about it. And you definitely shouldn't feel bad about when he was a kid. You were always so good to him.'

'Aye. But we couldae done more.' Dotty shook her head. 'It just makes me sad. The whole thing.'

'I'm sorry, Mum. I didn't know you felt like this.'

'Aye, well. I dinnae like tae make a fuss.' Dotty screwed up her nose.

'You're allowed to have feelings, Mum.' Tara thought that, in a strange way, she would have liked it if her mum had cried in front of her before now.

'I know. But you're my daughter. I'm supposed tae be the one that helps ye, dries yer tears. No' the other way around.'

'No, you're a human, just like anyone else. And I'm not a child,' Tara said, gently.

'Aye. But I hope ye know how hard it was tae ask for your help in the first place.' Dotty let out a long breath.

'I do know. And I'm grateful to be able to help you,' Tara said, realising that it was true. There had been a distance between them for a long time: a wound, really, that neither of them had addressed. Tara knew they had both been hurt by what had happened with Ramsay. Tara had always felt resentful that Dotty hadn't addressed it with her, she supposed. They'd never particularly talked about it, and she'd wanted to. But when she'd tried, Dotty had brushed it off and avoided the topic.

Tara, now having stepped into her mother's shoes at the Inn, saw for the first time that Dotty's life as the landlady at the Loch Cameron Inn had given her the habit of making the best of everything: always being positive, always putting a brave face on things. It was what you had to do as part of the job, and maybe she'd felt that it was the only way to deal with Ramsay leaving, and Tara being depressed and bereft without him. Dotty had felt that it was best left: she didn't want to upset her daughter by talking about it.

But, Tara had really wanted to talk about it, and she realised that she had avoided coming home very much in the past ten years, partly because she felt a distance between her and her mother because of what had happened with Ramsay.

'I'm grateful fer yer help, believe me, hen.' Dotty squeezed her daughter's hand. 'I'm sorry. I just felt so sad when I woke up. I think I had a dream aboot ye when ye were a bairn. I remember holdin' ye in my arms when ye were born an' vowin' I'd never let anythin' or anyone hurt ye. An then, I did.'

'Mum. Life is horrible sometimes. I know you think you could protect me from everything, but you can't. Some things are out of your control.'

'Hmph. Not somethin' I like tae hear.' Dotty chuckled wryly. 'Yer father knows that I like tae be in control always.'

'Ha. Well, you are, most of the time. But no one can be in control of everything. You tried your best, Mum. And that's more than enough. What happened with me and Ramsay – and what's happened now – isn't your fault. There's nothing you can do about it, apart from be here to give me hugs.'

'I hope ye know I'm always here fer hugs.' Dotty smiled. 'Shall we have one now? I could do with one.'

'Of course.' Tara hugged her mum gently. 'I love you, Mum.'

'I love ye too, poppet.'

Tara hadn't wanted to come back to Loch Cameron for the summer. But, being here with her parents had meant that she was spending more time with them than she had since she was a teenager. And, it was a shock to see, suddenly, that Dotty wasn't as relentlessly practical and as closed off as she'd thought.

The experience of 'being Dotty' at the Inn had given Tara an insight she hadn't had before: it was hard to be Dotty. And, seeing her mother break down over the hurt that she too had carried all these years made Tara sad, but it also made her realise that Dotty had a deeper emotional life than she'd realised. And, for that realisation, and knowledge of Dotty as a woman – a fallible, vulnerable person, just like everyone else – she was grateful.

TWENTY-TWO

'It's so good to see you, babe.' Carla enveloped Tara in a hug in the doorway of the Loch Cameron Inn. 'So, this is the hood? Very nice. I approve.'

'Thanks. Come on in.' Tara led her flatmate into the bar: it was a quiet night with just a few locals in. Eric was chatting to Angus, one of the regulars, a tall, greying redheaded Viking of a man who lived up on Queen's Point.

'Oooh. It's so quaint. I love all the wood. And the beams.' Carla pointed to the black wooden beams on the ceiling of the bar. 'Original?'

'I think so. There's been an Inn here since the 1700s, I think. Not the same building – this got built in 1855 or so. Dad would tell you.' She nodded to Eric. 'That's him, over there.'

'Ah, I see a resemblance. Daddy Ballantyne. How's it been, with your folks?' Carla dropped her backpack and collapsed into one of the high-backed upholstered chairs.

'It's been okay. They've been keeping me busy. G&T?'

'You're an angel. The train was packed and then the taxi took forever. I'm parched,' Carla sighed.

'I've got some casserole on the go as well, if you want some,' Tara said, over her shoulder as she lifted up the wooden divider that separated the end of the wooden bar and allowed access behind it.

'That would be amazing, babe. Thanks. And thanks for letting me stay! I didn't expect to be here, but it's cool to see where you're from.'

'No bother.' Tara poured two gin and tonics and took them over to the table by Carla, then went back to the kitchen and reappeared with a steaming bowl of chicken casserole and a crusty bread roll. 'Here you are, Miss World Travels. So, come on then. Where's Craig?'

'Haha. What, d'you think I've got him in my rucksack? He went back to his.'

'How was Paris, then? And Berlin?'

'And Amsterdam. We went a bit mad.' Carla sipped her drink and closed her eyes blissfully. 'Ahh. That's the stuff.'

'So, you're still... an item?' Tara asked, grinning. It was good to see Carla. She'd missed their talks.

'Yeah. Just giving him some time off for good behaviour. And it was *very* good, if you catch my drift.' Carla gave her an exaggerated wink.

'I can see that. You're glowing.'

'It's more likely dirt. I'm desperate for a shower.' Carla rolled her eyes good-naturedly, but Tara could see that her friend was happy, and that made her glad.

'I'll show you up to your room in a bit. It's got a really nice shower and a big bath. I've booked you in for a week. Free of charge, of course.'

When Carla had called to say that she was thinking of visiting Loch Cameron, Tara had insisted that her friend come and stay as part of her extended summer holiday. It was a brilliant idea: she'd missed out on the Berlin trip, but it didn't mean that she and Carla couldn't spend a bit of time together when she wasn't working. Seeing Carla now made her feel a thousand per cent better.

'You are an absolute angel,' Carla sighed. 'So. What's going on with you and Ramsay?'

'Oh, god. Nothing.' Tara put her head in her hands. 'I mean, we've had some mortifying run-ins and then I found out he was married with a kid, and had declined to tell me. You know it all.'

'Hm. I just wondered if there had been any developments.' Carla spooned some casserole into her mouth. 'Yum. This is delicious.'

'Thanks. Made it with my own fair hands. No, no developments,' Tara sighed. 'I guess I'm just keeping out of his way now, until I come home. Mum told me this whole story I didn't know about his past, with his dad. That was kind of heartbreaking, but it doesn't change the facts.'

'No, but your feelings aren't facts,' Carla said, breaking off some of the crusty roll and dipping it in the sauce.

'True. But, facts are facts and he's married with a kid. So, we could be friends, but I'm not really ready for that.' Tara made a face. 'Sorry. Can we talk about something else? I'm sort of Ramsay-ed out. I'm so sick of crying about it, but I will cry if we talk about it.'

'Dear me. That sounds intense. All right, what else has been going on?' Carla spooned more of the casserole into her mouth. 'Not that you can't cry in front of me, of course.'

'I know. Errr, well, we've got the fundraiser here next week, for the local primary school. They've asked me to take a job there, actually.' Tara raised her eyebrow.

'Really? You do hate Loaded Primary,' Carla said. 'But you'd have to live here. I get the feeling you don't really want to, what with everything that's happened.'

'Exactly. I mean, I wouldn't live here with Mum and Dad long term. I'd get my own place. There are some really nice places up on Gyle Head, now, for instance. But it's more the whole, *living in the same village as the love of your life and his perfect little family* thing. Doesn't appeal.'

'Fair. Shame, though. It's a gorgeous little village.'

'It is. I mean, it would be really sweet to teach at such a tiny little school. Loch Cameron has a lot of things going for it. Don't get me wrong. But... seeing Ramsay around, all the time? Having to teach his kid? I don't think I could.'

'Yeah, I get that.' Carla frowned. 'It really is a shame.'

'It has been lovely being back and rediscovering all of my old haunts. The nature is stunning up here. When I was a teenager I used to read *Wuthering Heights* in the woods, or up on Queen's Point, overlooking the loch,' Tara admitted.

'Haha. That's so emo. Who knew you were a mini goth? I thought you were this apple-cheeked sporty type. Girl next door.'

Tara hugged her friend spontaneously. It was so good to have Carla here: it made her feel more like her old self. She realised she'd really missed their evenings watching the soaps, doing the silly accents and gossiping. She'd missed the nights in the pub with Carla's fellow teachers from St Clare's.

However, being in Loch Cameron had given her a sense of grounding and a calm she hadn't felt for a long time. Earlier that day, after she'd done the breakfasts and cleaned a couple rooms where guests had checked out, she'd walked up to Queen's Point and found her special ring of oak trees and sat there for half an hour, feeling their reassuring, aged wisdom enveloping her.

She hadn't stayed long: she knew that she had to strip the beds, put the sheets on to wash in Dotty's extra-large washing machine, and get on with the hundred and one other duties that a day at the Inn involved. But, for that brief time, Tara had felt herself root into the ancient land. She'd felt herself connecting with something deep in the earth of Queen's Point. Something that said *you belong here. You are safe.*

'I was. But you can be that and still like gothic romance novels. Speaking of which,' Tara went behind the bar and got Agnes' copy of *Jane Eyre* out of her bag, 'check this out.' She handed it to Carla.

'*Jane Eyre*. Nice. Looks old.' Carla nodded.

'It belonged to my great-aunt. She probably inherited it from her parents, looking at the date it was published. But the interesting thing about it is all the little notes she wrote in it.'

'Oh, no way. Let's see.'

Tara opened the book to where she had read up to.

'There's this series of notes about a J. I don't know who J was. Agnes – that's my great-aunt, she was a teacher at the primary school here, back during World War Two and after-wards. She had this ill-fated affair with the headmaster, who was a bit of a piece of work, but his name didn't begin with J. I'm sort of hoping that she had better luck with someone else.'

'Ooh. What does it say about this J, then?' Carla sat forward, finishing the last of her roll. 'Bravo on the casserole, by the way, babes. A triumph.'

'Oh, thanks. It's my mum's recipe, though. I just followed it.' Tara flicked back in the book to some of the pages where J had been mentioned. 'Well. We know it's a he because she says *Just like J. Hot-headed* and then she says *I will never understand him.*'

'Hot-headed. Got it. She could be talking about a family member though. Maybe a brother. What else is there?'

'Here she says *J's eyes are piercing and make me feel like I am the only person in the room.*'

'Okay. Probably not her brother then.' Carla raised an eyebrow. 'Hot, though.'

'Yeah. And then this: *I will always remember our first time. His lips on mine.*'

'Wow. Agnes had a secret romance, then? Or was this someone she married?'

'Not that I know of. My mum says she was a spinster. So, it must be a boyfriend, or a lover. I don't know if it was a long-term thing.'

'It's weird to think of people from the past having these sexy dalliances, isn't it?' Carla mused. 'Like, when you've only known someone as an old person, finding out about their life when they were young is kind of wild. Because, of course people did wild things. Especially in the wars. There was that threat of danger always in the air. You didn't know if you were going to live or die.'

'Yeah. It must have been horrible, but I guess it did lend a certain frisson to things.' Tara frowned. 'I wish I knew more. She was a really inspiring woman. She's inspired me, anyway. The affair she had with the headmaster went sideways really badly, from what I can read between the lines in the letter, but she had this amazing resilience. She was determined that she'd stay teaching at the school with the kids, because she loved them – despite the fact that she had to work with the guy who'd broken her heart, or at the very least, used her. And she outlasted him. He left the school a couple of years after their affair, but she stayed for the rest of her working life.'

'She had balls, then,' Carla said, approvingly. 'Or a more feminist way of putting it. Why isn't there a female equivalent of that? We should start something.'

'Yeah. Ovaries? Fallopian tubes. Breasts.'

'Ovaries the size of apples. Though that would be really uncomfortable. Probably a gynaecological issue.'

'Hmmm. It's a work in progress. Anyway, she was brave and strong. A role model,' Carla summarised.

'Yeah. She really was. And I guess thinking about Agnes has made me look at my past with Ramsay in a different way. And what's happened now. Yeah, it's not ideal. Did it hurt? Yes. Was I heartbroken for years? Yes. Did I survive? Also, yes. Maybe that's what I was always supposed to learn. Be more Agnes. Survive. Thrive.'

'I can see that. You're different. Stronger.' Carla nodded. 'Good for you, babes.'

'Thanks. I mean, I'd prefer to be Agnes 2.0, with a special someone in her life, and not alone forever, but still. That's why I really want to know who this J was.'

'Is there anything else about who he was in the book?' Carla asked.

'I mean, she's underlined a lot of romantic passages in the book, but I've had a good flick through and I can't see anything else.'

'Did she have any other books?' Carla asked.

'Yeah. All of those, actually.' Tara pointed to the shelf of leather-bound books above the fireplace.

'Have you looked at those?'

'Actually... no. That's a bit of a rookie error, isn't it?' Tara tutted at herself. 'I think I just got really into reading *Jane Eyre* again and sort of forgot there were others.'

'Come on, let's see what there is.' Carla got up and skipped excitedly over to the fireplace. 'Oooh! I feel like Nancy Drew!'

'Okay. You take Christina Rossetti, I'll take Robert Browning.' Tara handed one book to Carla and took one for herself. She opened her book carefully, admiring its gossamer-thin pages and tracing Agnes' spidery handwriting of her name on the top right hand of the title page again.

She started flicking through the pages: apart from a few underlinings, there wasn't anything. She shook her head and picked up another book: Collected Poems of Siegfried Sassoon. Not being a particularly romantic book, Tara didn't expect to find much in there about Agnes' secret love life, and, again, apart from some underlinings, there seemed to be nothing.

'Nothing in Browning,' Carla sighed. 'Maybe she just loved *Jane Eyre*.'

'Maybe it was just the Brontës,' Tara said, reaching for *The Tenant of Wildfell Hall*.

As soon as she opened it, something fell out.

'A letter.' She opened it and looked up excitedly at Carla. She opened the package; there were a number of pieces of paper folded together. 'More than one, in fact!'

'Read them!' Carla cried excitedly. 'Mr Ballantyne! Come and listen to this!' She beckoned Eric over, who had finished talking to Angus and sauntered over with an amused look on his face. 'Hello. I'm Tara's flatmate, Carla,' she continued.

'Ah, nice tae meet ye, darlin'.' Eric nodded. 'Yer stayin' wi' us fer a bit, aye?'

'Yeah! If that's all right. If you can fit me in.'

'Aye, o' course. Always room fer Tara's friends.' Eric smiled warmly. 'Tara, what's this aboot?'

'Dad! I found some old letters in one of great-aunt Agnes' books.' Tara opened the browned, brittle paper carefully. 'You know that I found that letter from her up at the school. And there are these mysterious notes in her books about this J that she seems to have been in love with.'

'Oooh.' Eric wiped a pint glass with a tea towel. 'Read on, then. I'd get yer mother down, but she's on the phone. Party line wi' the crochet coven. I daren't interrupt,' he chuckled.

'All right. This is the first one, I think.' Tara read the letter aloud.

Dear Agnes,

I have never known a woman like you. Every day apart from you is torture.

I miss Loch Cameron. My time there was so unexpectedly wonderful, because of you. I never dreamed that my work would bring me anywhere as lovely as the loch, but meeting you made it all the lovelier.

Every day, I sit at my desk and dream of you. Your soft hair;
your curious eyes; the way you smell like lilacs and fresh air.
Our times together have been so very sweet, dear Agnes.

Please write so that I may touch the paper you have
touched. That I may breathe in the ink that has been shaped by
your fingers. I remain, eternally,

Yours,

John xxx

'Wow.' Carla swooned. 'Loving John. John is a superhero.
Oh my god.' She fanned herself. 'So that's who J is.'

'Very romantic.' Eric nodded.

'I wish we could see what Agnes wrote back.' Tara turned to
the next letter and handed it to Carla. It was another letter from
John, though this one definitely had a sexier theme.

'Oh, my.' Carla put her hand to her chest and handed the
second letter to Eric, who read it and raised his eyebrows.

'Goodness.' Tara's leaned on the back of a chair and put the
glass and tea towel down.

'I know,' Tara said. 'Looks like Agnes and John were definitely an item.'

'Ye could say that.' Eric chuckled. 'Can I show these to your
mum? She'd like tae see them, I'm sure.'

'Of course.' Tara handed them to her dad. 'I'm definitely
going to look through the rest of the books now, just in case
we've missed anything.'

'Aye. But I'd suggest ye take yer friend up an' show her her
room.' Eric nodded subtly at Carla, who was leaning up against
the fireplace and had closed her eyes. She looked exhausted.
'Mebbe that dinner's taken effect, aye?'

'Oh, right. Carla.' Tara nudged her friend, who opened her
eyes suddenly, looking hyper alert.

'What? I'm here.'

'Come on. I'll show you your room. We can look at the books tomorrow,' Tara said, gently.

'Yeah. Okay, that might be good. I haven't really slept well in a couple of days.' Carla blinked and rubbed her eyes. 'All that travelling and sex is catching up on me.'

'Right, well, I better tidy up the glasses.' Eric blinked and bumbled off.

'Sorry I said "sex" in front of your dad,' Carla whispered.

'That's okay. He's heard the word before I'm sure,' Tara chuckled.

'Done it at least once,' Carla whispered, giggling.

'Ugh. The very thought.' Tara picked up Carla's bag. 'Come on. Follow me.'

TWENTY-THREE

'Emily, this is my flatmate Carla. She teaches at secondary. Carla, this is Emily. She's the headteacher at the primary school here.'

'Lovely to meet you, Emily.' Carla proffered a hand covered in pastry crumbs, which Emily shook, slightly doubtfully. 'Sorry. I've literally just now stuffed a chocolate croissant in my mouth,' she explained, swallowing indelicately. 'This food market is amazing!'

'Nice, isn't it?' Emily grinned. 'The bakery stall is remarkable. The fishmonger's got some amazing mussels in, if you're into seafood. And the natural soap and vegan candle lady is great.' Emily pointed across the way among the jostling crowds surrounding the market day stalls and their jaunty, striped awnings.

'Listen, ladies. I really appreciate you helping me out like this, ahead of the fundraiser. There are so many last-minute tasks and, you know what it's like. You think you've got everything under control and then, *wham*. Something comes out of the blue.' Emily rolled her eyes. 'Or, in my case, it was on my list, but I forgot to do it.' She handed Carla and Tara a stack of yellow leaflets each, a roll of tape and a staple gun. 'You're lifesavers.'

'No problem.' Tara took the staple gun and handed the tape to Carla: she probably wasn't to be trusted with anything vaguely dangerous. 'So, basically, just put these up everywhere?'

She glanced at one of the leaflets.

LOCH CAMERON'S GOT TALENT!
PRIMARY SCHOOL FUNDRAISER
LOCH CAMERON INN, SUNDAY, 3PM–LATE
CEILIDH, FOOD, ENTERTAINMENT
SINGERS, DANCERS – WE WANT YOU!!
GREAT PRIZES!!

'Please. Obviously be mindful of the environment, but yes.' Emily nodded. 'We just want to make sure everyone's got it in their diary, and you know what people are like. I put a notice in the local paper the last couple of weeks and a few notices on bulletin boards and what have you, but I thought we needed greater visibility.'

'What're the prizes? For the singing and dancing?' Carla asked.

'Umm. There's a box of meat for first prize. Cake subscription for a year from that bakery you just had a croissant from.' Emily pointed at the bakery stall which had a crowd three-deep around it, reaching for its towering piles of giant hot cross buns, buttercream-filled cronuts and cream horns with delicate, flaky pastry, covered in sugar. 'Voucher from Fiona's Fashions, that's the clothes boutique in the village. Very nice, actually. Voucher from the hairdresser's for fifty per cent off. That kind of thing.'

'Not gonna lie, a cake subscription sounds amazing.' Carla

gazed longingly back at the stall. 'I might just pop back there later. When the crowd's gone down a bit.'

'You can have a cake when you've done all your leaflets.' Tara tapped her flatmate mock-seriously on the arm.

'Oh, fine, okay, Mum.' Carla rolled her eyes.

'Thanks, again.' Emily tucked her hair behind her ears. 'I do really appreciate it. I'm going up to Gyle Head to put some up and put some through letterboxes. By all means do that too if you like, around the high street. There are some residential streets behind, and there's Queen's Point, if you want to get the cottages up there.'

'Sure. That's fine, we can go up there.' Tara nodded, secretly relieved that she didn't have to go up to Gyle Head and risk seeing Ramsay up there: he'd said he lived there. 'You'll like it, Carla. There's a fab view of the loch.'

'Cool. One of your teen hangouts.'

'Yeah. Come on, then. We'll see you later, Emily?'

'Sure. I'll pop into the Inn this evening if that's okay. I just need to finalise some stuff with your dad.'

'Great. We'll see you then.'

'Thanks again. You really are helping me out.' Emily kissed Tara and then Carla on the cheek before heading off towards the end of the high street, picking her way between the crowds.

'Right, then. Come on. You can do letterboxes, I'll find places to put up signs,' Tara suggested. 'We'll get off the high street for a bit and come back when it's a bit less busy.'

They turned off the cobbled high street and onto a narrow residential street, where a crowded row of cottage-style terrace houses jostled against each other. Each garden was neat and well-tended, and a group of children were playing catch with a stuffed animal at the end of the street.

'This is sweet,' Carla said as she went up to the first door, folded a leaflet and posted it through the letterbox. 'Loch

Cameron's really quaint, isn't it? You feel like you've gone back in time a bit. And then you look over your shoulder and there's the castle looming on the other side of the loch. So gothic.'

'I guess so. I'm used to it.' Tara smiled at the children as they squealed and giggled at the end of the street. 'When I was a kid, I thought all villages had a castle. In fact, I didn't really know that not everyone even lived in a village.'

'I bet. You and Ramsay must've had a lot of fun, playing like them. When you were kids,' Carla observed. 'I grew up in Romford. Not quite the same.'

'Hmm. Well, I'm sure Romford has its charms.' Tara smiled.

'Not many. But it's home. I'd kill to have somewhere like this to come home to, though.'

'Well, you're welcome anytime. My parents think you're great, and they're always hospitable.'

'I think they're great. Your mum's a legend. Like the Joan Collins of Loch Cameron.'

'Ha. I've never thought of her like that, but I guess she does have a certain diva quality,' Tara chuckled.

'Yeah.' Carla took in a deep breath of the clean air and let it go, a peaceful look on her face. 'You know, you're different here. More confident. More relaxed. I mean, you've always been great, but I always thought there was this inner sadness in you. You could be really shy at times, if we were out at the pub or whatever. Here, I feel like you're more yourself.'

'Really?' Tara walked along slowly with her friend to the end of the road.

'Yeah. This is your home, after all.' Carla shrugged. 'Makes sense. And you're a country girl at heart. I love the city. The hustle and bustle. But you're a bit of a gentle soul. It suits you to be out here, in nature. It soothes your soul.' She posted the final leaflet through the last house's front door and came back to the end of the pathway.

'That's a very poetic thing to say.' Tara gave her friend an amused smile.

'Yeah, well. I can be poetic, although, don't tell anyone.' Carla shrugged. 'And I'm observant. That's all.'

'You're a good friend, is what you are.' Tara thought for a moment. 'Yes, I like being back here. I do feel more grounded, more resilient, like I was saying before about Aunt Agnes and thinking about how I could be more like her. And since I've been dancing more, I've reconnected to that sense of being care-free that I used to have. I think I was sad because I lost that, as well as losing Ramsay.'

'I can see that. It was your joy. We're always sad when we lose our joy,' Carla replied.

'I guess so. It's hard to see that when you're inside it. I feel like I was inside a sort of grey place for a really long time.' Tara flicked through the leaflets in her hand, distractedly.

'Awww. Love. Come here.' Carla enveloped Tara in a fierce hug. 'I don't want you to be in a grey place. I want you to be in a bright place filled with rainbows and fairies and all that crap,' she said, her voice muffled in Tara's hair.

'Thanks. I want rainbows and fairies for you too,' Tara mumbled back. 'And, thanks for coming to stay. It's really nice, having you here. It's been a bit of a weird time and I really appreciate the support, if I'm honest.'

'You're welcome, daftie.' Carla stepped back from the hug, and then, without warning, grabbed the staple gun out of Tara's hand and ran to the end of the street with it. 'I have the power!!' she shouted, and disappeared onto the high street, brandishing her remaining leaflets.

Tara laughed out loud, making the children look up from their game and frown at her. She waved at them and pointed to the end of the street where Carla had reappeared, waiting for her.

'Kids. Tell your parents about the fundraiser at the Inn on

Sunday. There's going to be dancing and cake. Okay?' she called out, grinning. The kids nodded, seriously.

What it was to be a child, Tara thought, nostalgic.

Carla was right. She had had a wonderful life in Loch Cameron. And, she realised, all the years she'd been away, she missed it terribly.

TWENTY-FOUR

'And, I believe we have here with us tonight two national champions in Highland dance: Tara Ballantyne an' Ramsay Fraser, where are ye?' Hal squinted into the crowd, scanning it for them. Tara shrank back at the back of the room, not wanting to be seen.

No. No. No. Please, not this.

It was the night of the fundraiser, and everything had been going very well so far. Tara had prepared all the food and set it out on two large tables that she and her dad had arranged in the back room of the bar. Eric was manning the bar, and Tara was on general clean and tidy duties – collecting dirty plates and glasses and returning them to the kitchen and the bar. As well as that, June had organised a piper and a ceilidh band to provide music, and Hal Cameron, the laird of Loch Cameron, was acting as caller.

The crochet coven had already led a couple of dances, and Tara had joined in, enjoying dancing again. It was good to feel that adrenalin pumping through her, and move her body. She'd been continuing to dance, using the practice room at the community centre a couple of times a week, and her fitness was returning. It was *fun*. And, she realised, she had missed fun. As the ceilidh spun out around her, she had the sudden sense of being in the flow of the dance. That same feeling of being care-free bubbled up in her, and she found herself laughing out loud, just for the fun of it.

The coven had taken their classes seriously, but really, there was no judgement if you got the steps wrong in a ceilidh. All the fun was in the whirling around, giggling, the energy and the speed of the dance and the sense of everything happening in unison. Usually, by the ceilidh stage of the evening, everyone had had a few drinks and inhibitions were lower: Tara had always thought that there was something inimitable about being twirled and flung across the room by a bulky, inebriated Scotsman.

She'd seen Ramsay come in, and had avoided him. It wasn't hard to do in a room full of people, and she'd been busy. More than enough excuse to always be somewhere other than where he was. But, now, Hal was beckoning them both to the front of the room and there was nowhere to go to avoid him.

It was bad enough being in the same room as Ramsay, but there was no way that she wanted to dance with him. In front of everyone.

'Ramsay, there ye are. An' where's Tara? Come up an' show us how it's done,' Hal continued, cheerily, as the crowd clapped and whooped.

'Go on, hen. Get up there.' Tara had been standing next to her mum, who was enthroned in an easy chair at the side of the bar with her ankle resting on a pouffe like a queen. She'd been regally receiving visitors all evening.

Dotty nudged Tara in the back, impatiently.

'No, Mum,' Tara hissed. Ramsay had texted her a few times after their failed meet-up at Gyle Head, but she hadn't known how to reply, so she had said nothing. She knew that she should have, but what could she say? *I saw you with your wife and daughter and it broke my heart? I'm not over you disappearing out of my life with no explanation? I'm not over you? Why wasn't I good enough?*

'If she doesnae want tae, Dot, don't make her.' Eric had walked over from behind the bar, since there was a lull and everyone was watching Hal. He tapped Dotty lightly on the arm. 'Remember what happened between them.'

'Eric. I remember perfectly well. But she can still get up there an' give everyone a show,' Dotty snapped at her husband. 'She willnae break, darlin'. Stop babyin' her, she's no' a little lassie anymore.'

'Aye. So she can make her own decisions,' Eric said, firmly. Tara's dad never raised his voice. But he had a firm tone that he sometimes used – not often, but sometimes, when he thought the situation merited it – and when the firm tone was used, Dotty and Tara knew that was Eric putting his foot down.

'Hmph,' Dotty replied. She caught Tara's eye, and her face softened. 'Sorry, hen. I havenae forgotten our chat. It's just because I know ye love tae dance. But if ye dinnae feel comfortable dancin' wi' Ramsay, of course, I understand.'

'If ye want tae step oot for a minute, I'll say ye had a headache, hen,' Eric murmured in her ear, so she could hear him above the hubbub. 'But, if ye want tae leave, I'd say, go now.'

'Thanks.' Tara was grateful for her parents' kindness. She was about to duck out of the bar when she looked across the crowd and saw Ramsay, who had been shunted forward to the stage in front of the crowd. He stood there with Hal, looking self-conscious, and, despite everything that had happened between them in the past, her heart went out to him.

In that moment, Ramsay looked just like he had, all those years ago. He wasn't as skinny now – his collarbone didn't stick out in the way it once had, and his face wasn't as thin. Time had added meat to his bones and, she guessed, he didn't do as much exercise as he'd done, once. But the same vulnerability was painted on his face; it was the same look she remembered when he'd turn up at her house with bruises on his arm and refuse to say how he'd got them. It was the look he got when he'd look at her, before a competition. She knew what he was thinking. *I'm not good enough.* And she knew what she had to do.

'No. It's okay. I'll go,' she said.

Carla was standing by the stage; she'd been helping with cleanup. She shot Tara a concerned glance and mouthed *you okay?*

'Are ye sure?' Eric looked concernedly at her. 'Dinnae do anythin' that's goin' tae make ye feel bad.'

'Ye dinnae have tae do it for us,' Dotty interjected.

'I know,' she said, putting down her glass and holding up her hand. 'It's okay,' she repeated, and made her way through the crowd.

'I'm here,' Tara said to Hal, as she reached the stage; she touched Carla's arm in a gesture that said *it's okay, I'm okay*. Ramsay gave her a relieved smile.

'Hi,' he said, shyly.

'Hi. It's okay. We've got this,' she murmured to Ramsay, as she stood beside him. He looked surprised for a moment, and then smiled.

'Okay,' he said, softly, so that only she could hear.

Tara had always been the strong one. She got nervous before a competition too, but she was the one who could reach deep into her gut and pull out the competitive urge to win. Tara knew how to find that warlike push for glory; that pure, unfettered energy of victory.

We're going to win, she would say, taking Ramsay's chin in hers and staring defiantly into his eyes. *We're taking that trophy home because we're better than all these idiots. We worked harder. We're already the champions. Okay?*

Okay, he'd say, breaking into a smile. And, as long as Ramsay was smiling, she knew they would win.

Tara had the gumption for competing, but Ramsay had the most beautiful smile in the world. She knew that more than one competition judge had fallen for Ramsay's smile, in their years of competing. It wasn't even just his smile: it was his beauty in general. Tara was a pretty girl, but she never thought of herself as anything special. Ramsay Fraser, by comparison, was beautiful in the way of film stars of bygone eras; there was something fey about his high cheekbones and soft-lashed eyes. An indescribable glamour to him that made people love him.

'Well, we're delighted to have you both here.' Hal beamed at them both. 'I know that everyone would love tae see a Highland Fling, if ye had a mind?'

'It's been a bit of a long time,' Tara protested. 'We might not be that good. I mean, I haven't even warmed up.'

'Ah, go on!' Tara recognised her mother's voice in the crowd. 'Just a little! They were such a bonny couple to watch, Hal!' she added. The crowd laughed.

'Yer mother has spoken, Tara,' Hal chuckled. 'I've found, over the years, it didnae do tae disappoint Dotty Ballantyne.'

'I'm well aware.' Tara frowned at her mother, who gave her a double thumbs up in return. Dotty had clearly got behind the dance, now that Tara had decided she was going to do it.

'We love ye, Tara!' Dotty cried out, and Tara couldn't help but smile.

'Okay. Let me stretch out my calves at least for a minute.' She did some quick yoga stretches, falling straight back into her warmup prep as if it had been last week that she and Ramsay had competed in anything, and not over ten years ago. Ramsay took his phone and his wallet out of his pockets and put them carefully at the back of the stage, and unbuttoned his blue tartan shirt, taking it off to reveal a fitted black T shirt underneath.

He had filled out since their younger days. Tara caught herself staring at Ramsay's muscular arms and chest. *Goodness*, she thought, before looking away hastily. Ramsay was a man, now: no longer a boy. And she was disturbed to feel a rush of attraction towards him.

That's not okay, she reprimanded herself. *He's not yours anymore. Remember what he did. Remember that he didn't choose you.*

Tara hardened her heart, though it was difficult to be so near to Ramsay and not want to fall effortlessly back into their old ways.

You just have to dance for ten minutes, then this is over, she thought. *Focus.*

'Ready?' Ramsay asked, and she nodded.

'Do you remember the steps?' she asked.

'Yeah.' He placed his hands on his waist, his feet turned out like a ballet dancer's. Tara copied his stance, which was how the dance began, with a bow to the audience and then up on tiptoes for the first jump.

The Fling was danced solo, but it was common for dance troupes and couples to perform it together, aiming for as total synchronisation and accuracy as possible. In the practice studio, their teacher had taped a star comprised of eight bisecting lines to the floor, so that there was a central point for them to stay within as they jumped. Tara had been able to stay on a central point for the entirety of the dance, as had Ramsay. It looked easy when you performed it, but the strength and precision it took to make a dance look easy was hard won with hours of sweat, aching muscles and frustration.

Tara remembered the steps so well: they'd been imprinted on her brain forever. Point upwards with the hand, the other hand low. Jump on the right leg, left leg forward, back, forward.

That was a step called shedding, which began the dance. You repeated it on both sides, and then jumped whilst turning in a circle. Then it was back-stepping, then toe and heel, then rocking. Then, you repeated the back-step, followed by a cross over, then a shake and turn. Last, shedding again.

Some bagpipe music began, and they both bowed to the audience.

As soon as Tara took the first jump, she felt her body remember the dance. That was how it was: something like muscle memory, but there was something else too, when you were a dancer. The dance was a language that you learned, and, if you worked very hard, it became a spell that you could cast over the audience. Your body was the magic, and it could conjure something alive and exciting.

As they danced, Tara felt them synchronise to each other in the way that they were so used to. Her body knew how to follow the music and make sure that their feet hit the ground at exactly the same time. How to be in the same time, how to follow the same angles and movements so that their bodies were in perfect unison.

The crowd cheered and clapped to the rhythm of the music. Tara was taken back, in her memory, to the years past, competing at castles and on stages in the countryside, in community halls and everywhere in-between. Wherever they were, once the music started, that was all there was. The dance was the place that she loved to be. And, she loved the shared space that existed between her and Ramsay. It was a meditative, almost psychic space of just being, but, at the same time, working hard to make sure that they were as perfect as they could be. There was a flow state to it, when it was good: it felt effortless, even though they were working hard.

When the music stopped, Tara didn't know how long they'd been dancing. She bowed, following Ramsay, and the crowd clapped.

'Encore!' someone shouted. Tara laughed, the exuberance of the dance still with her. She took a few seconds to get her breath.

'Good job,' Ramsay murmured to her, wiping a sheen of sweat from his brow. 'You forget how hard that is, though. We must have been fit as dogs.'

'Haha. I guess we were. You did all right, though,' she replied.

'Thanks. I spend most of my exercise time in the gym these days. It's not dancing, but it's something.' He grabbed the hem of his T shirt and used it to wipe his face. Tara was unexpectedly faced with Ramsay's washboard stomach: wider than she remembered, and more covered in his dark hair. She cleared her throat and looked away.

'Ah, that was lovely,' Hal said, clapping them. 'Thank ye both. Now. I know yer both experts, so I willnae ask ye tae teach us anythin' too hard. But perhaps ye'll lead us all in the Gay Gordons? Most of us'll know that one.' he turned to the crowd. 'I think we all fancy a bit o' a dance, now that you've inspired us, eh?' Hal asked the crowd, who cheered.

'Oh. Right, okay.' Tara had thought they were done with the dancing, but apparently they weren't. She couldn't very well refuse this, so she took Ramsay's outstretched hand.

'The Gay Gordons?' Ramsay asked Hal, who grinned.

'Aye, why not?' he said, walking offstage and bowing to one of the ladies in the audience, who blushed and giggled at the Laird, in his kilt and T-shirt, asking her for a dance. 'Right. Partner up, everyone! An' follow Ramsay an' Tara,' Hal called out, and the music began again.

'Umm... sorry about this,' Ramsay said, as they started to promenade forward, his left hand holding hers and their right hands joined above their heads.

'Not your fault,' Tara said, keeping a smile on her face as

they reversed their hands and repeated the same four steps, walking backwards. 'When the laird says dance, we dance.'

'Yeah. You were good, back there,' he said, as they went forward again. 'It was weird doing it again though, after all this time.'

'It *was* weird,' she agreed as they went backwards again, and then allowed Ramsay to twirl her under his uplifted arm.

'So, how have you been?' he asked, as his hand found her waist, and they began the last stage of the dance sequence, which was a standard ballroom-style skipping step. 'I was sad not to see you at Gyle Head.'

'Fine, thanks,' Tara replied by instinct, although she was seriously distracted by the sensation of Ramsay's hand on her waist. It was warm and it felt good: as if it belonged there. 'Yeah. I'm sorry about that. Something came up at the last minute,' she said, finding something to say that wasn't technically a lie.

'Well, we should still talk,' he said.

The music came to a climax, and then the couples started the whole sequence again from the beginning. Tara released Ramsay's hand for a moment as she helped a nearby couple with the transition of the turn: they were getting muddled somehow and halting the progression of everyone else in the dance, and giggling maniacally.

It was good to have a distraction; she didn't know how she felt, being in such close proximity to him. And, she also didn't feel ready to talk. Not about his wife and daughter. About her feelings, which were uncomfortably close to the surface.

They danced a few more rounds, and the music drew to a close.

'Ah, that was fun, eh?' Hal clapped his hands to get every-one's attention. 'Now then – the refreshments are ready, I believe, so let's all have a break, and thank ye tae Ramsay and Tara!' he boomed. Tara curtseyed and Ramsay made a deep bow.

'So,' Ramsay said, as the dance ended, and everyone clapped. 'It would be nice to go for a coffee, or dinner, or something.' Ramsay held onto the tips of her fingers for a moment before releasing her hand. 'Since we didn't get to do it the other day.'

'Oh. Umm...' she mumbled, smiling to the other villagers who were nodding to them. Some were watching them curiously: mostly older residents of Loch Cameron, who would have remembered the pair as children and teenagers. Tara wondered what people were thinking. They all knew that Ramsay Fraser had disappeared without a trace. And, they all presumably knew that he was now married with a child. Were they going to gossip behind her back now? That she was a homewrecker, a whore, trying to go after someone else's man?

'I'd love to spend some more time with you,' he continued, but Tara couldn't meet his eyes. She knew that if she opened herself to the full force of that smile, she would be lost. And she didn't want to be lost. She had been so deeply in love with Ramsay. So far gone that she had committed all of her heart to him: all her hopes and dreams were woven with his. And when you lost someone you were that deeply meshed with, it hurt so much that you thought you might die.

I can't do that again, she thought, knowing deep in her bones that it was true. *I can't survive Ramsay Fraser a second time. And I'm not a homewrecker. How dare he flirt with me like this. Use me, when he knows how I must feel.*

'Sure. Maybe. I have to go,' she said, knowing it was abrupt, but not being able to help herself. Tara's self-preservation instincts were suddenly on high alert, and she needed to get out.

'What? You're not staying for the evening?' Ramsay frowned. 'Aren't you... living here now?' He gestured at the walls of the Inn, which had been hung with bunting and banners saying things like SAVE OUR SCHOOL and DONATE NOW. Dotty had a flair for the dramatic; Tara had wanted to ask her if she'd made any banners that said WON'T SOMEBODY THINK OF THE CHILDREN but she knew Dotty would give her a withering look if she did.

'Err... yes. But I need to pop out.' Tara excused herself, knowing that it was the thinnest of thin excuses, knowing that she seemed cagey, but she just couldn't be here anymore with Ramsay and with the locals looking on. She imagined she could feel their disapproval. 'I forgot I need to run an errand for Mum.'

'Right... Okay, well, I'll give you a message or a call. Find a time to get together for a proper chat,' he said, looking rather unsure of her.

'Sure... okay,' she said, and practically ran out of the Inn and onto the street outside, which was mercifully quiet.

I can't. I just can't her brain was yelling at her. *No.*

Tara ran to the edge of the loch and down the stone steps from the high street, flinging off her shoes and rolling up her jeans. Thankfully, she walked into the loch – just far enough for the water to go up to her ankles – but she knew it was what she needed. The calming waters of Loch Cameron had helped her on many occasions in the past when her feet were exhausted from dancing. Time was, she would come and stand in the freezing water after a long practice session and let the cold water act in the same way as ballet dancers used an ice bath.

But, sometimes, she also needed to walk out into the water and let its freezing stillness calm her heart and her mind, as well as her body. When she was younger and still lived at home, Tara would walk out into the loch if she was in a bad mood or worried about something, and let the cold waters wash away her problems until she felt her heart lighten and her mind clear.

Tonight, she needed the calm of the loch. She needed to feel the composure she had felt before she had seen Ramsay Fraser again. Before that moment in the market, life had been simple. But, now, her heart was on fire, and Tara didn't know what to think.

Please, she asked the waters of the loch, as she bent forwards to trail her fingers in its silky, cold surface. *Please bring me calm and clarity. Please don't let my heart burn again.*

Perhaps the loch heard her, or perhaps it was just the cold of the water, but, after a few moments, Tara started to feel a little better. She took in a deep breath and let it go, slowly.

Calm and clarity. Calm and clarity.

It's okay. Nothing has to happen, she rationalised.

Her phone pinged, and she reached into her pocket to answer it.

Hope you're okay. Would be great to catch up soon. Ramsay xx

Tara's heart pounded again, returning to its state of panic.

Leave me alone she replied, quickly. *I know you're married, or at least with someone. You had your chance with me, Ramsay. It's over.*

She put her phone back in the pocket, trying to regain some composure, but it seemed to have left her. Rather than calm, her feet just felt numb in the cold.

She waded back to the sand, and sat down on the stone steps, staring into the loch.

What was she going to do about Ramsay Fraser? She couldn't trust herself around him – her body reacted to him so strongly that if she'd have stayed next to him for any longer, she probably would have done something she'd have regretted.

Perhaps the only rational thing was to ignore him and avoid him as much as humanly possible until she left Loch Cameron at the end of the summer holidays. *I have to protect myself*, she thought. *And, he's married now. Or, at least, he's with someone. So, what was he doing, flirting with me? Where was she, when all that was happening? Where was his daughter?*

Tara imagined Ramsay's wife and daughter, at home, perhaps in one of the cosy little cottages in Loch Cameron. Snuggled up on the sofa, watching a movie while Daddy was out, flirting with his ex-girlfriend. She felt sick.

She deleted his message, and felt like throwing her phone into the loch while she was at it. Whoever he had used to be, Ramsay Fraser was no longer a good man, and she wanted absolutely nothing to do with him, ever again.

TWENTY-FIVE

'Pass the potatoes tae Carla, Eric.' Dotty waved her hand imperiously at her husband. 'She'll waste away. No' a speck on ye, dear,' she added to Carla, in a confidential tone. Tara could see Carla subdue a giggle.

'Thanks, Mrs Ballantyne.' She took the large blue ceramic bowl, heaped with mashed potatoes, and spooned some onto her plate. 'It's so kind of you to have me staying with you.'

'No' a bit o' it.' Dotty smiled warmly. 'It's grand tae spend some time with Tara's flatmate. We hear so much aboot ye.'

'Oh. All good, I hope.' Carla made a face at Tara.

'Aye, of course, dear,' Dotty chuckled. 'Did ye have a good time at the fundraiser? I saw ye have a bit o' a dance.'

'Yeah. I've never been to a ceilidh before. It was awesome. I think I've pulled a few muscles, though.' Carla winced as she shifted in her seat. 'I hardly do any exercise, and then suddenly I'm being thrown around the room by a mountain of a man in a kilt.'

'Ha. That was Angus, wasn't it? Lovely fella. Enthusiastic dancer. No' that I was allowed, this time.' Dotty pouted. 'Shame. I do love a dance.'

'Next time, hen,' Eric said, quietly, from across the table. 'Ye cannae stand very well yet, let alone dance.'

'Aye, I suppose,' Dotty sighed, and elbowed Tara. 'Mind ye, someone looked good dancin' wi' Ramsay Fraser. Just like auld times.'

'Mum. I didn't choose to do that. Hal called us up to the stage. I could hardly say no,' Tara protested.

'Aye, but it looked like ye were enjoyin' it.' Dotty raised an eyebrow.

'She's right, Tar. You did look like you were having a good time, once you started dancing,' Carla added.

'Well, I don't want anything to do with him. Flirting with me when he's married and has a child,' she said, vehemently. Dotty blinked.

'I didnae know that,' she said. 'Still, I havenae been oot and aboot, so I'm a bit behind on the news. Married, ye say?'

'Well, I assume so. Or at least, partnered with someone. I saw them at the park together,' Tara said. Eric raised both eyebrows, but said nothing.

'Poor Ramsay,' Dotty sighed, as though Tara hadn't just told her that Ramsay had a child and a – at the very least – serious girlfriend. If you had a child together, then whatever your marital status, then that was game over, in Tara's eyes. 'Ye know I feel bad we didnae do more for him.'

'Poor Ramsay?' she echoed her mother. 'I know he had a bad time as a kid, Mum, but he lied to me.'

'Aye, I know, hen. But I told ye aboot about Jack Fraser. Pure mean, he was. An' Ramsay's poor mother left when he was just young. Poor wee mite.' Dotty and Eric exchanged glances.

'He was a drinker. Used tae use Ramsay as a punchin' bag when he was drunk, which was a lot,' Eric interjected. 'This was Ramsay's dad, when they were young,' he added, for Carla's benefit.

'Well, Ramsay never talked about his dad, but I knew he

was mean.' Tara frowned. 'But... a *punching bag*? How regularly was this? Why didn't you ever tell me?'

There was a big difference between Ramsay having a dad who was in general unpleasant to be around – moody, shouty and often drunk – and Jack Fraser using him as a *punching bag*. That was something she had never been aware of. Yet, as soon as she thought that, Tara remembered her eleventh birthday, and realisation overtook her with its looming shadow.

'I mean... there was that time at my birthday party. Something had happened, but he never told me. But I wasn't stupid, I knew it was his dad. Don't you remember? He said he'd been making too much noise wrapping up my present and his dad couldn't hear the football.' Tara had never forgotten her eleventh birthday, because it had been the day when Ramsay had given her the heart necklace.

'Aye. Gave that boy a black eye, an' the rest,' Dotty said, darkly. 'We kept things breezy because it was yer birthday. But the poor lad could hardly breathe. If his ribs weren't broken then they were definitely bruised, that time.'

'That time?' Tara leaned forward, her dinner forgotten. 'That implies that there were other times.' She swallowed hard, feeling sick.

'D'you really want tae know, darlin'?' Dotty looked away, evasively, as she always was when talking about Ramsay's past. 'I mean... Carla, you don't want tae hear this...' She trailed off, but it was Eric who cleared his throat.

'Dot. The girl needs tae know. We've kept it from her long enough,' he said, kindly, but in the tone of voice that meant he had decided, and there was nothing that was going to stop him. Dotty nodded, reluctantly.

'Go on, then,' she said.

'Aye, well. One day, Ramsay was here playin' with ye – ye were oot in the garden, runnin' around, an' he fell. I went oot tae pick him up – ye were aboot seven then, I think – an' he cried out so loud when I put my hand on his little arm.' Eric's voice was steady, but Tara watched his face as he told the tale, and could see how difficult it was for him to say the words. 'I thought it was because he'd hurt himself fallin', but when I rolled up his sleeve, his whole arm was purple.'

'Oh, no.' Tara's stomach clenched. A sense of dread overcame her, even though her dad was telling her something that had happened over twenty years ago.

Tears sprang to Dotty's eyes, and she took Tara's hand across the table.

'I took him inside. I was very casual, I just said, *let's make sure ye dinnae need a plaster*, or somethin' like that. I took his shirt off, and his whole arm an' his shoulder was black an' blue.' Her father let out a long sigh. 'I remember, on his back, there was a handprint. Adult sized. I cannae even imagine how hard ye need tae hit a child tae leave a handprint.' Eric shivered. 'I still think about that poor wee lad's bruises. Even now.'

'Oh my...' Tara swore under her breath. 'I knew his dad was mean. But he never wanted to talk about it. Not even when we were older.'

'Aye. Wanted tae forget it, I dinnae wonder.' Dotty wiped her eyes with a tissue from a box at the side of the table. 'Sadly, that wasnae the end o' it. We agreed that we'd have Ramsay here as much as we could, after that.'

'What happened to Jack? Is he alive now? Is he still in the village?' Tara hadn't even considered the possibility until now. She could count on one hand the number of times that she'd ever met Ramsay's dad, even though she and Ramsay had grown up together.

Tara's phone, on the table next to her, lit up.

Tara. Would still love to talk. Let me know. Ramsay x

Tara picked the phone up and read the message. *Speak of*

the devil, she thought, but of course, Ramsay Fraser wasn't the devil. That was his father, judging from Eric's story.

Her fingers hovered over the screen, but she didn't know how to respond. She still didn't know what to say to Ramsay.

'He's still alive? Jack Fraser?' Tara prompted her parents, wondering if Ramsay was living with his dad, now that he was back in Loch Cameron. It seemed unlikely, but you never knew. She didn't even know at this point whether Ramsay was here for good, or whether he was just visiting, like her.

'No, thank the Lord.' Dotty crossed herself with her free hand. 'An' I don't say that lightly, but there wasnae a worse man in the village for a long time, in my view.'

'What happened to him?' Tara took a bite of her sausage, remembering that there was a meal in front of her. Carla had been sitting, agog, as the story unfolded around her. When she saw Tara eat, it seemed to remind her that she too had food in front of her that was going cold, and she started eating again.

'Heart attack, in the end.' Dotty pursed her lips. 'Happens tae drinkers. Not least, cirrhosis of the liver, cancer, all of that. He wasnae old. Ye drink that much, ye want tae die, that's what I think. Maybe he felt guilty aboot what he did tae that poor wee lad.' Dotty shook her head, angrily. 'Some people, ye feel sorry fer. Some, we've seen in the bar, over the years, hopeless. They've had a rough time. A drink's all they can find tae escape.' She sighed. 'But Jack Fraser, he wasnae like that. He mightae had a rough upbringin', but didnae we all?' Dotty stared out of the window for a moment. 'No. He was pure mean.'

'Aye,' Eric said, grimly. 'Come on, Dot. Ye know that's not all.'

'Aye, all right.' Dotty pulled her lips tight. 'It was some years after the bruisin'. It still happened, but no' so much. I'd gone up tae see Jack wi' yer faither, an' we'd had a wee chat.'

'What did you say to him?' Tara asked.

'I told him that I knew what he'd done tae Ramsay. He said it was an accident. Said Ramsay had pulled a chest o' drawers onto himself an' Jack had had tae pull him out from underneath.' Dotty's expression was furious at the memory. 'I said if anythin' happened tae Ramsay like that again, I'd report him tae the police.'

'You should have reported him then,' Tara argued. 'That was serious abuse.'

'Aye, hen. I know,' Dotty sighed. 'But we thought, if we let Jack knew that we were keepin' an eye on him, that would be enough. We were naïve, I suppose.'

'So, it didn't work?' Tara wondered what else she didn't know about Ramsay's past. 'Mum, I can't believe you never told me all this.'

'I'm sorry, darlin'. Your dad and I thought it was best we protected you from it.' Dotty shrugged. 'An' then we thought, when he disappeared, what's the point now? He was ootae yer life. Ye were upset enough.'

'So? What happened?' Tara prompted her mother.

'Ah, goodness. Well, some years after I had a word wi' Jack Fraser, don't ye remember, Ramsay broke his collarbone? An' ye had tae bow ootae that regional competition?'

'Yes. He did it swimming. He slipped on the steps by the loch. Fell badly.' Tara remembered it so well; Ramsay calling her on the phone a few nights before the competition. He'd been so apologetic. Tara remembered telling him over and over again that it was okay, it was just an accident.

'No, he didn't, Tara.' Dotty met her daughter's eyes.

Tara's hand flew to her mouth.

'Oh, no,' she said, horror filling her from her toes, into her thighs, her stomach, her chest. It felt as though all her blood was turning to wet sand.

'Jack got home that night, drunk outtae his mind,' Dotty

continued, grimly. 'He started on Ramsay. He was, what, four-teen at the time?' she asked Eric, who nodded.

'Aye. Bigger than a wee bairn, but still no' a man yet. No' as big as his dad – Jack was a big fella, too – but big enough tae think he could stand up tae him, I guess.' Dotty let out a long breath. 'They had an argument an' Jack hit him wi' a cricket bat. Must've been Ramsay's from school. Broke his collarbone an' a couple o' ribs.' Dotty started to cry.

'No,' Tara breathed, not believing what she was hearing.

'Oh my god,' Carla said, at the same time.

'I'm afraid so, hen. Ramsay got tae the phone an' called the ambulance. Poor wee lad had tae go on his own tae the hospital tae get fixed up. First thing me an' yer dad heard aboot it was the day after. Bill, who drove the ambulance, popped in an' told us. He knew you and Ramsay were friends, an' that we'd been keepin' an eye on the lad.'

'I can't believe it,' Tara repeated. 'So what did you do? Report Jack to the police?'

'Aye. I did it myself. Poor Ramsay didnae want me tae, but I had tae.'

'Good,' Tara said. 'So, did he get arrested?'

'No,' Dotty said, in a faux light tone that she used when she was particularly angry. 'I'm afraid he didnae. The police abso-lutely failed poor Ramsay. They said they could put him in care, but that wouldae meant he'd have had tae move ootae the village. He didnae want tae leave ye, sweetie.

'So, I asked the police what we could do, an' that was the point that yer dad an' I stepped in an' made up the room for Ramsay here, an' he moved in. The authorities let us take him in, sort of unofficially, I suppose.'

'Wow. You wouldn't be able to do that now,' Carla said. 'If I think about the children in care in my school... I mean, it's very different.'

'Right. I knew that he came to live with us, but I guess I just thought it was because he was unhappy at home and you were happy to have him. I'm surprised you could sort of adopt him, that way. It wasn't that long ago. Surely things were supposed to be official. He was a minor,' Tara added.

'I know, hen. But Loch Cameron's a small place, an' we promised the Laird an' the local police we'd look after Ramsay. An' they all knew we would. An' we did. Got him off to university, just like ye. We were so proud of ye both.'

'I guess you've been a part of the community so long that people would trust you. More than his dad, anyway,' Tara said, trying to take it in.

'Aye.' Dotty paused for a moment. 'There is somethin' else.' A dark look passed over her face.

'What?'

'Well, after that time, with the collarbone, your dad an' some of the fellas from the village went up tae see Jack. No' me that time.' Dotty's face took on a hard expression. 'They persuaded Jack tae leave the village an' never come back.'

'What do you mean?' Tara turned to her father. 'You threatened him?' A curl of dread unfurled in her stomach.

'Jack Fraser left Loch Cameron that night an' never came back. I heard he died a few years later. Couldnae have happened to a nicer fella,' Eric said, shortly.

'What does that mean?' Tara asked, incredulously.

'It means what it means, hen. We dinnae stand fer hurtin' kids, no' in Loch Cameron.' Eric's voice was low, and his expression was uncharacteristically hard. Tara was used to her dad being so sweet and gentle that it was strange, seeing him like this.

'I didn't know that. I thought... I dunno. That his dad was working away or something,' Tara said, furious that this secret had been kept from her. 'He never said.'

'I guess there was a lot of things that went unsaid,' Eric mused. 'Dunno if we did the right thing by runnin' Jack ootae town, but Ramsay was better off here. I'm just sad it took until he was fourteen tae do it.'

Tara stood up and started pacing the room.

'I don't know what to do with this information,' she said, running her fingers through her hair.

'Well, it's the truth.' Dotty picked up her knife and fork and started eating again.

'*Mum*. What am I supposed to say to him now?' Tara felt terrible for having been so mean to Ramsay now. Even though he had still done what he'd done to her. But this new knowledge changed things. She couldn't feel the same. Everything had shifted. 'I was – I am – still so angry at him for what he did.' She lowered her eyes, thinking about what she'd done. The thing that had tortured her for so long.

She had to say it out loud.

'I did something. I never knew if he hated me for it,' she said, looking down at her plate. 'If that was why he left.'

'What, poppet?' Dotty looked concerned.

'Oh, god.' Tara put her hands over her eyes. 'Okay. I tried to find his mum. That first term we were away at university.'

'His mum? How? Why?' Dotty asked, her eyes wide.

'I knew he missed her. He'd been talking about his mum a lot around that time. I guess because we were about to leave the village, this whole new life was going to start. He had said a couple of times that he wondered where she was. That he missed her. That I was so lucky to have you and dad around to support me.'

'We treated him like our own,' Dotty said.

'I know, Mum. And he was so grateful for it. But I guess he always knew that he wasn't really yours, no matter how much you made him feel like part of the family.' Tara sighed. 'Anyway, I asked around, and there were a couple of people who had been friends with Mrs Fraser. I wanted to ask you. Mum, but I didn't know if you'd think it was a good idea.'

'Ah, darlin'. I wouldae helped.' Dotty frowned.

'I know. Anyway, I got a phone number. I called it, but she didn't answer, so I left a message. That was all that happened – I did try her again a few times, but there was never a reply. But there was an answerphone message, so I do think it was the right number. She just didn't get back in touch, for whatever reason.'

'Nothing at all?' Carla asked. 'I would have thought, if you'd had to leave your child... you'd want to see him again, wouldn't you?'

'I know. I thought so. But then, about a week later, she texted me,' Tara continued. 'It was really short, but she asked me for his number, so I gave it to her. And then I never heard any more from her. I was going to tell him – explain what I'd done – and I was so hopeful that they'd reconcile. That Ramsay would have his mum back again. But then, I got that note from him and he disappeared, and that was that for ten years.'

'Oh my goodness.' Carla put her hand on her chest. 'No offence, but that is straight up soap opera territory drama.'

'I know. But it's been weighing on my mind for all this time. What if... I don't know? He didn't want to hear from her, and it was a huge betrayal of trust? Or, what if she did get in touch with him and it turned out badly? That she was abusive as well, and I unwittingly re-introduced this toxic element back into his life? The fact that it was at the same time as that note, and the time he disappeared... I've just always worried about it. I felt like... maybe him disappearing was my fault.' Tara's heart contracted, and she wrapped her arms around herself.

'Oh, Tara. I'm sure none of that's true.' Dotty leaned over and gave her daughter a huge hug. 'You shouldae said somethin'. All these years, you've been worried aboot that?'

'Yeah. But don't you think it's a huge coincidence?' Tara said, her face smushed into Dotty's cardigan.

'Yes, darlin'. I do. That's exactly what it was. A coincidence, nothin' more,' her mother said, placatingly. 'You did a nice thing for the lad. No, we don't know how it turned out. But he certainly wouldnae have done what he did because of that. I'm sure of it.'

'But, how can you be sure?' Tara pulled away from the hug.

'I just am,' Dotty replied. 'Trust me. Do you trust me? Yer wise auld mother?' She gave Tara a gentle peck on the cheek.

'Of course I trust you, Mum,' Tara replied.

'Well, then. We'll have no more talk aboot all this bein' yer fault,' Dotty said in her no-nonsense voice.

'Talk tae the poor boy, Tara,' her dad added. 'Just talk to him, okay? Promise me you'll do that.'

'I will, Dad.' Tara let out a long breath. 'I will.'

'And, I agree. I don't think him leaving was your fault at all,' Eric added. 'Your mother is right. As always.' He twinkled his warm smile at Dotty, who reached for his hand over the table and squeezed it.

It's not your fault. The words rang in her head, and reverberated in her heart like a bell, sonorous and deep, disrupting the old truths that had lodged there for so long.

Could Dotty and Eric be right about this, like they were – as it pained Tara to admit – usually right about most things?

Could she really let go of the guilt she had been holding for all these years?

TWENTY-SIX

Tara was packing the last of her things into her wheelie suitcase when there was a knock on her bedroom door.

Since she'd been staying in her old room, she'd done some tidying up: she'd taken down the posters of the bands that had been hanging up since she was in her early teens and put her old stuffed toys in a bag to donate to the community centre.

As for the dancing trophies, she had packed a couple to take home to her flat. They were nice things to keep: she had lots of good memories about her dancing career.

Carefully, she had mended the old silver necklace after tearing it from her neck in anger, and stored it in a small jewellery box. She stared at it for a moment before putting it in her pocket. It would always be a part of her life, and, despite the sad memories attached to it, there were many good ones, too.

Carla had gone home the week before. It had been good, having her to stay at the Inn. Part of Tara was looking forward to getting back to the flat, and their old life together. She was looking forward to re-establishing herself in her real life; where she had a real job, and she could rely on the fact that she wasn't going to run into old memories or old lovers around every corner. Being back in Loch Cameron had been exhausting, both emotionally and physically. Tara didn't think she'd ever worked as hard as in the last few weeks at the Inn, from making up rooms to breakfasts, lunches and dinners and the thousand and one other tasks that running the Loch Cameron Inn demanded.

But she was also dreading going back to Lomond Primary. Yet, she'd learnt something from Agnes, and that was resilience. If Agnes could stand to work alongside the man who had treated her so badly, then Tara could manage working in a toxic workplace. At the very least, she could look for something else, if she decided that she really wasn't happy.

She had gone down to the loch, earlier that morning, to say goodbye to it. The haar was down, and the whole village had been blanketed in a heavy mist.

Please, she had asked the waters of the loch again, trailing her fingers in its silky, cold surface. *Please bring me peace.*

She had taken in a deep breath and let it go, slowly. *Calm and clarity. Calm and clarity* she had repeated, like she had done before.

Then, she'd walked up to Queen's Point and hugged each oak tree in the circle that was her special place of peace. *I'll miss you*, she'd thought, as she'd pressed her cheek against each tree's rough bark. *Thank you.*

She would miss the loch and the oak trees. She would miss the view of the castle across the loch, with the narrow blue bridge that led to it, and the morning haar that sometimes snaked through her open window, like a ghost.

She would miss the food market, the bread and cakes that she bought there, wrapped up in paper bags, which smelt so good when she unwrapped them.

She would miss the crochet coven, and all the kindness of the people of Loch Cameron, who had accepted her back into the community as one of their own, as if she had never left.

Tara resolved to come back and visit more often. Now that

she had settled things with Dotty a little more, she felt easier about coming home.

'Come in,' she called, looking up.

'Tara, darlin'.' Her dad pushed the door open, but stayed in the hallway outside. He looked a little uncomfortable.

'I'm just coming,' she said, zipping the suitcase.

'It's no' that, hen.' Eric made an awkward scuffing motion with his shoes on the carpet.

'Dad?' Tara frowned, wondering what was wrong.

'You've got a visitor, downstairs,' Eric said.

'Who?' she asked, confused. 'Can't you just say I'm leaving in a minute? If it's one of the girls from the crochet coven, I've got their numbers. They know I'm going today.'

'I think you'd better just come down, hen,' Eric repeated.

'Okay...' she replied, nonplussed. Her dad was being uncharacteristically vague. 'Can you bring my suitcase down, then?' she asked her dad, who nodded.

'Course,' he said.

Tara walked down the stairs, half wondering who could have popped in and why it demanded so much mystery on her dad's part, and half thinking about how strange it would be to leave the Inn and go back to her real life. Because, since she'd been here, she'd been reminded of how Loch Cameron felt like home. Was her life in Glasgow her real life? Yes, she'd missed teaching, and she missed the children at school. But, she had to admit that most of the rest of her life in Glasgow was a little underwhelming.

She'd made friends in Loch Cameron and reconnected to the land here. And, while she didn't necessarily want to live with her parents for much longer, it had been nice to spend time with them again.

'Hi, Tara.' Ramsay Fraser looked up as she walked into the bar.

He was standing next to one of the comfy chairs to the right of the bar, with his hand resting awkwardly on the back on it, like he was about to take a formal photograph.

'Ramsay,' she said, warily. Eric, who had followed her down the stairs with her suitcase, cleared his throat noisily.

'Well,' he declared. 'I'll just put this in yer car,' he said, and disappeared into the hallway leading off the bar. Tara heard the front door to the Inn open and close: her dad was obviously giving them some space.

'What are you doing here?' she demanded. 'I'm leaving in a minute.'

'I wanted to catch you before you leave.' Ramsay gripped the top of the easy chair. 'Your mum called me. Said we should talk.'

'Oh. Did she indeed,' Tara said, looking around for Dotty, who was nowhere to be seen. In fact, Dotty was getting around a bit better now, and Eric had got Kathy from the crochet coven to take over from Tara, now that school was about to start again.

It'll just be short term until Mum's fully back on her feet again, Eric had said, giving Dotty a squeeze around her shoulders. But Tara suspected that Eric would be persuading her to take it easier from now on, and she didn't think that was a bad thing at all.

She supposed that she should have seen this coming, after her talk with her parents and Carla over dinner, a week or so ago. But they hadn't mentioned it again, and, knowing that she was going back home, she'd thought that perhaps everything was better left alone.

Clearly, Dotty hadn't been able to resist interfering.

'Can we talk?' Ramsay repeated.

'Umm... I suppose so,' she said.

'Can we sit down?' Ramsay asked. The Inn wasn't open for customers yet: Tara had planned to leave about ten thirty in the morning.

'Okay,' Tara said.

They sat down, opposite each other.

'So.' Tara wondered how to begin. She knew that he had some things to explain, but her confession weighed on her mind, too. She'd decided that she wasn't going to say anything, but now that he was here, she felt suddenly nauseous at the idea that she would have to tell him what she'd done – contacting his estranged mother, and prompting whatever chaos that had or hadn't manifested in his life.

'I need to talk to you,' Ramsay repeated. He'd pressed his hands together into a tight ball, and Tara could see that the knuckles were white.

'I need to talk to you, too,' she sighed. 'Can I go first?'

'Sure.' He looked surprised, but leaned forward, his hands on his knees in a curiously nervous-looking posture.

'Okay.' Tara took a deep breath, and repeated what she'd told her parents the week before. Ramsay's eyes widened as she told her story, but he didn't look away for a second.

'So, I suppose I always wanted to know what happened between you and your mum – and whether that was the reason you disappeared so suddenly,' Tara finished, trying to keep her tone level. She wanted to stay calm, but her stomach was a ball of nerves. She had worried about this for so long.

'Wow. Okay. Well, I guess the first thing to say is, that wasn't the reason I cut ties with you. With everyone.' He sighed.

'Why did you then?'

'Umm. I don't know where to start. The beginning, I guess,' he sighed. 'Okay. Before I tell you what happened with my mum, we need to actually have a conversation about what happened when I left Loch Cameron,' he began, and Tara's stomach tensed even further. What was he going to say?

'When you left me, you mean?' she asked, unsmilingly. It was still so raw, and even though she had her anxieties about the part she'd played in it all, that pain had cut her, deeply.

'Yeah. I guess so.' Ramsay let out a breath. 'Listen. When we went away to our different universities... I mean, it was fun, but I missed you like crazy. We had that big argument just before I went away. Do you remember that? And for the first time, I was without you. And I hated it.'

'Of course I remember,' she said, quietly. 'It was what made me try and get in contact with your mum. You were so uptight. I thought... I thought it would help.'

Tara remembered exactly what they'd said; where they'd been, even what she was wearing, that day. It was just a couple of days before they were due to leave for university. She had been wearing a green jumper that Dotty had crocheted for her, and jeans. She and Ramsay had gone out for a walk along the loch. It was the last week in September and it was freezing, even for Scotland at that time of year.

Tara had bundled herself up in her dad's sheepskin coat and a knitted hat. Ramsay – who was always warm, had worn a navy-blue sweater and a scarf, jeans and his old hiking boots.

I sometimes wish I could talk to her, he'd said, out of the blue. *I wish I could ask her why she didn't take me with her.*

Tara had known that Ramsay had been talking about his mum.

I'm sure she would have taken you with her, if she could, Tara had replied, hesitantly. *Maybe she couldn't.*

Why couldn't she? He'd turned to her, the question burning in his eyes.

I don't know, babe, she'd replied. *But you know Mum and Dad love you.*

They're not my parents, he'd replied, uncharacteristically darkly.

Well, they think of themselves as your mum and dad, she'd replied. A little hurt by his tone.

Not everyone is as lucky as you, he'd replied, sharply.

I know that, she'd replied. *Why are you being like this? You're pushing me away.*

Like what?

You don't want to talk. You've hardly kissed me recently. Or anything else.

It was true: Ramsay had been keeping to his room at the Inn, saying that he had reading to do ahead of the course. Usually, they had spent all their time together, walking, dancing, kissing under the stars and talking about the future. He had been withdrawn.

You're imagining things. I'm here, aren't I?

Yes, you're here, in body, if not soul, she'd said, trying to be patient. *Tell me what's wrong.*

Nothing's wrong.

Fine. Go and live your new life without me, then Tara had said, crossly, her temper rising up.

Fine. I will.

But, after that, they hadn't really spoken for the rest of the day, and then Ramsay had left early to go to university, saying that he had things to do. It was then that Tara had decided to try and find his mother, thinking that might have helped cheer him up.

'I hated myself after that argument. But I felt like you wanted to be away from me. That was what I was so upset about, that day. It was like you'd decided there was no room for me anymore,' she said.

'I didn't want to leave you, babe. But we got accepted at different universities,' Ramsay said, carefully. 'I felt like you were pushing me away. You said something like, go and live your new life without me. I was hurt, so I said, fine, I will.'

'It was a long time ago. We were just kids,' Tara sighed. 'I felt the same. I thought you were pushing me away, so I guess I thought, I'll just let you go.' She took a moment, then continued 'But, then, when you came back, and we got back together, and you proposed at New Year... I was so happy.' Tears had sprung to her eyes, and she wiped them away in irritation. 'Then you were gone, just a few weeks after that. It didn't make any sense.'

'I know. I can only imagine how that must have been for you, Tara, and I'm sorry.' Ramsay sounded so full of regret; even though Tara wanted to be anywhere than here, having this conversation, her heart still hurt for him.

'When I left for uni, it was a huge change for me,' he continued. 'I just want you to understand where I was, at the time. I'm not making excuses. Okay?'

She nodded, not trusting herself to speak.

'Right. Well, we'd both only ever lived here, in Loch Cameron. And then, suddenly, I realised I wasn't going to have you or Dotty and Eric to depend on, and I sort of felt at sea,' Ramsay explained. 'Can you understand that? With... my family background, and everything? You and your mum and dad were all the family I had. And I had to leave all of you. It was tough.'

'I know. I do understand,' Tara said, softly. 'Mum's told me some things about your dad that I didn't know when we were younger. You never talked about him.'

'I didn't want to. He was a cruel bastard.' Ramsay's expression darkened. 'I didn't want to scare you, or make you feel sorry for me. I just wanted not to think about him, most of the time.'

'He passed away, Mum said,' Tara said. 'I'm sorry.'

'Yeah.' Ramsay let out a long sigh. 'I've been in therapy the past couple of years, and it's helping me deal with it. Because I'm still mourning him, which seems nuts. Like, shouldn't I be delighted he died? But he was still my dad, you know? And, there's a part of me that's mourning the life I could have had, too. If he'd have been a decent father. Maybe my mum would have stayed. Maybe I would have made better choices. I could have had a happy home life, like yours. Not always been thinking about how I could get away, or, if I had to be there, if he was going to come home drunk. And, then, how drunk. Would he just fall asleep on the couch, or would he come at me with the poker, or his belt.' Ramsay put his head in his hands.

'What your parents did, taking me in... I never forgot that. And I'll talk to both of them, too, because they deserve an apology.' He sat up and put his hands back in his lap.

'I'm sure they just want to know what happened. Like me,' she said, pointedly.

'The thing was that I meant it. When I asked you to marry me. It was always what I'd imagined for our future. We talked about it all the time. And then when I went away to university and I realised how much I missed you – it was like a piece of me that I'd left behind. It physically hurt, being away from you. And that was why I proposed. I just couldn't be away from you,' he continued.

'But then, you were. For ten years,' Tara said, the same teary frustration welling up in her as before. 'And I *still* don't know why.'

Ramsay sighed deeply.

'Please don't judge me for what I'm about to say, Tara. It's taken me a really long time to have the courage to say this to you,' he began, slowly. She nodded. Any closure was better than none, and she had waited such a long time to hear this. Whatever it was, it had to be better than not knowing.

'In that first term, after we'd broken up, I was really lonely,' Ramsay began, shakily. 'I'd never not spoken to you for a day, and suddenly, we were miles apart, and we'd split up. Well, we hadn't really spoken after that argument and we never argued. I didn't know what to do with myself. I found it really hard to cope. I started drinking.' He stopped talking for a moment and took in a deep breath.

'It was something I swore I'd never do. Because of my dad,' he said, raking his fingers through his hair. 'But I did. I drank heavily. Passed out a few times. And there were a couple of uni parties. You know, fresher's month, all that.'

'I know.' There had been similar parties at Tara's university, all aimed at getting the students to know each other. She'd gone to a couple – they were all right, although Tara had never been much of a drinker.

'Well... I met a girl at one of the parties,' Ramsay continued.

Oh no. As soon as he said the words, dread balled its fist in Tara's tummy and started to punch upwards to her heart.

'And?' Tara asked, not wanting to know the answer, but needing to hear it.

'We slept together. A one-night thing. Neither of us had been drinking a lot that night. She was in one of my classes, and we'd said a few things back and forward here and there. So, I knew her to say hello to but that was about it. The party was raging but I had a hangover and I wasn't drinking. I was just about to go back to halls – parties where everyone's drunk except you are awful – and I saw her and said hi. She'd been thinking the same thing. Anyway...' he let out another long breath. 'We ended up sleeping together.'

'Oh.' Tara didn't know what else to say.

'Yeah.' Ramsay balled his fists together again.

'So, you left me because of her?' Tara tried to keep her tone even, but she couldn't hide the confusion she felt. 'A one-night stand. But this was *before* I saw you that Christmas. And you *proposed.* Oh, my god, Ramsay. You asked me to marry you. *After* that.'

'You and I had broken up. It... sleeping with Sarah – it was a mistake. When I got home at Christmas I realised that I wanted – needed – to be with you forever. It was always you, Tara.'

'No. It wasn't. Because clearly, whatever you had with this Sarah changed everything,' Tara snapped. Sarah. She remembered the cute woman at the park, with the blonde bob. How

Ramsay had smiled and waved at her. Her stomach twisted with jealousy.

'Yes. It did. But not in the way you think, Tara.' Ramsay leaned forward. He paused, looking as though he was thinking about what to say next. 'On that night, Sarah got pregnant.' He closed his eyes, as if he didn't want to watch her face as he said the words. Or that he could. 'I didn't love Sarah. I don't love her now. But I do love our daughter, Kelly.'

TWENTY-SEVEN

'What?' Tara gaped at Ramsay. 'I don't understand. I saw you with your daughter at the park a couple of weeks ago, and a woman. I assumed you were married, or at least together with the mother.'

'No. Sarah and I are in touch, but we're not together. She lives in the next village. I have joint custody of Kelly.' He frowned.

'Who were you waving to at the park, then? With the blonde hair?' Tara was so confused. She'd already worked out for herself that Ramsay was a dad, and she didn't know why he hadn't told her. This was why.

'When?' He looked confused.

'The day you asked to meet me to talk, up on Gyle Head. I went to meet you, and I saw you with Kelly and a woman then. You were playing with your daughter on the slide, and you waved at her. She was watching you from a bench.'

Ramsay looked blank for a moment.

'When you didn't turn up? That day? You said you'd had to work at the Inn.'

'I made an excuse. I saw you there, part of this happy

family... you hadn't mentioned either one of them. What was I supposed to do?' Tara shot back. 'It was an ambush.'

'No, it wasn't.' Ramsay shook his head. 'Yes, I was going to tell you about Kelly. And all of this. But a woman...' He looked blank for another moment. 'Wait, with a blonde bob? That's Brianna. Her daughter and Kelly are friends. We must have just been waving hello.'

'So, that isn't your wife? You're not with anyone at all?' Tara was trying to take it all in.

'Brianna? No. She's an acquaintance. I'm on good terms with Sarah, but we're not together. We tried it for a couple of months after Kelly was born but it soon became clear we were very different people. I've never loved anyone, apart from you.' He reached for her hands across the table.

'Ramsay. This is a lot to take in.' Tara withdrew her hands and put them in her lap. She wasn't ready for connection yet.

'I know. I'm sorry.' He looked downcast.

'So, you disappeared from Loch Cameron when you found out that Sarah was pregnant?' Tara was trying to make sense of it all.

'When I found out Sarah was pregnant, I didn't know what to do. I couldn't tell you. Just the thought of it... I knew it would break your heart. And I didn't know what was going to happen with the baby. I felt that I should be there for Sarah, despite the fact that it was obvious after a certain period of time that we weren't going to be a couple.'

'You broke my heart by disappearing from my life, Ramsay.' Tara was trying not to cry: she held her hand up to her mouth to hide the cry face that she knew her face wanted to pull.

'I know. I know! It's something I've turned over in my head a million times. I'm sorry. Tara, I'm so sorry.' Ramsay started to cry, and it broke her heart even more. 'I never wanted to hurt you. But I didn't know how to tell you about the baby. And I knew that I wanted to raise her, and that I would have to sacrifice my life with you to do that. But I guess I felt...' He trailed off and wiped his eyes. 'My home life was so terrible, Tara. And here was this new life being given to me to look after. She was like a little angel just appearing in my life. I just felt like, this is my chance. This is my chance to have a family, to break that cycle. I wanted to be a good dad. I wanted to be there for her, not run away and leave her.'

'You could have told me,' Tara said, quietly. 'You didn't have to disappear. I know you sent that note, so we knew you were alive, I guess. But... our relationship could have survived you having Kelly,' she said.

'Maybe it would. I don't know. I'd like to think so, now, yes. But at the time... we were young. I was young, and I panicked. It took me a long time to know that I should have told you.'

'So why did you come back to Loch Cameron?' Tara asked.

'Sarah moved to a village nearby. Aberculty. Coincidence, really – we met at uni, and then we both stayed around Edinburgh until about a couple of months ago when Sarah moved out here with her new partner. I didn't want to be that far from Kelly – Sarah and I have always co-parented and stayed local to each other so that Kelly could see us both all the time. So I moved back to the village.'

'Not your dad's old place?'

'Goodness, no. That was rented anyway, and he's long gone. No, I rent one of the new places on Gyle Head.'

'Oh. So that playground's right by your house.'

'Yup. Kelly loves it. Though she's getting a bit old for swings and slides now. She's nine.'

'Right.'

There was a silence. Tara didn't quite know what to say next.

'I know you're going home. I... I just wanted to explain. Finally,' he said.

'Well, thank you. Finally,' she sighed. 'I wish I'd known all of this a long time ago. And I know that mum and dad will want to know, too.'

'I know. I'll tell them.'

'What happened with you and your mum, though?' Tara asked. 'Did you ever reconnect with her? I gave her your number and then I never heard anything more. It always worried me, that it had been the reason why you left. I didn't know what had happened. But I really did care... I thought I was helping.'

'You did. She called me, and we went for coffee a few times. We were able to put some things in the past to rest, and I'm really grateful for that. We stay in touch, I see her about once a month or so. She's got another family now. She remarried – a really great guy, nothing like my dad. They've got two kids. She loves Kelly.'

'That's great. I'm so relieved.' Tara let out a long breath, and felt a tension leave her shoulders and her heart. She'd been holding on to that worry for such a long time and it felt strange and wonderful to let it go.

'Well, you know, it's kind of all down to you that Kelly even knows her grandma. So, thank you. Truly.' He looked shy. 'And, I also wanted to say that I'm so proud of you for becoming a teacher.'

'Oh. Thanks. Well, I'm proud of you for being a dad,' she said, because she was. 'You always wanted a family. And now you do.'

'I always wanted a family with you,' he said, taking her hands in his. This time, she let him hold them. 'I'm sorry that didn't quite go to plan. You were always my family. I still...'

'Now then, what's all this?' Dotty appeared in the doorway to the bar, before Ramsay could finish what he was about to say. 'Tara. Are you all right?'

Tara wiped her eyes with her sleeve.

'It's okay, Mum. I'm all right,' she said, but Dotty flounced into the bar – as best as she could flounce now, with her mobility impaired – and put her arm protectively around Tara's shoulders.

'Hey, now,' she said, handing Tara a hanky from her pocket. 'Blow yer nose, darlin'. It's all right.' She moved her gaze to Ramsay, who had stood to attention as soon as Dotty walked in. 'An' I hope yer not upsettin' my Tara, Ramsay Fraser. I think ye've done quite enough o' that fer now.'

Tara was taken aback to see the change in her mother. Dotty had always been a loving parent, but she had always tended towards a brisk approach with Tara. Yet, she was taking Ramsay in with a gimlet stare and her hands on her hips. If she had a tail, it would have been swishing, Tara thought.

'I tried not to,' Ramsay replied.

'Hm. Tryin's no' good enough for my girl.' Dotty wagged her finger in his face. 'Now, you listen, my lad. Don't think I'm no' delighted tae see ye back in Loch Cameron, because I am. We missed ye fer all these years. Ye know yer like a son tae us.' Dotty's voice cracked a little. 'But I willnae have ye comin' here an' upsettin' Tara. Ye've got nae idea what it was like fer that poor lassie when ye up sticks an' fair disappeared. No idea at all,' Dotty continued. 'She was absolutely heartbroken. Never been the same since. Her dad and me, we've always worried about her since then.'

'Have you?' Tara asked, genuinely surprised.

'Aye, o' course. Ye retreated intae yerself after Ramsay left. Ye used tae be such a fun-lovin soul – aye, ye were bookish, but ye were a happy girl. After he disappeared, ye hardly came home anymore. Ye just focused on yer work, never much of a social life. Never danced again.' Dotty tutted. 'That's why I'm so happy tae see ye get involved in the fundraiser, dance, make some friends. Ye've got happier since bein' here, I can see it.'

Dotty turned to Ramsay and stabbed him in the chest with her forefinger.

'So. I dinnae what ye've been tellin' her, but don't you dare try an' undo all the good things that've happened since she's been home,' she finished.

'Dotty, I would never knowingly hurt Tara,' Ramsay said, quietly. 'I've been explaining something that I should have explained a long time ago. And I owe you the explanation too,' he said, and waited while Dotty sat down in one of the floral upholstered easy chairs.

'Eric needs tae hear this, then.' Dotty tapped Tara on the hand gently. 'Darlin', could ye pop out an' get yer dad tae come in? He's just outside.'

'Sure.' Tara went out into the reception area and opened the heavy Inn door, going outside to find her dad smoking an illicit cigarette in the car park.

'Don't tell yer mum. As far as she knows, I gave up in 1998,' he said, with a wry smile.

'Dad. I think she would have worked it out by now,' Tara chuckled.

'Nah. I just pop in a breath mint every time. Works a treat.' Eric looked past Tara at the Inn door. 'What's up?'

'Mum says can you go in please. Ramsay wants to talk to you both.'

'Oh. Right.' Eric frowned and looked up at the Inn. 'I was thinkin' I might get the ladder out an' do the windows,' he said, but Tara shook her head.

'No chance. She's got her "I mean business" look on.'

'Oh. Fine, fine. Right ye are,' Eric sighed, and stubbed out his cigarette on a corner of the wall. 'How is the lad?' he asked Tara quietly as he followed her inside.

'He's all right.'

'Bein' grilled by yer mother, nae doubt.'

'Err. Yeah.'

'Ah. Well, she's fierce over ye.' Her dad nodded. 'As am I. I dinnae get fierce aboot many things, but you're one o' them.'

Tara reached for Eric's hand.

'I love you, Dad,' she said. 'And I've really enjoyed spending time with you and Mum this summer. It's made me see you both in a new way, honestly.'

'Aww. I love you too, Tara,' he said, stopping and enveloping her in a hug. 'Always have. And it's been lovely havin' ye home. Ye've been such a huge help wi' yer mum laid up. I really couldnae have done it without ye.'

When Tara walked back into the bar with Eric, Dotty and Ramsay were also hugging. When she saw them, Dotty stood back and wiped her eyes.

'We've had a good blether,' she said. 'Ramsay's told me everythin'. Eric, I'll fill ye in.'

'All right.' Eric frowned. 'I willnae ask ye tae repeat yourself, Ramsay. If Dotty's happy, I'm happy. Is everythin' okay, hen?' he asked his wife. Tara remembered what her mum had said about Eric getting a group of the local men together and running Jack Fraser out of town. He had always been a gentle man. Always the quieter one, letting Dotty do the talking.

'Aye. Everythin's okay.' Dotty nodded. 'I've reminded him what we always said. We're his mum and dad, always have been, always will be. An' he should bring little Kelly round tae visit.'

'Aye.' Eric broke into a warm smile. 'That's yer little one, is it? We'd love tae meet her. Ye know that regardless of whether ye were with Tara or not, yer family, Ramsay,' he continued. 'And as long as Tara's happy, and Dotty's happy, then I'm happy. Okay?'

'Okay,' Ramsay agreed. 'And, yes, I'd love to introduce you to Kelly. She'd love to meet you, I'm sure.'

'Well, that's that then.' Dotty planted a kiss on Ramsay's cheek and gave Eric a meaningful look. 'Now. We'll leave ye young un's tae it. Come on, love.' She gestured for her husband to follow her out into the kitchen; Tara watched them go, then heard the kitchen door open and close.

'They're giving us space,' she observed.

'Yeah.' He stuck his hands in his pockets.

'Did Mum give you the third degree?'

'Not really. She just listened, and let me explain. She's always been great. So has your dad.'

'They really do think of you as the son they never had,' Tara reminded him.

'I know. I'm so grateful to them. And I love them.' He looked down at his shoes. 'Tara, if you can find it in your heart to forgive me, one day, I would be so grateful. I know it'll take time, and that's okay. But... I want things to be okay between us. I know that you're going back to Glasgow, and you've got a whole other life there. But it would be great to be friends again, at least. If you can forgive me. I'm so very sorry.'

'I forgive you now,' Tara said, quietly, taking his hand in hers. 'And I'll never not be your friend.'

They stared into each other's eyes for a long moment, and Tara felt the heat build between them. It was intoxicating, being this close to him: familiar and unfamiliar at the same time. And there was that same sense of groundedness, wholeness, that she was perfectly where she needed to be. There was no sense of being lost anymore.

'Friends is good,' he said, his gaze unwavering.

'Yeah,' she murmured.

Gently, he pulled her towards him, and she gazed up into his eyes. *Those eyes*, she thought. *I've always been powerless when he looks at me like this.*

'Tara. I missed you so much,' he breathed.

'I missed you too,' she murmured, and couldn't help her sigh when his lips finally met hers.

TWENTY-EIGHT

They kissed and kissed, losing themselves for what felt like hours, until Tara had heard her mum and dad come back in. Dotty and Eric made what Tara knew were noises specifically aimed at letting Tara and Ramsay know that they were back in the building; she grinned up at Ramsay when she heard her dad's careful cough.

'They don't want to walk into anything inappropriate,' she whispered.

'Hey. Hands strictly above the waist here,' Ramsay murmured, grinning. 'Hi, Dotty. Hi, Eric.'

'Look at these lovebirds! Together again!' Dotty trilled. She was glowing with joy. 'I just want to hug you both! If you knew how much I dreamed of this moment!' she chattered.

'Dot. Leave them be.' Eric guided his wife into the back room of the bar. Tara could hear her mother bickering gently with her dad, and she smiled to herself.

It was nice to see her mum happy. She didn't know what would happen with Ramsay: where it would go, whether it would look anything like what Tara had thought it would, once upon a time. But, for the first time in a long time, she felt complete and right.

It had always been wrong, when Ramsay was missing from her – but, also, when he was missing from her family. Ramsay had been a Ballantyne, even though they had never got married. He'd been in Tara's heart for always, just like the two hearts pendant. But he'd also been in her family's heart, too.

'Come and see something.' She led him to the fireplace and took down some of the books from Agnes' shelf. 'These belonged to my great-aunt. Beautiful, aren't they?' She handed one to him: *Villette* by Charlotte Brontë.

'Gorgeous.' Ramsay took the book and opened it gently. 'Agnes Smith. That was her?'

'Yes. She had a difficult relationship with the headmaster at the time. But she was dedicated to looking after the children in her care, and she did look after them. She had a really long career at the school. She became headmistress and she ran the school for like 40 years.'

'That's awesome. Like you.'

'Well, I haven't had as long a career. But, yes, hopefully. The other thing that Carla and I found in these books – that's my flatmate, by the way. You'll love her – were some love letters between Agnes and this guy called John. I'd just love to know whatever happened between the two of them.'

'When were the letters dated?' Ramsay stepped forward and peered at the shelf on top of the fireplace. 'You know there's another book back here? Wedged behind the rest? Wait, I'll get it.' He removed some of the books and set them down on a chair, gently freeing a larger, brown leather-bound book.

'Oh goodness. No, I didn't know that,' Tara breathed.

'Looks like a scrap book or something.' Ramsay opened it and handed it to her.

'Oh, my goodness,' Tara repeated, taking the book. 'Look! It's Agnes!'

The book opened with a black and white print of a young Agnes. Unlike her school headmistress photo, the Agnes in this picture sat with her back against a tree, shading her eyes from the sun. She was wearing a tatty straw hat with a ribbon and a summer dress. She looked carefree and was grinning into the camera.

'That's up on Queen's Point. Look, you can see the loch behind her,' Ramsay said, softly.

On the next page, there was another picture. It was Agnes again, and a handsome young man in a light shirt and dark slacks. Underneath the picture, Agnes had written

John and me, summertime

'That's him,' Tara gasped. 'Wow. They look good together.'

'They look happy,' Ramsay said.

Tara flicked the pages. There were mementoes stuck to the pages, some of them labelled: an aged black feather on one page, under which Agnes had written *Our friend Carruthers the Crow*. On another page there were a handful of vintage train tickets, all dated 1942.

'Clearly they spent a good bit of time together,' Ramsay said. 'These are day trips to the coast... look, here's Orkney. That would have taken a week or so, don't you think? A trip there?'

'Probably, yes.' Tara nodded. 'So they had some good times together. It seems like he really loved her. And look how happy she is.'

Tara flicked the pages. There were some photos of landscapes, beaches and trees: the kind of scenes that clearly meant a lot to Agnes, but whose meaning was lost in time. Tara felt a warm glow of satisfaction that Agnes, though to all intents and purposes had remained a spinster in the eyes of her family and of Loch Cameron, had loved, and been loved.

Finally, Tara turned to a page at the back of the notebook,

where a handwritten letter had been pasted in. It was John's handwriting.

Dear Agnes,

This is the most difficult letter I have ever had to write.

I have been posted to the Eastern Front, and I leave next week.

I know that we had been looking forward to a weekend together, but I'm afraid that is not to be. The only way that I can evade being called up is by deserting, and I will not do that. Dear Agnes, you and I will have to wait for each other.

I thought that my work would protect me from active service, but my boss, Mr Andrews, says that they are getting desperate for troops on the Front now, and are recruiting any young men that they can get, and the older ones too. Mr Andrews is fifty and has a bad leg and is a father, but I know he too is dreading getting his papers.

I am frightened. I have heard terrible things about the Front, not least the weather and conditions, but I will try my hardest to come back to you, my darling Agnes.

Fate brought us together, and I refuse to believe that it will tear us apart.

Be strong, my darling: as strong as I know you are. Look after the children in your care. They need you.

Forever yours,

John xxx

'Oh, no.' Tara's heart wrenched, and tears sprang to her eyes.

There was nothing else in the book, apart from the page after the letter, where Agnes had simply written –

NEVER GONE, ALWAYS WITH ME

'Do you think he survived?' Tara turned her face up to Ramsay.

'I don't know, babe. Maybe.' Ramsay stroked her hair. 'But the book stops there. I feel like there'd be more if he did.'

'That's so sad.' Tara pressed the book to her heart. 'I wanted Agnes to be happy.'

'But she was happy,' Ramsay said, pulling her to him in a deep hug. 'Listen. Agnes had a rough time with that head-teacher guy, right? But she also had this John, and John definitely loved her. John was crazy about her.'

'Yes, but then he probably died in the war. And she had to be alone for the rest of her life.' Tara's voice cracked a little. 'That's sad.'

'But, Tara. Agnes loved her work. She was headmistress for like forty years, you said? She loved those kids. And she was loved. All right, maybe not for her whole life, but she still had something beautiful with John. Think of that. Don't think about what she lost. She might not have thought that she lost anything.'

'Maybe,' Tara sniffed. 'But I lost you for ten years. That was terrible.'

'I know. But then we got a second chance.' Ramsay met her eyes with a steady gaze. 'And, anyway, look at what else you have. You've got your family. Your friends. A job you love.'

'And dancing. I've rediscovered that. Agnes inspired me to remember the things that make me happy, and be resilient,' Tara added.

'Exactly. You're lucky. We're lucky. Let's honour her memory by remembering her and John every single day. And honour her by loving each other, and living our lives joyfully, and knowing how lucky we are.'

'All right.' Tara nodded, and laid her head on his chest. 'We are lucky to get a second chance.' She was filled with gratitude;

everything Ramsay said was true. If she was like Agnes, like Dotty had always said she was, then she could take the best parts of Agnes' example: her ability to love, her dedication to her children and the school, and do as she had. But, at the same time, she could be grateful for the circumstances that had brought her love back to her. And, perhaps, somewhere, Agnes would know, and be happy.

Her hand found the jewellery box in her pocket and she drew it out. 'Ramsay? Would you help me with something?' She opened it and took the necklace out, gently. 'I stopped wearing it... but I'd like to wear it again. If you didn't mind.'

'Of course I don't mind.' He took it from her gently and fastened it around her neck. 'Back where it belongs,' he said, and kissed her.

TWENTY-NINE

'Kel. You can have crisps or biscuits, but not both,' Ramsay said as he and Tara stood at the snack bar and waited while Kelly regarded the range of snacks there with a deeply serious gaze. Finally, she pointed shyly to a pile of luscious-looking flapjacks on display under a glass dome.

'Good choice. Let's all have one,' Ramsay chuckled, and asked the friendly-looking woman in the booth for three flapjacks. 'Coffee?' he asked Tara, who nodded.

'Cappuccino, please,' she asked, and smiled at Kelly, who was holding Ramsay's hand. 'Shall I have chocolate sprinkles? That's the question.'

'Oh, most definitely. Kelly likes to drink the foam from my coffee, and it's even better with chocolate,' Ramsay chuckled.

'Oh! I will, then.' Tara winked at Kelly. Kelly broke into a goofy smile.

'Yummy!' She giggled.

Tara understood that Kelly was feeling shy. It was normal for a nine-year-old when a new adult was introduced, even though she and Ramsay were taking things very cautiously.

Tara had been back in Glasgow for a few weeks, and she

was back visiting Loch Cameron on a sunny weekend in late September. This was the first time she'd met Kelly, and she'd been nervous about it. It was silly, she told herself: she taught nine-year-olds. She shouldn't be scared of one. But, this was different. This was Ramsay's daughter.

The day they'd kissed at the bar, Tara had realised that she wanted to be with him. All the doubts and fears she'd had had been put into perspective. It wasn't that she didn't have those feelings, still: she didn't know what was going to happen in the future between them. But she wanted to be with him. And that was enough for now.

'Come on. Let's get a bench.' Ramsay pointed to one that was free, and they made their way over to it, Kelly skipping ahead as they walked. Tara was reminded of that day she had come to Gyle Head and mistakenly thought that Ramsay was married.

'I could have saved myself a lot of confusion if I'd just stayed and talked to you, that day,' she said, as they sat down.

'When?'

'When I came here to meet you and then ran away. I should have given you the benefit of the doubt.' She took her coffee as he handed it to her. 'Thanks.'

'Ah, maybe. But it's understandable why you didn't.' He took a flapjack out of a paper bag and handed one to Kelly. 'There you go, poppet. I've got the water bottle if you want it.' He took off a backpack and slung it next to the bench.

'You came prepared, I see.' Tara nodded to the bag.

'Ah. Yes. Dad backpack. Sorry.' He looked a little embarrassed.

'Don't be sorry. It's practical. I've always got wet wipes, snacks and hand sanitiser.'

'Then you know.'

'Daddy? Can I play?' Kelly had taken some bites from the flapjack, and had stood up, skipping on the spot.

'Sure, baby. Stay where I can see you, okay? And I'll come and watch you on the swings in a while,' he said.

'Can Tara watch me too?' Kelly asked.

'Sure, honey. I'll be right there,' Tara said, a warm glow enveloping her heart. Kelly nodded, handed Ramsay her half-eaten snack and skipped off.

'She's a happy thing. You're doing a good job,' Tara observed.

'Agh. I hope so.' He ran a hand through his hair. 'She likes you, I can tell.'

'She's sweet.' Tara watched Kelly as she climbed the central pyramid-shaped climbing frame with ease. 'Good that she's physically adventurous, too. Some kids – especially girls – you see their parents socialising them in particular ways from when they're little. You know, telling them they can't do things. I've seen parents stand at the bottom of climbing frames like that and yell at their daughters to come down, because they can't climb that high.'

'Oh, no. I mean, yeah, when she was younger, my heart was always in my mouth, watching her climb. But I'd never stop her. I was just there in case she fell. If she needed a hand, I'd get her, but she hardly ever did. I always thought about your parents, how they always gave me confidence about dancing. Tried to do the same for Kel.' He shrugged. 'Nowadays she's old enough for me not to worry too much. In a couple of years she'll probably be boy crazy, so I'm appreciating her still being a little girl for now.'

'Well, you should be very proud of her. And yourself,' Tara added. 'And, she'll always be your little girl. It's good that you're being such a good dad to her. Breaking the cycle of toxic parenting and all that.'

'I guess so. I mean, yes. I consciously wanted to do that. Not repeat what was done to me.'

'You would never do that.'

'I know. But it's a fear,' he sighed. 'Listen. I know this is all very weird. But I really appreciate you coming back to visit.' Ramsay turned his gaze to her. 'I know it was awful timing. Us kissing on the day you went home.'

'It's okay. You can't control these things,' she said.

'How's it been, back at school?'

'Ugh. Terrible, actually,' Tara sighed. She always loved her children, but things at Lomond Primary were worse than ever. There was a new Head, who had already sacked half of the staff, and Tara's morale was seriously low. 'And I missed you.'

'I've missed you too,' he murmured, and leaned in towards her, putting the tips of his forefingers under her chin. 'And I want more of that kiss.'

Tara's lips met his. This time, it was relaxed and unhurried, and she relished his touch: the way he tasted, the softness of his mouth on hers.

Of course, she remembered how Ramsay kissed. She'd kissed him thousands of times. But, it had been ten years, and he was a man now, not a teenager.

The urgency in his kiss took her breath away; the way he held her gently but firmly and the heat that rose between them as his hands caressed her cheek and then found her waist and pulled her to him. Finally, he pulled away, keeping his eyes fixed on hers.

'Well, that was...' she trailed off. 'Hmm.'

'Hmm, good?' Ramsay smiled that smile that had won them so many competitions. 'I'm hoping for good.'

'You know it was good.' She tapped him playfully on the arm. 'That was never a problem for us.'

'No, it wasn't,' he said, holding her gaze. She felt her cheeks flush, remembering how it had used to be between them. Their physical relationship had always been as harmonious as their dancing partnership – perhaps because of that, she didn't know. But lovemaking had always been fun, sometimes silly, always honest, always kind and in sync. Tara realised how much she'd missed being in Ramsay's arms. And how much she'd missed being intimate together, too. All those small moments, woven into the mesh of a relationship.

'I have something for you,' he said, letting go of her for a moment and reaching into his pocket. 'If you'll take it.'

'What is this?' Tara asked, alarmed, as Ramsay presented her with a small red jewellery box. For a moment, she wondered whether it was a ring. 'It's not my birthday.'

'I know. But I missed ten of them, so...' he shrugged. 'An update, then.'

She opened the box.

Inside, a gold heart locket sat on a delicate gold chain. She took in a deep breath.

'Ramsay! This is too much!' she stuttered, startled and taken aback. She took the necklace out and held it in her hand: it was a good weight, clearly well-made and expensive.

'Daddy!' Kelly called from the swings.

'Coming, baby,' he replied to his daughter, then turned to Tara. 'Not at all too much. As if anything would ever be too much for you. I thought it could replace the old one. And this is a heart in one piece. Not one, broken in two.' Ramsay stood up.

'Thank you. It's beautiful,' she breathed. 'I'll always treasure the old one, though. It has a lot of memories attached to it.'

'Of course. But some of those memories were bad, eh? We can start fresh with this one, I thought. And it's a locket, so you can put a photo in it. Of anyone, it doesn't have to be me.' He grinned and held out a hand for Tara. She took it, and followed him into the playground, thinking that if anyone was watching them, what a sweet little family they made. It was, of course, very early days, and she had to get to know Ramsay again, and build a relationship with Kelly too, if she wanted to be in a relationship with him. But, she found that she was willing to do that.

She couldn't believe that he'd bought her the locket. It was such a beautiful, thoughtful gift.

'Of course it'll be you. Us, maybe. A picture of us from way back when,' she said, smiling.

Her phone buzzed; she looked at it and saw that it was a text from Emily.

Sure I can't tempt you? she had written, with an attachment to a job advert for class teacher at Loch Cameron Primary.

What on earth am I waiting for? Tara thought. She replied with a smiley face.

OK. As long as there's good biscuits in the staff room, then I'm in she replied, and put her phone back in her pocket. She felt it buzz again and smiled to herself, anticipating Emily's excited reply.

'Okay.' Tara stood behind the swing as Kelly sat on it. 'Are you ready? Because this is going to go high.'

'Ready!' Kelly squealed excitedly.

Tara pulled the swing back by the chains and let it go, grinning at Ramsay as Kelly whooped, swinging high up into the wide, blue sky.

EPILOGUE

SIX MONTHS LATER

'Right. Who's going first?'

Tara stood in her newly built classroom at Loch Cameron Primary amid a group of nine-year-olds. All ten of them each held a piece of paper on which they'd written a hope for the future, and they were standing around a large coffee tin that Tara had found for the occasion.

Ten pupils was a much smaller class size than she was used to, despite the fact that Emily had told her about the bigger intake of children that were starting in Reception now, because of the new families that were continuing to move to Gyle Head.

'Robbie?' Tara asked a shy boy who she had helped with his time capsule message earlier in the day. They had taken time to think of their hopes and then decorated them with drawing, glitter and stickers in whatever way they'd wanted. Robbie's wish, like Ramsay's from so many years ago, was a simple one. He had wished for his mum to be happy, which had made Tara's eyes mist up a little and her throat tighten.

'Yes, Miss?'

'Why don't you go first? Yours is so lovely. As they all are,' she said, beaming at her little class.

'All right, then,' he said, and held the carefully folded piece of blue art paper above the open coffee tin. After a couple of seconds, he dropped it in, a sudden grin lighting up his face.

She had taken over the new class in January, and it was now March. In a couple of months, she felt as though she had got to know her pupils quite well, although she was still enjoying building relationships with them all.

She'd given in her notice at Lomond Primary as soon as Emily had called her, excitedly, later on that day at the park with Ramsay and Kelly, and assured her that the job was hers, whenever she wanted to start. She had worked until Christmas; it had been bittersweet, saying goodbye to some of the children. But, the new Head was on the warpath, and Tara knew that she would have been next to be moved or politely asked to leave.

As well as that, she and Ramsay had started a little dance school for the village children at the community centre. It was just a couple of evenings a week, but he'd suggested it after they'd both started to teach Kelly the steps to the Highland Fling. Kelly had taken to dancing like a duck to water, and Ramsay had said to her, afterwards, *you know, we could do this for other kids, too.*

As soon as he'd suggested it, Tara had loved the idea – and, like any plan that was meant to be, it had come together surprisingly easily. They'd started using the same rehearsal room she'd been renting out at the community centre, and they'd both spent some time cleaning it up, bringing in some nicer decorations and making leaflets that they'd distributed around the community. There had already been a lot of interest, and they now had ten pupils that were learning the basics of Highland dancing.

It gave Tara a great deal of joy to be passing on her dancing know-how, and it was even more of a joy to be doing it with Ramsay. They'd always been a great team, and, now that he was a father, Tara could see how great Ramsay was with children, too. He was a natural teacher: patient, kind, sweet. And, Tara could also see that teaching the little ones was healing something in Ramsay, too: perhaps every hour that he spent helping a child erased an hour that he had spent being abused and ignored, himself.

The time capsule had been her idea. She'd suggested it to Emily who had approved, and today, each class was making a tin of their hopes for the future, and burying them under the new flower beds that the local gardener, Christian, had dug for them.

She let all of the children drop theirs in, and then held out her own folded piece of paper.

'Are you going to put yours in now, Miss Ballantyne?' Aisha asked.

'Yes. Here it goes!' Tara said, and dropped her piece in ceremoniously.

'What did it say?' Aisha asked.

'Ah, that would be telling!' Tara replied, playfully.

'But we had to tell ours!' Aisha said, her bottom lip sticking out.

'I know. You're right. I wrote that I wish for happiness and safety for all of the children of Loch Cameron,' Tara said, placing a calm hand briefly on the top of Aisha's head. 'Now. Are we ready to bury the capsule?'

'Yes!' they shouted in unison, and Tara laughed.

'Okay, okay. Coats on, then, it's cold out.'

They trooped outside to the central playground, where a burly, bearded gardener wearing a khaki-coloured knitted hat waited for all the different classes to assemble. Some of the children waved and called out to him, and he waved back and chatted to the children that strayed over to see the seven holes he'd dug for the canisters, with seven fruit bushes – raspberries, loganberries and gooseberries – ready to plant in the holes on top of them.

'Now then, everyone!' Emily bustled to the centre of the playground and waved to get the children's attention. She started clapping in a recognised rhythm, and all the children followed it instinctively, quieting down immediately.

'Okay. Well done. Now, I know that today's an exciting day, and we've got Christian here to help us bury our time capsules. Thank you for coming today, Christian! And you've dug the holes ready, and you have the fruit bushes to plant over them?'

'Yeah, all ready.' Christian nodded and grinned, leaning on his spade. Tara had learned that as well as working on many of the gardens locally, Christian belonged to a local biker gang that did a lot of work for charity. He had offered to help with the time capsule project for free after Emily had happened to mention the project to the local hairdresser, Bel, when she was getting a cut and blow dry.

'Okay, then. Primary One, Bees, off you go!' Emily nodded to the teacher of the youngest class of four- and five-year-olds who led them to where Christian was standing. He hunkered down and gently helped the smallest member of the class – a tiny girl called Essie – place the time capsule into the hole. Everyone clapped.

'Primary Two, Butterflies, your turn!' Emily called out, and the next class took their turn.

As she watched the children excitedly clustering around the flower beds, and listened as they chattered with Christian, Tara thought of Agnes. She had loved the children of Loch Cameron so much, and had endured abuse to remain their teacher. What would she think of all this?

As Tara's class made their way over to the flowerbeds, Tara clapped her hands in the rhythm Emily had used just earlier, and everyone followed, looking at her expectantly.

'I just wanted to say something, while we're doing this,' Tara began. 'Not all of you will know this, but I went to this school when I was your age, many years ago.' She smiled at the little faces turned to her and the surprised expressions that statement elicited. 'And, part of the reason that Miss Jones and I thought that it would be a nice idea to bury time capsules is that we found a time capsule that I made with my classmates when I was here. Isn't that amazing?'

Tara looked around at the children of Loch Cameron, listening to her. She caught Kelly's eye, who was in the class above hers, and smiled.

'And, when we found that time capsule, we found an even older one too, which was from 1941. That's such a long time ago, isn't it? And we found a letter from the teacher in it and some toys and letters from the children, and the toys and the children's letters are all inside for you to see in Reception, in a special display,' Tara continued. She and Emily had taken the decision not to display Agnes' letter with the rest, as its contents were of an adult nature and weren't appropriate for children. Instead, they had framed it and hung it in the staff room, so that Agnes would receive the honour she deserved – and as a reminder that abuse and harassment would never be tolerated at the school.

'And in her letter from 1941, the teacher wrote about how much she cared for her pupils. Her name was Agnes Smith, and she was a teacher here from 1938, and headteacher here from 1943 to 1980. There's a photo of her in the hallway. Have you seen it?'

Some of the children shouted *yes!*

'Well, the other amazing thing is that Agnes Smith was actually my great-aunt. So, her memory is very special to me, and to all of us, because she was such a good teacher and she cared about every child she ever taught. So, I wonder if we can all close our eyes for a minute and just think about Agnes Smith and say a little thank you to her? I think that would be nice.'

There was a small silence, and then a host of little voices filled the playground.

'Thank you.' 'Thank you, Agnes Smith.' 'Thank you, Miss Smith.'

Bless you, great-aunt Agnes, Tara thought, closing her eyes briefly and recalling Agnes' sepia toned school photo. A stern-faced woman with her hair in a bun, wearing a sensible skirt and blouse, with a brooch at the neck, just like Dotty. *I'll always think of you, and remember you.*

But, Tara knew that stern school portrait wasn't all of who Agnes was. She had Agnes' secret diary, and she had copied and framed the pictures of Agnes and John, and Dotty had put them up in the bar of the Loch Cameron Inn. Now, she proudly told all the customers the love story of Agnes and John – having learned some of their letters off by heart – and had even started learning some of Agnes' favourite poems to read aloud to tourists.

Agnes had been a strong woman, yes. Just like Dotty, and just like Tara. Agnes had not taken any crap: she had decided that Paul McLeish wasn't going to break her, and he hadn't. She had won, and taken over as headteacher from him. And she had spent her whole working life at the school thereafter.

But it was Agnes' capacity to love that Tara knew was the most important thing. And she and Dotty had inherited that, as well as Agnes' strength. Tara wasn't particularly religious – she had been raised Church of Scotland, like most in the village – but she knew, deep in her heart, that Agnes and John were together again now, somewhere, in spirit. That kind of love endured the ages, and death was no competition for it.

Tara thought again of the *Jane Eyre* quote that Agnes had underlined – *I am no bird, and no net ensnares me: I am a free human being with an independent will.*

Agnes was a free spirit; an independent woman. She would not allow death to part her and John.

Tara wondered what Agnes would say about her and Ramsay. She hoped that Agnes would be pleased that they had found each other again. Agnes believed in love: her heavily annotated copy of *Jane Eyre* was testament to that. Despite losing John, she had believed.

Tara thought of Ramsay's own note from the time capsule. He had wanted a family, and to be happy, and Tara had wanted to help and inspire others. And, there was something about this process of burying the time capsule with these new hopes for the future which made Tara feel grounded here in Loch Cameron. Most of the time she'd been here, over the summer, she'd felt disconnected from what she thought was her real life, back in Glasgow. She'd felt odd, unmoored, being back in Loch Cameron and feeling like she was always running into the ghosts of her past.

But, now, Loch Cameron was home again, and life had looped backwards and forwards at the same time. She had made her home in the village again, and there would always be shadows of the past here. She saw them every day at the school: memories of her and Ramsay, in the classrooms, in the playground, running down the corridors and playing under the trees. But that was okay. She could hold and love those memories whilst knowing that she and Ramsay were making new ones with Kelly, with her new pupils, within the loving community of Loch Cameron that had always been there for both of them.

She felt that they had both achieved what they wanted, or were at least on the way to it. Something had come full circle, and as she watched Christian start to cover their capsule with earth, she said a silent thank you to Agnes and whoever else was listening. *Thank you to all the ones before me. Love to all before, love to all that will come*, she thought. *And may lovers always find each other again: in this life or the next.*

A LETTER FROM KENNEDY

Dear reader,

I want to say a huge thank you for choosing to read *Keepsakes from the Cottage by the Loch*. If you did enjoy it, and want to keep up to date with all my latest releases, just sign up at the following link. Your email address will never be shared and you can unsubscribe at any time.

www.bookouture.com/kennedy-kerr

I hope you loved *Keepsakes from the Cottage by the Loch* and if you did I would be very grateful if you could write a review. I'd love to hear what you think, and it makes such a difference helping new readers to discover one of my books for the first time.

I love hearing from my readers – you can get in touch through social media or my website.

Thanks,

Kennedy

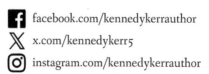

facebook.com/kennedykerrauthor
x.com/kennedykerr5
instagram.com/kennedykerrauthor

PUBLISHING TEAM

Turning a manuscript into a book requires the efforts of many people. The publishing team at Bookouture would like to acknowledge everyone who contributed to this publication.

Commercial
Lauren Morrissette
Hannah Richmond
Imogen Allport

Cover design
Emma Graves

Data and analysis
Mark Alder
Mohamed Bussuri

Editorial
Kelsie Marsden
Nadia Michael

Copyeditor
Claire Rushbrook

Proofreader
Tom Feltham

Milton Keynes UK
Ingram Content Group UK Ltd.
UKHW030739071024
449371UK00005B/351